THE LAST RUN

A PETER BLACK THRILLER

DAVID ARCHER

VINCE VOGEL

RIGHTHOUSE

ISBN-13: 978-1-63696-166-8

ISBN-10: 1-63696-166-5

Cover design by: Damonza

Printed in the United States of America

www.righthouse.com

www.instagram.com/righthousebooks

www.facebook.com/righthousebooks

twitter.com/righthousebooks

PETER BLACK THRILLERS

PROLOGUE

A BUNKER SOMEWHERE IN RUSSIA - 14TH APRIL, 12:37 (MSK)

IN THE DEPTHS OF AN UNDISCLOSED LOCATION, the president of Russia sits in his state-of-the-art underground bunker. Dominating the wall behind him, the Russian tricolor stands resolute and unwavering, its bold colors a striking contrast against the room's stoic grayscale. The banner casts a solemn shadow over the long, austere table where Vladimir Vladimirovich Putin sits alone, his presence lit by the somber glow emanating from an enormous telescreen adorning the wall in front of him.

Displayed on the colossal screen are the grim faces of his three main military chiefs, their expressions grave, their attention undivided. Each appears burdened with the toll of a war spiraling out of their grasp. The silence in the room is deafening, interrupted only by the quiet hum of unseen air filtration machinery and the sterilized, measured steps of the bunker's carefully selected staff as they hurry around the president.

In their white uniforms, gloves, and face masks, they move with precision, carefully maintaining distance from Putin as they serve him breakfast. One aide places a steaming cup of black coffee next to him, while another unveils a platter of warm croissants, their aroma subtly perforating the sterile air. Soon, they retreat with courteous nods, leaving Putin alone with his breakfast and the faces on the telescreen.

"Gentlemen." He addresses the somber assembly standing attentively on the screen, his voice reverberating against the cold, stark walls of the bunker. "Report."

The generals exchange weighted looks before a hard-jawed man steps forward. His voice carries a heavy truth. "Mr. President, we've lost significant ground in Ukraine. Our position is rapidly deteriorating... At the current rate, we risk losing the war within the next year, thus ceding the territory we gained in 2014, including the Crimea. We also see Ukraine becoming a full member of NATO by then, thus placing Western missiles on our own borders."

A palpable silence falls over the room, the devastating words hanging in the air like specters. Putin finally breaks the silence. "What about conscription? Mass mobilization of all able-bodied citizens aged eighteen to thirty?"

The generals wince. One by one, they shake their heads. "A draft of that scale would cause massive public dissent," one general admits. "Furthermore, it wouldn't come with guaranteed success... and with the current state of our ammunition and equipment supplies... It's not a viable solution, sir."

Putin steeples his fingers, his gaze darkening. He breathes in deeply, his waxen, immovable face showing nothing. There's a moment of silence before he straightens, his gaze hardening with resolve. "Then we must take decisive action, gentlemen," he barks. "Initiate Protocol X-9."

The order echoes in the sterile room, its significance palpable. No one argues or disagrees. The generals on the screen offer their silent nods, a grim acceptance marking their faces—which have lost all color. Something terrible has just been set in motion. The untouched croissants and coffee bear mute witness to the weighty decree that has just been issued in the bowels of the earth, unseen and unheard by the world above.

ONE

THE EARLY MORNING SUN CASTS A SURREAL GLOW over the bustling harbor of Red Hook Container Terminal, Brooklyn. The colossal silhouette of an oil tanker juxtaposes the calming hues of dawn as a matte-black SUV navigates its way toward it through the dockside maze of crates and machinery.

Driving is Michael Black. Beside him in the passenger seat, his petite girlfriend Mayu observes the busy scene with wide eyes. Seated quietly in the back is Michael's father, Peter Black, a kit bag on the seat beside him.

His gaze lingers on his son and the woman beside him, their hands entwined across the car. A pang of envy runs through him as he contemplates their unblemished existence, their simple pleasures. He longs for the normalcy they have, a normalcy that he has never known.

Michael parks the SUV near the towering ship. Killing the engine, he twists around in his seat to face his father.

"How're you feeling about your first day as a tankerman?" he asks.

"Nervous" is Peter's reply before he adds in a more serious tone, "Now remember, I don't want you two getting into trouble while I'm away."

"We'll be fine, Dad," Michael reassures him.

Peter looks at his son, his pride evident. "I'm glad, you know," he says softly. "Glad that we're all finally living normal lives. After what you've both been through"—he turns to Mayu—"you deserve to live like normal people." The note of finality in his voice has them sharing a sobering silence.

"You, too, Dad," Michael adds, Mayu nodding beside him.

His voice shaking slightly, Peter adds, "You'll be in college by the time I get back. Both of you."

"We'll still be in the same city. Our new apartment will only be a half hour on the subway."

Peter tries to smile but can only pull off a glum grimace.

"Look," Michael says, "don't go getting all sad on us. You don't want your shipmates seeing you like this on your first day. It'll be a couple months at sea, and then you'll be back. We'll spend plenty of time together then."

Peter finally manages that smile. "I'm looking forward to that," he says, and they embrace across the car.

As he walks away from the SUV, his heavy boots crunching against the gravel of the weathered dock, Peter looks back once to see Michael wrap an arm protectively around Mayu.

It's the two of them now, he thinks.

He turns, squares his shoulders, and walks up the gangplank.

The inside of the ship is a stark contrast to its exterior—less maritime, more clandestine. The inside is practically deserted, and the men who inhabit the ship don't make eye contact with Peter as he strolls past. No one asks for his papers, no one greets him, and no one tells him where to go. Peter already knows where to go. Because despite his son thinking he is going to be working on an oil tanker for the next few months, he is not.

Descending into the ship's belly, the first person to greet him is none other than Ben Knight of the CIA. The tall, lanky man with a mop of white hair, clad in a plain black suit, extends his hand, a subtle grin playing on his face.

"Good to have you back, Peter," he offers, his handshake brief and firm.

Knight escorts him to a secluded office nestled within the tanker's hull. Sliding into a chair behind a desk, he gestures for Peter to take a seat on the other side.

"What have you got for me, Ben?" Peter inquires, leaning forward with an air of anticipation.

"How does a trip to Spain sound?"

"Sounds nice. What's in Spain?"

"Pest control."

"That's what I'm here for. Who's the pest?"

"Cockroach by the name of Ali Hossain. He's got previous with al-Qaeda, ISIS, and anyone else who needs to blow up a bunch of infidels in the hope of progressing the international caliphate."

"Do we have his location?"

"Not yet. But we've got a lead. He's set to show up in Madrid. Our surveillance team has been tracking his crew. They're confident that they're planning something big in the city to mark the twenty-year anniversary of the Madrid bombing and that Ali Hossain will surface there within the next twenty-four hours to meet with them."

Peter nods, a hint of a smile playing at the corners of his lips. "Sounds like an easy first day back if all I am is the trigger man."

"Unless something big comes up and I need you for that."

"Well," Peter responds, an air of casual indifference in his tone, "here's to hoping nothing big comes up."

———

As those presumptuous words linger in the stale air of the oil tanker, across the globe, a long-dormant network of Russian sleeper agents spring to life. Triggered by a single phrase, lives are disrupted and ordinary façades peel away. A sequence of phone calls ignites a chain reaction. The message coming down the line is the same everywhere: "The dragon is released."

In the heart of Paris, within the clamor and aroma of a bustling fast-food restaurant, a man named Antoine receives the call. His supervisor begins complaining as he answers it, warning he shouldn't have his phone on him. All the while he listens, Antoine's hand hesitates over the sizzling grill, then drops the spatula when the call comes to an end. Without a word or backward glance, he strips off his apron and strides out of the restaurant, leaving behind the bewildered faces of his coworkers.

Half a world away, in the gleaming skyscrapers of Dubai, a businessman named Hamid is immersed in a high-stakes board meeting over the architectural design choice of a new shopping mall. His phone vibrates silently against the polished mahogany conference table. Excusing himself with a wave, he answers the call and steps into the corridor. Those same four words and he too is abandoning his post, his high-polished shoes tapping against the marble floor as he walks to the building's exit.

In São Paulo, a university professor named Helena stands in the middle of an engrossing lecture on the intersection between quantum mechanics and human consciousness. Her phone rings, the sharp trill cutting through her words as she explains Orch-OR theory. Pausing, she checks the caller ID and answers, listening with a furrowed brow at the front of the auditorium. Four words later and she is placing the chalk on the blackboard and striding out of the room, ignoring the baffled looks of her students.

Down under in Sydney, a taxi driver named Liam hears his mobile chime through the speakers of his cab.

"The dragon is released." And the call goes dead.

Liam's passenger watches in surprise as the affable driver's face turns serious. "Gonna have to cut this ride short, mate," Liam says tersely, pulling over abruptly. He orders the fare out, then speeds off, leaving the bewildered passenger standing on the curb.

Across the Pacific in Atlanta, a seasoned cop named Jackson sits in his cruiser, his partner chattering next to him. His cell phone rings, cutting through the idle banter. Recognizing the number, he answers. "The dragon is released," says the voice on the other end. Nodding, he hangs up, steps out of the vehicle, and begins walking away. His partner's calls fall on deaf ears as he disappears into the crowded street.

Thus, in cities scattered across continents, a chorus of seemingly inconsequential actions ripple through the mundane rhythms of daily life. Unseen and unknown, the sleeper agents have been activated. The dragon has indeed been released.

TWO

RUSSIAN FEDERATION MINISTRY OF DEFENCE, MOSCOW, RUSSIA - 14TH APRIL, 13:29 (MSK)

Sitting alone in his massive, shadow-laden office, Russian Staff General Vasily Ivanovich occupies a huge wooden desk. It is burdened by stacks of documents, photos, maps, and a neat row of fountain pens. The high-ceilinged room carries a thick silence that is only broken by the relentless tick-tock of an antique wall clock.

Perched in his high-backed leather chair, Ivanovich keeps his piercing, eagle-like eyes fixated on the clock as his typically calm hand rhythmically taps a finger upon the dark wood of the desk while his foot performs a nervous dance beneath the heavy furniture. The room feels charged and uneasy, and the decorated general's worry is palpable.

The clock strikes 1:30. Ivanovich springs to his feet. It is time. He moves swiftly to the door, his decorated chest catching a glint of dim light, and with a few hushed words to his secretary, he vanishes into the hallway, his mobile phone uncharacteristically left behind on his desk.

Half an hour of tense driving later, he leaves the cityscape behind and finds himself surrounded by the verdant countryside of the Moscow Oblast, the hills studded with scattered dachas. Ivanovich pulls his car to a stop in front of a nondescript wooden dacha, its privacy protected by the dark canopy of the surrounding forest.

The staff general's heart hammers in his chest as he fumbles with the padlock. The ever-shifting shadows of the trees fan the flames of his paranoia, looking like men playing out imagined threats in the benign tranquility of the woodland. He can't help stopping and glancing furtively around every so often, the padlock key slippery in his sweaty palms.

His mouth parched, he steps into the small wooden cabin.

Inside, the décor is simple, an embodiment of rustic Russian aesthetics: rough-hewn log walls, faded but richly patterned rugs over oak floors, an iron wood-burning stove. His footsteps reverberate in the silence as he navigates his way to the kitchen. He pulls away a plain rug, revealing a concealed hatch in the floor. There is a heavy click as the hatch unlocks, and he descends into a dimly lit stone basement.

A workbench is pushed against one wall, cluttered with tools and mechanical bits and pieces. He pulls open a drawer, and his fingers close around a small burner phone. His heart feels like it might burst out of his chest as he powers it on.

He's no traitor, Ivanovich. No spy for the US. This

phone is, and was, only ever a precaution. Just in case there was a reason he needed a back channel. Now is such a case.

Summoning his courage, he punches in a number that he's never written down but has committed to memory. It is answered after only two rings. An impersonal, unmistakably American voice greets him on the other end of the line.

"Yes?"

"This is Pablo," Ivanovich announces, his voice bouncing around the basement. "It has happened. The dragon is free."

A pause, then incredulity colors the American voice. "No... Are you for real?"

"I am. So you Americans need to make your move now," Ivanovich says, urgency creeping into his voice. He feels cold sweat trickling down his spine.

"How far is it gone?" the American asks, a tick of worry in his voice.

"It is happening now, right this second, Knight! Don't you listen?!" Frustration and desperation bleed into Ivanovich's voice.

"But you said there'd be enough warning."

"He surprised us all. So you need to move. Now!"

————

CIA HEADQUARTERS, Langley, Virginia, USA.
14 April, 07:10 (EDT)

THE NEWLY PROMOTED director of the Central Intelligence Agency, Sandy McLean, is standing in her bathroom, toothbrush in hand, when her phone erupts into a ring. It's a disturbing intrusion in her otherwise peaceful morning routine. She spits out toothpaste, grabs the phone, and answers, "McLean here."

"It's happened, ma'am," comes a voice she recognizes as Ben Knight.

Director McLean's brow crinkles up. "What has happened?"

The words coming through the line send a chill down her spine. "The dragon is free."

Twenty-one minutes later, Sandy McLean is racing through the corridors of CIA Headquarters, Langley, her mind already working on the implications of what is happening right now across the world. As she reaches a set of double doors, she pushes through into a buzzing conference room.

It is alive with activity; on a large screen at the very front, the head of the FBI, the chairman of the Joint Chiefs of Staff, the secretary of defense, and the national security advisor are all present on a secure video call. Their faces are grave.

"Has the president been informed?" someone asks.

"No, not yet," the secretary of defense replies, his voice heavy.

Director McLean takes a seat at the head of an oval table. Ben Knight is already there, having landed from New York only an hour before.

Leaning into him, she says, "Ben, please tell me your man in Sudan is ready."

Ben's "man in Sudan" was a Sudanese scientist who ostensibly worked for the Sudanese government. However, this was a cover. Really, he was working for the Russian Federation, developing viruses for their bio-weapons division in an underground lab.

"Our call time," Knight explains, "is eight Eastern Standard." He checks his watch. "Another forty-five minutes."

"You can't get to him sooner?"

"No. Eight is when he switches a burner on for fifteen minutes while he waits for his kid to come out from school. The Russians are listening in to every other phone line and have bugged his car, home, and office."

"What about the host?"

Everyone in the room is looking at Knight, including those on the telescreen.

"He has them under his control."

"And are they capable of producing the protein?"

Knight nods. "But he'll need to send us his research data, too."

"Then he needs to move—ASAP," Director McLean says with some force.

Almost forty-five minutes later, Knight exits the conference room, moving into a secure communications suite. There, his fingers fly over a keyboard, bringing up a secure line. He dials in a number, knowing that every second counts.

"Ibrahim, are you alone?" Knight asks urgently as the line connects.

The voice on the other end is hushed. "I'm with my daughter." Knight can hear the sounds of her in the background, the everyday noise of a little girl unaware of her precarious position.

"Ibrahim," Knight starts, his voice level, "I need you to move."

The panic is clear and immediate in Ibrahim's voice. "What?! No. I can't. Not yet. I mean, have you seen it here? We're minutes away from civil war."

"Ibrahim, listen to me. You have to."

"But why?" There's a tremor in Ibrahim's voice, an undercurrent of fear. "You said we should take it easy, not arouse suspicion. A month, you said."

"We haven't got a month."

"Why?"

"Because the Russians are releasing it as we speak."

The line goes deadly quiet. Knight can imagine Ibrahim absorbing the information, the magnitude of what he is asking him to do, and the weight that has just been placed upon his shoulders. The weight of the world.

Finally, after a long pause, Ibrahim speaks, his voice more resolved. "Okay. Okay. I'm due in the lab in the next hour. I'll fetch the bacteria sample for you today."

"What about the host? Can you move them?"

"Yes. I will be with the host when your men come to take us."

"Then I wish you luck, Ibrahim," Knight tells him.

The line goes dead, leaving Knight alone in the room, the weight of the mission closing in on him like a vise.

THREE

Ibrahim can't control the shaking. The air presses down on him so hard it feels like it's squeezing the life out of him.

Beneath the harsh sterile lights of the laboratory, he stands before a Class III Biological Safety Cabinet, an imposing monolith, his frantic heart matching the low hum of the cabinet's ventilation. Staring through the cabinet's glass screen, he is a man at the edge of a precipice, staring not just at the vials held within but into an abyss of invisible danger held at bay by the glass wall.

He slides his hands into the glove ports, the cold, detached touch of the metal handle through the rubber glove gripping his skin. The vial, a tiny vessel of devastation, rests within the cabinet, waiting.

Ibrahim's breath comes in ragged gasps as he maneuvers the mechanical hands toward the vial. His world shrinks to this singular, defining moment, a monumental endeavor demanding his entire concentration. Get this wrong and he could crack the vial, set off the detectors, the alarm system, and cause a shutdown protocol. End up stuck down here for the next three days while they perform quarantine. Not good. Not when you're trying to save the world.

The mechanical fingers close around the vial—secure, no crack. With extreme caution and precision, he guides the hands to deposit the vial into a shock-resistant case nested in the cabinet's drawer. His heart rebels against its bony cage as he nestles the vial within the foam padding and seals the case.

Withdrawing his hands from the gloves, relief seeps into his tense muscles. He moves to the adjacent drawer, eyeing the indicator light, willing it to flash green.

It finally does.

A newfound wave of resolution empowers Ibrahim. He seizes the case—the cold weight of it a grim testament to the lethal secret it harbors. Clasping it against his chest, he stows the case within his lab coat. The bulge beneath the pristine white fabric brands him a traitor, and he prays that the guards monitoring the facility aren't scrutinizing the corridor cameras with any real vigilance.

Drawing on his threadbare courage, he steps out of the lab, trying hard to maintain the picture of an unassuming scientist. But beneath this façade, his insides writhe with terror. He feels as though he's balancing on the edge of a razor, one misstep away from falling onto the blade.

Ibrahim slips through the maze-like environment of the lab, straining to retain his composure. In the changing room, within the sanctuary of the camera's blind spot, he stealthily secures the container within the false bottom of his work bag. In the elevator, he breathes a sigh of relief at being alone; maintaining his composure under the scrutiny of others would be a Herculean feat, given the explosive secret concealed in his bag.

Like normal, the guards don't inspect his belongings with any real effort, and he seamlessly passes through the turnstile, the two men wishing him goodbye as he leaves. His responses are automatic, the entire interaction shrouded in an aura of unreality, as if he's trapped in an unsettling dream.

Donning a pair of shades, he steps into the glaring desert sun, a lone figure navigating the desolate Sahara. To any observer—not that there are any all the way out here in the barren desert—it would appear that the man in the nice suit is walking out of a small military compound. One made up of nothing more than a single stone building where two guards block a turnstile that leads to nothing more than a set of elevator doors. Not a five story underground facility built by the Russians during the Soviet era and reestablished ten years ago under the Putin administration.

Upon starting his car, the radio crackles to life. It is filled with news reports on the imminent scrap that's about to happen in Khartoum, an added layer of tension on all of this. But the real news, of course, isn't out yet.

A minute later, as the compound recedes in his rearview mirror, Ibrahim hastily dials a number on the burner phone.

"Okay," he utters as soon as the call is answered. "I got it."

"Good," comes Ben Knight's succinct reply. "Now get the host and meet the extraction team at the airfield. And Ibrahim?"

"What?"

"You're a good man. Remember that."

His voice chokes with emotion. "Tell that to my family if they die because of me."

———

MILITARY TRUCKS BELONGING to the army rampage down the streets of Khartoum, as they have for almost a week now. The rebel Rapid Security Forces (RSF) are now entering parts of the city, all guns pointed on the good folk of Khartoum.

Ibrahim makes it back much quicker than usual. Ordinarily, the drive takes about an hour over the rough, gravel road. But today the needle doesn't drop below a hundred, the sharp din of gravel hitting the car's undercarriage a mere whisper against the clamor of his immediate worries.

Shaking his head, he looks up into the rearview mirror, casting an eye over his reflection. This is not how his life is supposed to be.

Dr. Ibrahim Bol is a towering figure, owning a mind as vast as the Sudanese savannah he hails from. A child prodigy who traded the dusty landscapes of Sudan for the esteemed halls of Cambridge, England, his genius is both his identity and an enigma. Thriving on the adrenaline of scientific discovery, Bol's relentless pursuit has led him to the uncharted realms of symbiotic research. His theories, once considered audacious, now thrive under the watch of his paymasters: the Russian Federation. With their money and the use of Facility Fifty-Five, he has changed how we view bacteria and its relation to man, turning them from simple organisms into allies, partners, potential saviors—or potential killers.

Once past the White Nile, the inevitable clog of traffic he meets in the inner city presents a maddening obstacle. He stares helplessly at the obstinate knot of smoking, honking vehicles. Fear like a relentless tide washes over him, bringing back the trembling. It's as if his blood is boiling in his veins.

A few blocks into the city, his wife's call pierces his anxious reverie.

"Amira?"

"Ibrahim, have you finished work yet?"

"Yes. Did you gather the children as I asked?"

"That's what I wanted to talk to you about. I forgot that Leila is at your parents' place today."

Ibrahim goes cold. Frustration flares. "I asked you to keep Leila at home," he retorts, the unexpected fissure in his plans threatening to widen.

"But she's only around the corner at your parents', Ibrahim. I can go pick her up now."

"No!" The word snaps out, frantic, his fear spiraling. "Don't leave the house. I'll pick her up. Stay put. Do not leave the house."

Just as he's about to disconnect, she breaks the silence.

"I know I've asked repeatedly," she says, "and you've told me not to worry repeatedly, but please, Ibrahim—what's going on?"

"I promise you, by the end of the night, my love, everything will be clear. For now, I need you to trust me."

He ends the call, fear constricting his stomach like a coiled snake. Sweat trickles down his face, even with the BMW's air conditioning going at full whack.

Navigating through a tangle of city traffic, Ibrahim reaches his parents' house in a lonely suburb on the outskirts. As he steps into their living room, guided by the maid, his mother's words puncture the tension-laden air. "You look terrible," she says.

Her face is etched with worry. Deep furrows accentuate her normally wrinkled brow. The television plays in the background, its screen displaying an ominous collection of images: army convoys, rebel soldiers, armored vehicles encircling the city, embassy evacuations. Lines of foreigners are shown boarding planes at Khartoum Airport, a last-ditch effort to escape before General Hemedti and his men storm the capital.

"Did you hear me?" his mother repeats, her voice piercing the room.

He shifts his gaze from the television to meet her anxious eyes. "I'm okay," he reassures her.

"Well, you don't look it. You're ill."

"Mom, please," Ibrahim groans. "I'm in a hurry. Where's Leila?"

Sighing loudly like she always does when she's annoyed, she replies, "In the garden with Papa."

She then guides him outdoors, into the vibrant embrace of the sun. They discover his father tucked away within the confines of a quaint greenhouse, diligently tending to a tomato plant. Beside him, Ibrahim's daughter, Leila, is playing her part in this humble act of cultivation. With an innocence only a child possesses, she assists her grandfather in repotting the plant, her small hands busily scooping in heaps of soil around the base, while the old man carefully supports the plant's delicate stem.

"Leila," Ibrahim calls out. "We need to leave right now."

The tiny girl raises her gaze, and her face brightens with joy.

"Papa!" she squeals.

Abandoning her task, she bounds over, the dirt from her small hands transferring onto his clothes as she throws her arms around him in an affectionate embrace.

"We need to get going," Ibrahim tells her as she pulls away to look up at him. "Your mother is waiting."

"Are you leaving so soon?" his father inquires, hoisting himself upright from his bent position. "Won't you stay for a cup of tea?"

The words hit Ibrahim like a ton of bricks. A thick lump forms in his throat. This will probably be his last encounter with his father. It wasn't supposed to be this way.

"I'm sorry, Papa," he says. "But Amira has dinner on the table, and you know how she is about being late."

His father smiles and nods, understanding a husband's plight.

With an urgency coursing through him, Ibrahim shepherds Leila out of the house and into his waiting BMW. As they drive away, he doesn't even check his mirrors to see his mother waving them off from the driveway.

A minute later, the sound of Leila's nursery rhymes fills the air of the car, a welcome respite from the grim news updates of the impending civil war. It is, however, in the midst of her singing and dancing that a call comes in. It's Amira, her voice trembling as she whispers into the phone. The words "They have guns" are followed by a short, snatched scream before a male voice takes over the line.

The stranger's voice paralyzes Ibrahim with fear.

"Ibrahim Bol?" he says. "If this is you, come home. Your family needs you."

The line goes dead, leaving Ibrahim in a state of terror, feeling like he's falling out of the sky.

Quickly composing himself, he stops the car at the side of the road and turns to his daughter. "Leila," he says as she stares at him, "do you know the way to Grandma and Grandpa's from here?"

The little girl nods.

"Are you sure?" he says sternly, giving her that look he gives Leila and her brothers if he thinks they may be lying.

She crosses her heart with a finger, a familiar tactic.

"How?" he asks to be sure.

She points behind them. "The alley. It takes you right there."

Ibrahim knows for sure she's done the journey with her mother and brothers a thousand times already in her seven years.

"Then I need you to go there. Not now!" he adds quickly as her hand snatches at the door handle.

She turns back to him.

"First," he adds, "I need you to trust me. Do you trust me?"

Leila nods immediately.

Ibrahim retrieves the case from under his seat and opens it. He removes the vial, looking at it a second or two. It is more than a liquid; it is the culmination of years of research, a microscopic army in a sea of hope. His fingers tremble as he takes a syringe and draws the precious cargo into it. All the while, the girl's big brown eyes stare at it.

"Leila," her father's soothing voice says, "I need to inject this into you."

"But I hate needles," the girl whines.

"I know. But you have to be brave." Looking her in the eyes, his expression as soft as he can make it, he says, "Can you be brave for Daddy?"

Her lip quivers, but she nods.

"That's my girl. It's going to be just like when Doctor Hammed gave you your shots. Okay?"

Another nod.

Ibrahim takes a deep breath. Every scientific principle he stands by, every ethical boundary he respects is now blurred in the face of a father's love. His gaze meets Leila's, her dark eyes wide and trusting. She understands little of her importance, only that she sometimes has to go to the lab to be tested.

As the needle pierces Leila's skin, she winces, a soft whimper escaping her lips. Ibrahim's own breath hitches in sympathy, the anxiety etched deep in his furrowed brow. There is no turning back now.

As the needle slides free, a solitary bead of crimson emerges. Tenderly, Ibrahim wipes Leila's arm, soothing the pinprick wound.

"You really are Daddy's brave girl," he tells her. "Now you must go straight to Grandmama and Grandpa's. Do not stop. Do not look back. I am counting on you, Leila."

They hug one last time, and she leaves the car, Ibrahim watching her disappear into the alley.

Alone now, he takes a deep breath, his heart heavy in his chest, and makes a call on his mobile.

"They know," he says when it is answered. "They are already at my house."

"Where are you?"

"Around the corner."

"Then turn around right now."

"I can't. They have my wife. If I don't show up, I'll be condemning her to death."

"But we need the bacteria sample. The host. Without it, we're blind. This will..."

"Knight!" Ibrahim snaps. "I have placed the bacteria into the host. I pray that my research is correct and that her unique genome will bind with the bacteria and give us the protein. If not, I have sentenced her to death."

"Who is the host?"

"It is my own daughter," Ibrahim replies, an element of regret in his voice. "She will be with my parents, Mustafa and Fatima Bol. Their address is 101 Al Abdi, Um Dalil. You need to move fast."

"Okay. I'll have the extraction team head there now. But I also need you to turn around right this minute. Go to your parents. Stay with your daughter. Wait for my team. Because we're going to need you, Dr. Bol."

"I'm sorry. I have to be with my wife."

And with that, Ibrahim Bol ends the call, swallowing down a dry lump.

A minivan is parked in his driveway as he walks on shaky legs to his front door. The oppressive heat and his overwhelming fear make him drop his keys multiple times along the way. As he enters the house, he's immediately seized by two waiting men, roughly hauled across his own hallway, and tossed onto the living room rug.

His wife is on the couch, sitting there in infinite terror. Ibrahim lands awkwardly on his knees, his eyes fixing instantly on her bruised, tear-drenched face. There is a man standing menacingly behind her who draws Ibrahim's attention. The man's red beret signals his affiliation with the Rapid Security Forces (RSF). Once a militia called the Janjaweed with links to the army, they are now in full rebellion for control of the country.

"Ibrahim Bol," the man announces in a threatening tone as he produces a piece of paper. "You have been placed upon a list."

Confusion sweeps over Ibrahim. "A list? What list?"

"A list of men who have betrayed Sudan. Whores of al-Bashir. Whores of al-Burhan. Betrayers of Sudan."

"You're not from the lab?"

The rebel commander furrows his brow at him.

"Did the Russians send you?" Ibrahim asks next.

The man shakes his head. Pointing to the ceiling, he says, "God sent me. To revenge his people." Flapping the paper, he adds, "You have been found guilty of betraying the people of Sudan by working with its former government. By using your intellect for your own benefit while your people live in poverty."

"This *isn't* about the lab?"

"No, Mr. Bol. This is about your work for our corrupt government."

"But I was only an advisor. I was never in the government. I never even received payment from them. I work for the Russians."

"And yet you are still on this list," the man in the beret says, rattling the paper.

"And so what? I'm under arrest?" Ibrahim ventures, hoping against hope for a relatively benign outcome. But as the man rises and gestures to his men, a cold realization dawns on him. The men raise their AKs, and the room fills with a chilling proclamation.

"You, Ibrahim Bol," the man in the beret declares, "have been found guilty of treason!"

"No! Wait!" Ibrahim yells, but it's too late. The men cock their weapons and let loose a volley of bullets. As his wife screams, the leader steps aside, and the men turn their smoking guns on her, transforming the two of them into bullet-riddled flesh.

———

At the edge of a dirt runway on the outskirts of Khartoum, four figures clad in tactical gear stand resolute against the biting onslaught of sand and heat. A Lockheed Martin C-130J Super Hercules, a monolith of gunmetal gray, stretches out behind them.

Bulging veins trace paths of anticipation along the men's sun-kissed forearms, hands tightly gripping the lightweight, battle-tested bodies of M4 Carbines. They stand there like silent statues, their minds and hearts racing with the pulse of the mission, ebbing and flowing with each tick of the unseen clock.

This is Ben Knight's extraction team.

The omens are poor: Trouble is coming. As the horizon swallows the dying embers of the day, a brewing desert storm of dust and dread is closing in on the airfield, painting the vast sky a muddy swirl of browns and grays.

A call comes through on their Iridium 9575 Extreme satellite phone, but due to the storm, the line is bad. Its static-laced message scratches against the eardrums of Jameson, the extraction leader, as he presses his ear to the speaker and frowns, getting only fragmented words like "city," "target down," "retrieve," "daughter"—the words ghosting through the airwaves. The frown etching its way onto Jameson's face mirrors his confusion, the half-understood message doing nothing to alleviate the tension that has them all on a razor's edge.

"Repeat that, base. I didn't get it all."

His request for clarity hangs unanswered, swallowed by a relentless torrent of static—which is then interrupted by the sharp, distinctive crack of a sniper's bullet that slices through the gloom and finds its mark: Jameson.

As soon as the bullet hits, the rest of the team knows they're in deep trouble. Blood spouts like a fountain from the hole in Jameson's neck, his body collapsing heavily onto the hard dirt of the ground. The dust it kicks up swirls into the air.

"Move, move!" Alvarez, the point man, shouts, the urgency in his voice betraying his usually calm demeanor. The two other remaining men, Turner and Castillo, react immediately. All three of them half-crawl, half-run toward the yawning mouth of the Hercules' rear.

They scramble into the cover of the ramp as the thunderous barks of AK-47 gunfire, the weapon of choice for the RSF, fill the air, the bullets ricocheting off the Hercules' reinforced steel body, each one a deadly echo in the night.

Turner, a hulk of a man with biceps that look like they could rip the wings off a plane, turns back to provide cover fire, his M249 SAW light machine gun coughing out rounds. Castillo, the team's medic, drags Jameson's lifeless body up the ramp, his face a mask of determination and fear.

"Get us the hell out of here!" he screams into the mic of his comms, the words barely discernible over the cacophony of gunfire. The pilot, a seasoned vet, doesn't need to be told twice. The four engines of the Hercules burst into life, a monstrous crescendo that drowns out the ongoing firefight.

The plane shudders as it lurches forward, the wheels straining under the load. The heat of the engines kicks up a dust cloud, which combines with the incoming storm and reduces visibility to near zero. But the pilot has done this a hundred times. He knows what he's doing.

Suddenly, a convoy of rebel pickups materializes from the dust, men riding on the backs of them, balaclavas over their faces, guns blazing as they lean them on the rooftops of the cabs. Bullets ping off the plane's fuselage, each one a reminder of the deadly threat they are under. But the Hercules, as if alive and defiant, thunders down the runway.

Within moments, the plane is airborne, the ground falling away beneath them. The relentless gunfire follows them all the way up, a few bullets managing to find their mark on the underside of the plane as it rises beyond their reach. And they are away. They've escaped the jaws of death, leaving behind the chaos of the battlefield and an extraction mission gone terribly wrong.

As they glide into storm-ridden sky, Castillo lifts the radio to his mouth, his voice raw and ragged. "We're aborting! Repeat, we're aborting!"

FOUR

CIA HEADQUARTERS, LANGLEY, VIRGINIA, USA - 14TH APRIL, 11:07 (EDT)

OVER SEVEN THOUSAND MILES AWAY ACROSS THE Atlantic Ocean, Ben Knight finds himself anchored to a chair in a sterile conference room, his mind reeling from the disastrous turn of events. His hopes of retrieving the girl any time soon have just crumbled to dust. His big hope after losing Ibrahim was that the extraction team would enter the city and retrieve everything. Now that, too, is in ruins.

Director Sandy McLean, a formidable woman even in her stillness, exclaims beside him, "What just happened, Knight?" The words reverberate in the high-ceilinged room.

Her usually chalk-white complexion now appears ghostly, as though the stress of the situation has leeched away the last vestiges of color from her face.

Knight's gaze locks on to the high-tech digital wall map showing hotspots around the globe, the LED marker over

Khartoum pulsing. He forces himself back from the precipice of despair, reigniting his resolve. His voice cuts through the stifling silence, steely yet measured. "Okay," he starts, eyes fixed to the map, "I've got someone nearby, currently on assignment just over the border in Egypt. I can have him in Sudan by dusk."

McLean's gaze locks on to Knight's, her icy blue eyes reflecting the gravity of the situation. With a grim nod, she replies, "Then for God's sake, Knight, make it happen. Time isn't on our side."

———

PORT SUDAN, Sudan.
14th April, 20:06 (EAT).

THREE HOURS LATER, the salty brine of the Red Sea fills the dark air as a small cargo boat makes its discreet entry into the murky waters of Port Sudan under the cover of night. Perched at the bow, CIA operative Kamal Osman's hardened gaze overlooks the bustling port, the glow of his burner phone the only light that illuminates his grim face.

With the device pressed to his ear, his deep baritone cuts through the rhythmic lapping of the waves against the boat's hull as it motors into port. "Knight, I'm in," he relays into the receiver. "Almost at the port now. My contact will be waiting for me in town."

"Who is he?"

"Hashim Iqbal. Nicknamed the Rat. I've worked with him before."

"Can you trust him?" comes the cautious inquiry from Ben Knight, thousands of miles away.

The briefest of smiles curls at the corner of Osman's lips. "Can you ever trust a man with a nickname like the Rat?"

"Then it could be too risky to involve him," Knight suggests.

"No. I need his knowledge of the place and his contacts. Plus, Hashim's got a nose for money. He's loyal to that. As long as I can keep the faucet running, he won't bite."

"Does he know you're Agency?"

"Not a chance. The little bastard would want a higher price if he knew that. No, he thinks I'm a journalist."

"Good," Knight says. "Keep your cover at all times."

"I will." Kamal's voice betrays his nervousness. He knows how important this mission is. His biggest yet. By a long, long way.

Ahead, the port city begins to separate from the darkness. Swirling dust particles catch the scattered floodlights, creating an almost ethereal haze around the dockyard as they motor toward a distant quay.

"I know you mostly work surveillance, Kamal," Knight goes on. "But so long as you don't catch too much heat, this should be relatively simple. Think of it as a classic package pickup job."

"But if it does get violent, sir, I am ready."

"I know, son. I know."

"I've done my time on the range."

"And your scores are good. But you're relatively new to this, Kamal. Two years in surveillance won't have fully prepared you for what you're about to find in Sudan."

"It looks pretty peaceful from here."

Unlike Khartoum, there are no crackles of gunfire, no thud of bombs. Port Sudan is still under the control of the Sudanese Armed Forces (SAF), the regular army. The RSF are all currently in the west, away from the coast. Instead of gunfire and explosions, the discordant racket of honking vehicles, metallic clangs of cranes loading and unloading ships, and human voices emanate from the bustling port.

"Remember." Knight's voice breathes in his ear. "Keep as low a profile as you can, trust this Rat guy only with the bare essentials, and get to the package. Contact me then, and we'll make arrangements for extraction. I don't need to tell you what we have riding on this, Kamal. Good luck."

"Thank you, sir."

The call disconnects with a low beep, the sound swallowed by the noise of the vast dock around him. Now nearing the end of the journey, Kamal moves to gather his belongings, ready to blend into the city's fabric.

He steps off the boat onto the worn wooden planks of the quay, papers clutched in his hand. British passport under the name Daniel Burns. A borrowed identity in a dangerous land. Two soldiers block the stone steps of the harbor wall. They give him cursory glances, his unassuming demeanor matching the BBC press pass he flashes at them.

Kamal is soon out of the dock, disappearing into the heart of the shadow-laden alleys. A few blocks on, the pulsating neon blue lights of a small café appear, a peculiar oasis in a pitch-black street with no streetlamps. He strides into the establishment, his eyes quickly adapting to the dim interior.

A figure rises from the far corner booth, the wisp of his cigarette smoke and a sly grin the only visible features. He's tall and athletic, but not bulky. He walks over, and Kamal stretches out a hand, meeting the other's firm grip. "Hashim," he greets.

The man nods, a glint in his eyes. "Or the Rat," he corrects, the nickname rolling off his tongue like a well-worn tale.

"Whatever you prefer," Kamal states.

"Call me what you want, so long as you pay me. Which reminds me: Where's the first payment?"

Kamal eyes the handful of men sitting in the café drinking tea.

"Don't worry about them," Hashim says. "They are friends."

"Can we at least sit down?"

"Sure, sure."

At the booth, Kamal places the rucksack on the table. As he unzips it, he glances left at the café owner and his two other customers. They are all staring straight at them.

Sighing, he pulls out a thousand dollars wrapped in plastic. He hands the money over, Hashim practically snatching it.

"You'll get another thousand when we reach Khartoum," Kamal says as Hashim counts the money. "It's all in five-dollar denominations, like you requested."

"Good. Good. Larger bills attract suspicion that they have been forged."

"The rest of the money," Kamal goes on, "will be..."

Hashim has a hand up. "Yes, yes. You explained on the telephone. Not until you're out of the country will I get all the money."

"Right. So, anyway," Kamal adds, glancing around, "I told you I was in a hurry. So we need to go."

Pocketing the money, Hashim gets up, and the two men leave the café to climb into a dust-ridden, beaten-up Toyota pickup. The engine coughs to life, and just like that, they ride off into the night, Khartoum another eight hours of driving away. That is, of course, if they don't run into trouble—and currently, Sudan is a whole lot of trouble.

———

AND SO IT BEGINS.

In Paris, Antoine finds himself guided by the GPS on his phone. It leads him thirty miles away from the French capital's urban sprawl and into the tranquil depth of the remote woodland of Fontainebleau, a shovel over his shoulder. Now involved in the single most important thing of his entire existence, his ordinary life as a fast-food worker seems a lifetime away.

In Dubai, Hamid strides confidently into a nondescript apartment building on the edge of the city, a large tool bag slung over his shoulder. A key grants him access. Inside, he descends to the basement and into the boiler room, the drone of machinery filling the air. Without a moment's hesitation, he pulls an electric jackhammer from the bag, plugs it in, and begins to break apart the concrete floor.

In São Paulo, under the cover of darkness, Helena stands waist-deep in a hole at the center of a deserted park. The rhythmic sound of her shovel digging into the earth fills the quiet night. Suddenly, she strikes something hard, metallic. Her eyebrows rise in expectation.

In Sydney, Liam hauls a heavy metal container from a hole in a plot of derelict land on the edge of the Sydney Basin. With a rag, he wipes away years of accumulated dirt from it, revealing its once gleaming surface.

Across the Pacific in Atlanta, Jackson, the former cop, carefully opens a similar container while kneeling next to a freshly dug hole. Inside, cushioned in protective foam, several clear glass tubes nestle. Pulling one out, he holds it up to the beam of his flashlight, his eyes narrowed as he scrutinizes the seemingly harmless object. It appears empty, housing nothing more than air, but this, Jackson knows, is untrue.

Back in Paris, Antoine emerges from the woodland, the heavy metal container secure in his grip. He stows it away on the backseat of his car, his glance repeatedly returning to its reflection in the rearview mirror as he drives off.

All the way in Dubai, Hamid, now covered in concrete dust, drives with an identical metal container secured on his passenger seat. His journey, mirrored by those of his unseen comrades, continues undeterred.

In Sydney, as Liam pulls into a motel parking lot, a towering airliner roars overhead, signifying his proximity to Sydney Airport. The thunderous sound punctures the silent anticipation of his mission.

In Atlanta, Jackson sits on the edge of a motel bed, the room lit only by the distant glow of runway lights shining in through the window. He gazes out of it, his eyes following the planes as they take off from Atlanta airport, the glass tube still in his hand.

He glances down at it. X-9. That's what they call it. Part of Jackson's training was to study video files on the virus so that he knew full well what was inside those tubes. In them, a scientist explained all about the virus and what it did.

Upon entering a host's body, X-9 selectively infects neurons inside the brain and spinal cord. The viral payload includes genes that, when integrated into the host's DNA, cause a massive overproduction of certain neurotransmitters, leading to neuronal hyperactivity and disruption of normal brain function. The host initially experiences flu-like symptoms, such as fever, chills, and fatigue, making the virus hard to identify in the early stages. As it progresses, the host then begins to experience severe headaches, hallucinations, loss of motor control, and eventually paralysis. This then leads to respiratory failure as the neurons controlling the lungs become overwhelmed. The host doesn't last any more than three weeks after infection.

The reason he has to know this is because he will himself invariably become infected by it. At some point during the next week as he travels the world, he will begin to show symptoms.

But Jackson doesn't care. Looking up from the vial as the lights from another plane flood the motel window, he smiles. Soon, like the others, he will be making history.

From the ordinary to the extraordinary, these once unassuming lives have pivoted on an axis, set into motion by one narcissist's need to avenge himself upon a world that rejects him. As the Earth continues to turn on its axis with the entire population oblivious to the gravity of their actions, the dragon stirs, unseen, yet increasingly present.

FIVE

Perched on a Madrid rooftop, Peter lies in wait, nestled behind a Barrett M82, the sniper rifle a cold, weighty presence in his hands. Below, the city buzzes with life, oblivious to the unfolding drama high above.

Through his scope, Peter watches a two-story house hidden from the street by a high wall—essentially a compound. It is an anomaly amidst the otherwise serene neighborhood of La Latina. The neighboring houses, vacant shells of what they used to be, stand on either side of it in silence.

Peter's crosshairs wander over the worn façade of the house, skimming past wooden shutters and cracked windows until he settles them on a balcony, a set of bead curtains open on to the room beyond.

Inside, three men with long, inky black beards are gathered around a cluttered table. Their hands move with a practiced, chilling efficiency, their attention laser-focused on the task before them. They're assembling a bomb. The casing, already laden with packed explosives, waits open. One of them meticulously wires the trigger mechanism while the others prepare the deadly shrapnel, pieces of scrap metal and nails, that will magnify the devastation when the bomb goes off.

Peter's finger rests lightly on the trigger, a whispered promise of violence. But not yet. He's waiting for one man in particular, their leader, a man by the name of Ali Hossain. This is Hossain's party, and every tick of the second hand on Peter's wristwatch resonates in his ear as he waits for the main man to arrive.

Without warning, a soft buzz rumbles in his earpiece. He tenses, his gaze never wavering from the scene unfolding through the scope.

"Azrael," comes the icy voice of Ben Knight. "Update?"

"Anticipating contact," Peter murmurs, the compound's view held in the crosshairs of his rifle.

Knight's voice crackles again. "Expected time?"

As if summoned by the question, a sleek black Range Rover emerges around the corner. It fits the intel on Hossain's preferred mode of transport. "Possibly moments," Peter whispers.

"That's good," Knight shouts, "because I've got something much bigger for you."

Peter's gaze locks on the Range Rover slowing by the compound's gate. "What?"

"I need you in Sudan."

"What's in Sudan?" Peter asks as the Range Rover accelerates, bypassing the compound. It's not Hossain. He relaxes.

"Two hours ago," Knight's voice cuts in, "an agent of mine was entering Khartoum to retrieve something very important when he went cold. He was supposed to call in via his burner, but the burner is now switched off."

"GPS?"

"Dead."

Peter arches an eyebrow at this just as two men round a corner on foot about fifty meters from the compound. He removes his crosshairs from the bomb makers, drops them on the two men, and searches their faces. "Doesn't sound good," he says, releasing his breath when he realizes neither man is Ali Hossain.

"No. It's not," Knight says. "Not when the package he went in to retrieve is just about the most important thing in the world right now."

"What is it?"

"A little girl."

Peter frowns. "A little girl?"

"Look, I'll brief you on the plane. Get your ass to the airport. Leave the job you're on. This has top priority. I repeat..."

Knight's words fade into the background. The white Mercedes that is creeping into the street matches the description of another one of Hossain's cars, and the man inside matches Hossain, though the baseball cap and sunglasses make a positive ID impossible.

"Just give me two minutes," Peter breathes.

"I need you to pack up Madrid now. Get to the airport."

Peter goes to say something when the Mercedes stops at

the gate. A figure steps out from the car and walks up to it, opening the thing so that it whines on its hinges. Peter's finger tightens around the trigger. It's Hossain. "See you soon. Azrael out."

His gaze doesn't waver from the target as he ends the call. The sounds of the city reemerge: the hum of traffic, distant chatter, cicadas singing in the night. His crosshairs follow Hossain as he enters the building, then follow his journey along the cracked stucco until he appears in the living room via the balcony. That's when Peter's crosshairs land on the bomb resting on the table. Hossain is in sight. He breathes in, holds it, and then...

The compound explodes, shattering the night's relative tranquility. The ensuing chaos is deafening as a thousand car alarms go off at once. As dust rises, obscuring the moon, Peter has already disassembled his rifle. Vanishing into the night, the next task is already on his mind: Sudan.

SIX

THE MISSION IS ON. HAVING SPREAD ALI HOSSAIN and his fellow jihadis across a four-block radius in Madrid's La Latina district, Peter hopped on a motorbike and rode to the airport, where he boarded a Lockheed MC-130, the plane of choice for the traveling CIA operative. Next move is to disembark at Abéché Airport in Chad and board a C-23 Sherpa run by a private company that flies internally in East Africa. That way he won't arouse suspicions that he's CIA when he lands inside neighboring Sudan. That would draw the attention of the Russians, who are sure to be watching.

Right now, he's being briefed by Ben Knight as they fly to Chad for the plane exchange. High above the pharaohs, the hulking military aircraft cuts through thick clouds. Inside, the dimly lit cabin resonates with the low hum of engines. Peter's cold eyes are riveted on a dossier, while Ben Knight sits opposite.

Knight leans forward in his seat, briefing Peter with a sense of urgency that ripples through his gravelly voice. "Have you ever heard of the Aurora Abyss project?"

"Can't say I have," Peter replies, looking up from an aerial satellite image of a small compound in the middle of the desert.

"The Aurora Abyss project," Knight states with robotic precision, "is a relic from the Soviet era in which underground labs were built in proxy nations. It was a way for the Russians to keep an outbreak away from the homeland."

"So what?" Peter says, looking down at the photo. "That's what this is?"

"Yes. That's Facility Fifty-Five in Sudan. They engineer viruses there. About a month ago, we received intelligence about a new, potentially catastrophic viral strain that they had developed at that lab. They call it X-9."

"And what—the Russians are going to release it?"

Knight's reply chills the air of the plane's cabin. "They already have. Backed into a corner in Ukraine, Putin has chosen this as his most desirable form of backlash. More discreet than nuclear weapons."

"Surely you can stop it?"

"We've been unable to fully infiltrate their network of sleeper agents," Knight tells him. "We found a few, but we're sure as many as five still exist."

"And, what, these sleepers are currently..."

"Dispersing X-9."

A stretched few seconds follow as Peter ponders this. Then, "The mission?"

Knight sighs. "We had a man on the inside. The same man who designed X-9 for the Russians before his conscience woke up. He was to be extracted with his family, but..."

"But what?"

"He was killed during the RSF attack on Khartoum."

"Bummer," Peter remarks dryly.

"Then, with the rebels and the army both bombing anything out of the sky around the city, my extraction team only managed to escape by the skin of their teeth. So with Sudan a no-fly zone, I had to send someone in by foot. My nearest guy was just over the border in Egypt monitoring an al-Qaeda cell in Shalateen."

"Wait," Peter stops him. "Monitoring? Do you mean to say he was working a reconnaissance job?"

"Yes. Kamal was, I mean is surveillance."

"You sent a watcher into a war zone for a high value package extraction?"

"I had no choice," Knight says as he sits in the dim lights of the Lockheed MC-130. "My original extraction team had been attacked, my contact was down, and the package was somewhat lost."

"And now he's missing, along with the package."

"Yes," Knight replies, his pallid face going glum.

"What do you know about his last moments?"

"He used a local to get him into Khartoum," Knight explains. "Met him in Port Sudan. They traveled together from there. He made contact once they arrived in the city. The fighting was pretty strong, and they had to continue on foot as army checkpoints were stopping all vehicles."

"Who's the local?"

"Page thirteen," Knight tells him.

Peter flicks through the dossier until he reaches the

mugshot of a dark-skinned Sudanese with a scraggly beard and a mean look.

"Hashim 'the Rat' Iqbal," Knight says.

"Sounds like a trustworthy guy," Peter comments dryly.

"He'd probably steal the tits off his own mother if he could get a price. It looks like he may have double-crossed my man."

"I'd say that was highly likely."

Peter flicks the pages past Hashim 'the Rat' Iqbal and lands on the picture of a seven-year-old girl with big eyes and braided hair. "This the package?"

Knight nods. "Yeah. That's her. Listen—" His voice becomes a low, gravelly whisper. "She is more important than you can ever imagine."

Peter places the file beside him, sits back, and folds his arms, his face inscrutable. "I've been wondering what a little girl has to do with all of this."

"And I'm about to tell you."

"I'm all ears."

"Leila, she… she's special. Her father, Ibrahim Bol, was the mastermind behind the symbiotic research of viruses. Of how we come to live alongside them. Bol created a unique strain of bacteria that can live in harmony within a human host. Symbio-B, they called it."

"And this Symbio-B has something to do with the cure for X-9?"

"More than just something. It *is* the cure. You see, this bacteria produces a protein, Protein Zeta. It's the only thing that can neutralize X-9. And it works as both a cure and a vaccine."

Peter frowns. "And the girl? Leila?"

"Leila is the key. Bol performed gene therapy on her, his own daughter, in Facility Fifty-Five, no less. He made her a host for Symbio-B—one of the only people in the world capable of hosting it because of her unique genetic code. In other people, it dies, but in Leila, the bacteria thrives, and she... she can produce Protein Zeta."

"But why a child? Why his daughter?"

"That's where it gets twisted. You see, the Russians... they wanted to control the vaccine."

"And Leila is their insurance?"

"No. Leila is *our* insurance."

Peter is yet again arching an eyebrow.

"Let me explain," Knight says. "The Russians have produced their own hosts. They'll be using them in Russia to produce Protein Zeta. Keeping it to themselves and happy in the knowledge that the rest of the world can't synthesize a vaccine or a cure. Eventually, when the rest of us are on our knees, they'll claim a miracle breakthrough and offer to sell us the vaccine."

"And I'm guessing the price for that will be Ukraine?"

"Oh," Knight begins, his voice grave, "it will be much more than just Ukraine."

"So when you said Leila was our insurance, you meant that Dr. Bol produced her separately?"

"Yes. At great risk to himself, he made sure that the rest of the world would have the ability to fight X-9."

"And now that ability is lost somewhere in the middle of a civil war."

"Yes."

Peter is silent for a long time, his mind grappling with

the enormity of it all. "We have to find her. We have to keep her safe."

Knight nods. "We do. Because right now, that little girl is the most important person in the world."

Peter picks the file back up and flicks the last few pages.

"This my in?" he asks, holding the page up.

It is a photocopy of an advertisement placed on the dark web by a man named Frank. Frank runs a securities company based out of Africa—essentially running a team of mercenaries.

"Yes. I managed to get you a job. See, whatever has happened out there, it's brought Hashim the Rat to the attention of someone willing to pay this guy Frank a lot of money to catch him alive. An hour ago, we intercepted chatter between several groups of mercenaries working out in east Africa. Someone has placed a hundred thousand US dollar price on the Rat's head, and every hunter in the area has homed in."

"And I'm to be one of them," Peter muses aloud.

"That's right. Whatever happened to Kamal and the girl, he knows about it. And the guys you'll be meeting with have already secured a location on him. It won't be long before they've gotten him."

SEVEN

SAYYAH, NUBIAN DESERT, SUDAN REPUBLIC - 15TH APRIL, 10:11 (EAT)

UNDER THE MERCILESS, WHITE-HOT GLARE OF THE Nubian sun, a solitary pickup truck carves a straight line across a vast, sun-scorched sea of sand, leaving in its wake a plume of dust that billows and twists in the wind. Ahead of it, jutting from the barren landscape, is the only thing to break up the monotony of the flat desert for at least fifty miles. A mosque, ancient and crumbling, stands in quiet dignity, its once grand minarets now no more than gnarled teeth pointing skyward. The modest building is a testament to a forgotten time when devout miners from a nearby nickel mine would emerge from underground to worship inside.

The truck skids to a halt at the edge of the mosque, stirring up a dust cloud that temporarily shrouds the vehicle. The men inside remain still for a moment, swallowed by the heat and the pulsating silence of the desert. The anticipation in the cab is as thick as the dry air. Then, as if stirred by some unseen conductor, they move. Doors creak open, and the three men emerge, silhouetted against the harsh desert light.

Each man carries a SIG MPX carbine, the compact firearm a brutal contrast against the austere beauty of their surroundings. Their leader, a lean, predatory figure with eyes that reflect the harshness of the desert, lifts a gloved hand and signals, his movements sharp and precise, slicing through the oppressive heat. His comrades respond, their training taking over, and they fan out, circling the mosque with grim determination, their boots grinding against the sun-bleached stone, their figures swallowed by the mosque's cavernous shadow.

One by one, they circle the structure, moving with deadly elegance. The only sound belongs to their cushioned footfalls and the occasional whisper of wind sweeping up against the decaying stone of the mosque. With each step, they trace the perimeter until they reach the main door, a weathered wooden entrance barely hanging on its rusted hinges.

Without exchanging a single word, the men take positions on either side of the door, their bodies rigid, their MPXs tight to their shoulders, the carbines extensions of their intent. With the leader's final nod, they push through, filing into the mosque's mysterious interior.

The sunlight barely reaches within, making the rooms almost pitch black, the interior swallowing them into a cavernous belly, filled with darkness that throbs with unseen threats. They move through the rooms with precision, their eyes rapidly adjusting to the dim light. The air is much cooler in the mosque, the stone floor cold beneath their boots, each room filled with a heavy silence that is as comforting as it is intimidating.

One by one, they reach the prayer room.

The grand chamber, once a place of tranquility and devotion, now lies silent and desolate, draped in shadows and layered with years of desert dust. A few prayer mats lie scattered about. The mihrab is half fallen down, its detailing faded and worn.

Their breaths shallow, they step lightly, their every move charged with a deadly grace, their SIG MPXs sweeping across the room in methodical arcs.

The place seems deserted, but it can't be. Their intel said he would be here. The Rat would be here.

Suddenly, a creaking sound ruptures the silence, like a scream in the void. The men freeze, every muscle, every nerve tensed to its limit. The sound comes again: It is above them. They pivot, their gazes shooting upwards, their weapons following suit, their eyes tracing the wooden beams, scanning the dim outline of the ceiling.

And there he is: the Rat. Perched up in the rafters, waiting, silent and invisible, until now. His hands grip the cold steel of two pistols, a grin playing on his lips as he stares down at them, his intentions as clear as the desert sky outside.

In the mere split of a second, the men are outgunned. Even as they start to lift their weapons, the man in the rafters beats them to the punch. He takes advantage of his aerial position and pulls the triggers of his twin pistols, the deafening reports ricocheting off the walls of the mosque.

His aim is lethal. The first man is hit square in the neck,

the bullet tearing through flesh and vital vessels, the sudden gush of blood hitting the dusty floor. He falls, his body crumpling in a hushed thud as the life ebbs out of him, replaced by the inevitable cold grip of death.

Another round meets the second man, a devastating blow to his cheek and throat. He barely has time to register the shock, the pain, before his world fades into obscurity. The brutal efficiency of the strike robs him of his life almost instantaneously, his body toppling over onto the worn stone floor.

The third attempts a desperate lunge for cover. But the Rat's bullets are quicker, remorseless. Three shots rip through his side, shoulder, and lower back, forcing a strangled gasp from his lips as he stumbles onto his front, blood staining his clothes and the ground beneath him.

With the grace of a panther, the Rat drops from the rafters, landing softly on the cold stone floor, only a pair of beady eyes poking from beneath his blue litham, a cloth veil that is wrapped in the local Sudanese style to protect their nasal and oral cavities from the invasive desert dust.

Those beady eyes fix on the crawling figure.

He stalks up behind him, like the eerie silence of death, his boots touching quietly, keeping pace with the dying man's labored breaths and the slow, steady smear of blood that trails behind him as he drags himself along.

When he is over the bounty hunter, the Rat speaks, his voice almost drowned out by the man's whimpers of pain. "Sorry," he says, a solitary word filled with neither remorse nor joy. And then he pulls the trigger one last time. The gunshot lingers in the air of the deserted mosque, a haunting epitaph to the fallen man.

The task done, the Rat turns away, leaving the mosque, its quiet halls now a tomb of death. He runs out into the harsh sunlight, his boots kicking up dust as he sprints toward the men's vehicle. Vaulting into the driver's seat, he offers a silent prayer of thanks as he finds the keys still dangling in the ignition. With a roar, the vehicle comes alive, and he drives away, leaving behind the mosque and heading back into the wilderness, to be swallowed once more by the unforgiving desert.

The Rat is on the run.

EIGHT

AL FASHIR AIRPORT, NORTH DARFUR, SUDAN - 15TH APRIL, 11:08 (EAT)

CURRENTLY THE ONLY SAFE AIRSPACE THIS FAR west in Sudan is al Fashir airport—an airport in pretty much name only, being that it consists of no more than a couple of runways, a concrete block building to the side of it, a single radar tower, and some dilapidated sheds that act as hangars.

Inside the rickety husk of one of these sheds, three figures linger in the relative coolness of its partial shade. Dressed in desert camouflage, they wear pistols strapped snugly against their thighs in holsters, and their faces are partially concealed by lithams. The wind carries with it a ghostly lament as it sweeps through the skeletal structure, causing the rusted metal sheets to creak and flap above them like some forlorn, metallic canopy.

As the three men stare out of the hangar, the harsh Sudanese sun suddenly bounces off the polished, reflective surface of a descending aircraft, scattering shards of light onto the sandy terrain below. The plane's wheels graze the rugged dirt runway, and a dust cloud billows up, momentarily shrouding the aircraft in a gritty haze.

"This his plane?" inquires one of the men, his voice barely above a murmur, yet resonating in the hollow emptiness of the hangar.

His companion, evidently the leader of this motley crew, inclines his head in affirmation. The aircraft, a robust C-23 Sherpa, meant for military transport, taxis into the semi-shadowed refuge of the hangar. It comes to a gradual stop, and the trio instinctively shifts to the back of it, their stances poised and ready, like predatory animals anticipating their prey.

The rear hatch slowly descends, revealing an isolated figure holding a sports bag at its peak. The fingers of the three men twitch, their tips grazing the cold metal of their holstered weapons in a subconscious readiness for action.

Bathed in the stark contrast of light and shadow, the figure at the head of the ramp radiates an intimidating presence. Even from their distance, the three men can discern his well-toned physique, an image of raw, compact strength. His eyes, a piercing gray, narrow as he takes in the sight of the three-man welcome party.

"Peter?" the lead man asks.

Peter narrows his gray eyes at him. "Frank?" he questions back, his voice filling the hangar's vast emptiness.

The leader of the crew shakes his head, the slightest of movements, yet laden with significance. "Frank sent *us*," he says.

The solitary figure, identified as Peter, glances toward a

dust-covered Toyota pickup parked inconspicuously in the corner of the hangar. With the compact cab space barely sufficient for four passengers, a realization dawns upon him.

"Is that your ride?" Peter queries, gesturing toward the incongruous vehicle.

The leader follows Peter's gaze toward the vehicle before returning his attention to the man himself, saying nothing, just staring up at him dumbly.

"It's too small," Peter suggests.

"And what if it is?" the lead guy retorts in a cockney accent, a challenge hidden within his curt response.

"We're supposed to take the target alive, aren't we?" Peter presses, his voice laced with an edge.

"Uh-huh." The affirmation is nonchalant, almost indifferent.

"Well," Peter explains, his tone cool and matter of fact, "that pickup can barely fit four of us. Including the target, we'd be five. Meaning it's too small."

The leader of the three seems unfazed by this revelation. "So what?"

Peter sighs, an exasperated undertone in his voice. "*So* we can't all fit in the front. Is one of us supposed to ride in the back? I mean, I don't want to sound pedantic, but we're in the middle of a desert. In this sun, anyone riding in the back will be roasted before we even reach our destination."

The leader grins, a grotesque display of yellow, tobacco-stained teeth. "Spot on," he says. "Either we need a larger vehicle or a smaller team. And a smaller team is exactly what we have in mind, me ol' mucker." His voice carries an ominous undertone.

The confirmation of Peter's suspicion sends a chill down

his spine, and he mutters an inaudible curse under his breath.

The leader continues, his grin widening, "Our boss, Frank, made some enquiries about you while you was on your way. Spoke with a mate of his in the Navy Seals. Bloke what can get him information and such. Cuz in this game you gotta make enquiries."

Peter curses under his breath a second time.

"He reckons," the leader goes on, "that he's never heard of a Peter Black, and Frank's computer guy couldn't find much on record either. So who are you, mate?"

The first mistake of the mission had been made. Knight hadn't expected such a thorough job being done on Peter's resumé, so he'd half-assed it. Did enough to get him in. Or not, as it now seems.

"Listen," Peter begins, taking a step down the ramp, allowing the stark Sudanese sunlight to illuminate his features, his countenance a blend of determination and conviction, eyes locked firmly on to the three men. "The only thing I'm looking for here is a job. Let me work, and then you'll see if I'm good enough."

The trio exchange cautious glances before steeling their gazes back on to him, an unspoken understanding lingering in the air.

The leader gives a dismissive shake of his head. "Let's get this straight. Frank doesn't trust you. His orders are clear: Ensure that you're back on that plane, airborne and out of Sudan before noon. It's half eleven now."

Peter absorbs this, the silence enveloping him briefly before he lets out a measured breath. "So does that mean you're not going to get a bigger truck?"

Their brows crease as mirth fills their expressions, a shared chuckle hanging in the air around the hangar. The lead man retorts, "Are you hard of hearin', mate? The point is you need to get straight back on that plane. Frank wants you as far away from this operation as is humanly possible. He's got a tight bounty hunting network going on here. He doesn't need some pretender poking around."

"Pretender? Me?" Peter parries, tapping his own chest incredulously.

"That's right. That's what Frank's sources relayed. You're some dreamer that thinks because he can shoot a gun on a range he can shoot one in real life."

Peter takes another slow, deliberate step forward, never breaking eye contact with the lead man. "Let me assure you, gentlemen," he states emphatically, "I am no pretender. I am more than qualified for your little hunt. I reached out to your boss, Frank, and presented my background—Navy Seal. Nevertheless, I didn't give your boss all the correct details. I apologize, but in my experience, it's best to hide at least a part of yourself. I'm sure we can tidy this clerical mess up later. However, for the time being, one thing is for sure."

"Oh, and what is that?" the lead guy wants to know.

Peter points at the truck. "That that vehicle is inadequate for our team. Either we secure a larger mode of transportation, or one of us is going to be left behind."

Frowning, the leader steps forward. "Yeah, one of us *is* gonna be left behind. You!"

Peter lowers his eyes at him. "So no bigger vehicle, then?"

"Mate!" the leader rages. "Are you fuckin'—humph!"

Without wasting a second, Peter has flung his hefty bag

straight at him. The unexpected missile thuds heavily against the lead guy's chest, the force of it knocking all the air out of his lungs and propelling him backwards, his eyes wide with shock. Before the other two can react, Peter springs into action, his nimble frame bounding down the final steps of the ramp in an agile leap.

The second man reaches for his holstered pistol, but Peter is faster. His muscular arm snakes out, his fist connecting with a solid punch against the man's jaw, an audible crack reverberating in the hollow expanse of the hangar. The man stumbles, the world spinning around him as he tastes blood in his mouth.

Simultaneously, the third man makes a dive for his own firearm. However, Peter, anticipating this, pivots sharply on his heels. A swift roundhouse kick sends the man sprawling onto the hard concrete floor of the hangar, his pistol skidding uselessly away from his outstretched hand.

The leader, now recovered from his initial surprise, charges at Peter with a grunt of fury. He's an experienced fighter, his body hardened by countless violent confrontations. But Peter is better. With an uncanny sense of timing, he dodges the first swipe, then another, effortlessly sidestepping each potentially brutal blow.

Using the leader's momentum against him, Peter delivers a punch to his solar plexus, knocking the wind out of him. He buckles over, gasping for breath. Peter doesn't let up. He strikes again, his elbow connecting with the man's cheekbone with a sickening crunch. The leader collapses, incapacitated but conscious, writhing on the floor in agony.

Peter turns his attention back to the other two men, the adrenaline pumping in his veins as he engages them again.

He moves with a lethal grace, ducking, weaving, and striking with a precision born of rigorous training and relentless discipline. The third man lunges at him, wild-eyed and desperate, but Peter effortlessly sidesteps the attack. With a swift, savage twist, he seizes the man's arm and bends it at an unnatural angle. The sickening snap of bone fills the hangar, followed by a scream of agony. Peter steps back, leaving the man writhing on the ground, the arm hanging limply by his side.

Having incapacitated all three, Peter collects his bag, motioning to the relatively unhurt man to pick up his whimpering leader. Wordlessly, the man complies, heaving him up from the ground. Reaching the Toyota, Peter gets into the driver's seat and grabs ahold of the keys dangling from the ignition. Then, before he twists them, he faces out the window and says, "Now you can agree or not, but I vote we leave the guy with the broken arm. What do you say?"

NINE

SOMEWHERE UNDERNEATH MOSCOW - 15TH APRIL, 12:24 (MSK)

IN A DISMAL, WINDOWLESS ROOM, THE STENCH OF fear and sweat clings heavily in the air. Staff General Ivanovich, a once formidable figure, is suspended from the ceiling by a chain. His naked body is a patchwork of purple and red, every bruise and gash a testament to the punishment he has endured. His tormentors, two brutes, stand on either side, catching their breath.

"Hold his head up." A chilling voice cuts through the dank air. The command is issued from a man lounging in a chair across the room, his appearance in sharp contrast to the grim surroundings.

With a cruel tug, one of the brutes hauls Ivanovich's drooping head by the hair, forcing the general to lock eyes with the man in the chair.

Even despite the pain, there's a spark of defiance in Ivanovich's gaze.

"Now tell me, General," the seated man drawls, his voice barely concealing the venom underneath, "who did you call while you were at your father-in-law's dacha?"

"You've all gone mad," Ivanovich rasps, the words spilling out in a pain-laden gasp. "You should be happy I've tried to stop it. What has become of us, huh? Is Russia no longer capable of anything other than murder? Where has our humanity gone?"

The man rises from his chair, crossing the room in three measured strides until he stands inches away from Ivanovich. "And where has your loyalty gone?" he taunts, pulling out a phone from his pocket and holding it in front of the general's face.

All color drains from Ivanovich as he takes in the images on the screen. His eyes widen in dread, and he averts his gaze, turning back to face the man. "No," he mutters, his voice hollow.

"Your grandchildren seem to be living a carefree life in these photographs," the man remarks, his tone eerily casual. "It would be such a tragedy if their happiness were abruptly cut short... if they were whisked away to an orphanage, their parents exiled to a gulag in Kamchatka."

The threat hangs heavy in the air, sucking out the little life that remains in the room. As the implications of the man's words sink in, a look of resignation clouds Ivanovich's face. He has been defeated not by physical torment but by the threat against his innocent kin, a vulnerability he cannot protect. "Okay," he splutters. "I'll tell you what I know."

Ten minutes later, the general sobs as he hangs in the

center of the room, the noise resonating in the cramped chamber. The man in the chair is on the phone. "Yes, sir. A code eleven breach. The Americans supposedly have someone inside Fifty-Five." He listens while his superior speaks. "Don't worry, sir. I will put my best man on the job."

————

St. Petersburg, Russia
    15th April, 13:44 (MSK).

IN THE OPULENT heart of a grand St. Petersburg mansion, golden chandeliers shimmer from high ceilings, illuminating the plush surroundings with a warm, ambient glow. The scent of aged whiskey and polished mahogany fills the air, a stark contrast to the scene unfolding below. On a luxurious leather couch, a hooded figure lounges, his demeanor unsettlingly casual. Opposite him, in a finely upholstered chair, sits another man. Not so casual—bruised, beaten, and bound. Blood slowly trickles from cuts on his forehead, each droplet staining the plush carpet beneath his feet, and his swollen, bloodshot eyes are filled with terror. In the background, the soft notes of a classical piano piece play on a stereo, the music a haunting accompaniment.

Bathed in the subtle glow of ambient lighting, the features of the hooded figure remain enigmatically hidden in shadow. Subtle movements, however, occasionally betray glimpses of a face covered in mottled scarring—the melted skin a testament to a harrowing tale of flames, pain, and a narrow escape. Another testament is the sinister metallic claw where a human left hand should reside, the appendage glinting under the chandelier's radiant dance. His icy, discerning eyes remain locked on to the bound man, relishing every involuntary shiver of terror that ripples through him.

"I-I swear," the man stutters, "I... I know nothing about the order to stand down in Rostov... The men who have given you this information are liars..."

"None of it matters anymore," the scarred man interrupts. "Your fat-headed friend Prigozhin is dead. Your attempts failed. Now the inevitable fall of the—"

He holds a finger up, having just been interrupted by a phone's ring. With a swift, almost mechanical movement, he reaches into his coat using the claw, deftly retrieving a sleek black device that he holds between his pincers.

"*Da*?"

"Semyon," comes the voice of his superior, "how is the mission?"

He looks into the terrified eyes of the man opposite and says in an even tone, "Almost done."

The bound man swallows, his Adam's apple rising and falling along his throat.

"Well, get it done quickly," his superior tells him. "I need you in Africa."

"Africa?"

"Yes. I have recently come into information regarding American knowledge of our Aurora Abyss project. In particular, Facility Fifty-Five in Sudan. The torture of yet another traitor—"

"Another?" Semyon Mikhailovich blurts out, his eyes burning at the man opposite. "Who this time?"

"Staff General Vasily Ivanovich."

"Another general," Semyon murmurs.

"Yes. We caught him using a location he thought was safe. Caught him tipping the Americans off and learned they know a little more about things than we thought. Our spies inside Sudan have since spotted CIA activity in the area."

"It could be the civil war," Semyon suggests.

"No. A well-known scumbag by the name of Hashim Iqbal, also known as the Rat, was seen taking a CIA operative into Khartoum a day after our lead scientist at the facility, Ibrahim Bol, was murdered in the city by those idiot rebels."

"But if their contact's dead, then what would the CIA be looking for in Sudan?"

"That's what we are wondering. I had security at Facility Fifty-Five run a check of all lab procedures. They called back a minute ago. A sample is missing. Ibrahim Bol took it. And not just that, but our people in Sudan claim that the rebels chased a military plane filled with armed men off an airfield on the edge of Khartoum the same day Bol was killed. We think it was a CIA extraction team."

"Sounds like too many coincidences to be a coincidence."

"That's what we think. So I need you to head to the airport. There's a plane waiting to take you to Sudan. How long have you got left where you are?"

Looking dead into the tied-up man's eyes, he says, "No more than a minute."

"Good. Then get yourself on that plane."

The call cuts off.

There is a moment of silence, nothing but the light

sound of the piano music playing in the background. With the two men locking eyes, Semyon lifts the metal stump. The man opposite begins breathing heavily. "Please... No... PLE—"

Semyon releases the three-bladed claw. It zips through the air, embedding itself in the man's throat.

He shudders on the chair, blood gushing from his neck, the detachable rod of the claw sticking out of it, the three pincers buried in his windpipe and carotids as he gurgles and splutters. Semyon, unperturbed, rises leisurely from the leather couch. With a casual nonchalance, he advances toward the man, who gazes up at him in horror as blood spills from his throat. Coming over him, Semyon thrusts the stump forward, connecting it to the end of the claw protruding from the neck, the rod slotting into a hole in the stump.

With a slight twist, it clicks. Then, placing a boot against the man's chest for leverage, he tugs it out brutally, the guy gasping as a jet of blood gushes from his wrecked throat. His body convulses with the last few pumps of his heart, then goes still.

"You forgot one thing, my friend," Semyon sneers at the dead man. "In our game, silence isn't just golden—it's survival. Maybe next time you plan a coup, you will learn to keep it quiet." And with that, he turns and leaves, the staccato of his boot heels echoing through the vast rooms of the mansion, a chilling endearment to what has just happened.

TEN

NUBIAN DESERT, NORTH DARFUR, SUDAN - 15TH APRIL, 14:34 (EAT)

BAKED UNDER THE UNFORGIVING MIDDAY SUN, THE Nubian Desert sprawls over western Sudan, its expanse a relentless plateau of scorched earth.

Perched on top of rocks with a commanding view of a dirt track that snakes past down below, a man lies hidden beneath a camouflage net. A Remington M700P sniper rifle pokes out the end of the netting, the man and his weapon invisible to the untrained eye, yet not invisible to the desert heat. He is roasting under there.

"Are we certain he's using this route?" he whispers into his comms unit as he wipes yet more sweat from his eyes.

"He has to," comes the curt reply of the leader. "There's no other way. He'll show up soon. Have faith."

A pause ensues, then, "Do you reckon Frank will be pissed we didn't get that guy back on the plane?"

"More than likely. But if we deliver Iqbal and his bounty, Frank should cool off."

"I..." the sniper starts, then interrupts himself, "Wait. I see a dust cloud. He's on the way."

A pickup truck rumbles around the bend, emerging from a corner of the rocks. The sniper lines his eye up with the scope, takes in a cool hard breath, and steadies himself.

The air shatters with the explosive sound of a gunshot; a front tire bursts, then another explosion, another tire. The vehicle swerves, lurches, and slams into rocks, its front end rearing upward, the pickup getting trapped. Smoke and steam billow from the crumpled hood.

The driver clambers out. Like prey leaving its hole, he scans the hills around him. Another gunshot rings out, a warning shot that whizzes close over his head, so near he senses the air's displacement before the bullet slams into the wrecked pickup.

The man retaliates, taking his pistol and unloading a barrage of bullets toward the rocky outcrop. But another shot, dangerously close to his feet, causes him to stumble and drop the gun. He attempts to retrieve it, but a stern voice rings out. "I wouldn't if I were you. There are three of us."

Looking up from the gun, he spots two men closing in on him, one from the road, the other descending from the rocky hillside, both holding pistols aimed at him.

He feels the need to raise his hands.

While the other keeps his distance, the one from the road approaches, an eye scanner in one hand, the other hand steadying a pistol that is aimed right at his forehead.

"Stay exactly where you are," he hisses as he comes up to

him and positions the scanner before his eye, waiting until it beeps.

"Bingo!" the guy says, glancing at the screen, then at the man he holds it in front of. "We got him. Hashim Iqbal, the Rat—or whatever they call you, I'm not sure whether you know this or not, but your face is rather valuable—worth at least a hundred thousand US dollars."

A round of smug chuckles fill the air as the two men secure Hashim's hands behind him with zip ties, the Rat not saying a single word throughout the whole process.

"Bring the truck," the leader instructs into his earpiece.

A billowing cloud of dust heralds Peter's arrival in the men's Toyota pickup. With a swift three-point turn, he swings the vehicle around.

They manhandle Hashim into it via the passenger side, but before they can get into the pickup themselves, Peter has the truck in gear and is speeding away with their bounty, leaving a spray of dust in his wake.

They aim their pistols and shoot off a few rounds, but within seconds, the pickup is out of range.

"Grab your rifle!" the lead man yells.

The sniper, still draped in camouflage, gestures helplessly up the hill. "It's all the way up there."

Cursing under his breath, the lead man watches as Peter and Hashim disappear into the desert.

Half a mile away, Peter comes to an abrupt stop, jumps out of the truck, shuts the passenger door, and then swiftly continues on. All the while, Hashim Iqbal, the Rat, regards him with a mix of wariness and disbelief.

"Is this a rescue?" he finally asks as they drive away.

"You speak English," Peter responds nonchalantly. "That's good. It'll come in useful."

"Useful?" Hashim presses, confusion furrowing his brows. "Useful for what?"

"You'll see."

———

HASHIM IQBAL, the Rat, finds himself fastened to the front of the pickup, his arms pulled taut along its width and his wrists bound securely to the vehicle's grille by zip ties. An opportune piece of cord, discovered by Peter amidst the truck's detritus, loops around his waist to further secure him, leaving his feet to dangle from the vehicle's bumper. Laid bare before him, an expansive desert valley unfurls, the truck poised precariously three meters from the edge of a precipice, beyond which a sharp plunge awaits onto the jagged embrace of rocks thirty feet below.

At the side of the open driver's door, Peter stands, one hand casually stretched into the vehicle's interior, latched on to a stick poking out of the steering wheel terminal.

"The beauty of these old Toyotas," he muses aloud, "is having the parking brake on the wheel. It means you don't have to be all the way inside to let it off."

The insinuation dangles in the arid air, filling Hashim with the phantom images of the Toyota tumbling down the precipice with him shackled to it, his body being crushed like a rotten watermelon between the front of the pickup and the unforgiving rocks.

"Let's cut to the chase, Hashim Iqbal." Peter's voice

carves through the tense atmosphere. "Where is Daniel Burns?"

Peter hopes Kamal stuck to his cover story and wasn't stupid enough to reveal his real name to this man.

Feigning bewilderment, Hashim cranes his neck. "I have no idea who you are talking about."

Peter counters with a smirk, pulling out his phone to reveal a snapshot of Kamal. "This doesn't ring a bell, huh? Here, take a look."

The phone screen is thrust before Hashim, whose eyes flicker over it before he shakes his head vehemently. "I've never seen him before in my life."

"You hardly looked at it," Peter retorts.

Hashim squints at the image once more. "There, satisfied? I've never crossed paths with this man. I swear it on the prophet."

Peter's wry smile unfolds at Hashim's vow. Tucking the phone back into his jacket, he casually drops a revelation. "You know, I had a good look at your file en route here." A scornful tut leaves his lips. "Having combed over its contents, I'm not exactly inclined to buy your prophet-invoking assurance. No offence, Hashim, but your reputation for deceit precedes you."

He inclines his head into the vehicle, his foot finding purchase on the brake pedal. As the parking brake relinquishes its hold, he guides the truck forward, the sloping gradient coaxing it toward the cliff's edge.

"Hey! Hey!" Panic surges in Hashim's voice as his feet graze the dusty ground, the void of the drop yawning ever closer. "Come on! Come on, man! I promise I don't know him."

With that, Peter brings the truck to a halt. Hashim's toes hover over the precipice, the ground falling away just beyond them, the circling vultures shrieking in the sky above.

"Only a day ago," Peter begins, his voice low and unyielding, the edges of his words like the very precipice Hashim's toes cling onto, "he paid you several thousand dollars to get him through the fighting and into Khartoum. Since then, he has disappeared, and you're out here in the desert being chased by bounty hunters. So, Hashim, enlighten me—where was Daniel Burns the last time you set eyes on him?"

Hashim's eyes flicker to the rocky drop beneath his feet, then to Peter, his heart hammering in his chest. He struggles to swallow, eventually managing to utter, "I... I don't know any... Wait! Wait!"

Peter has already slipped halfway into the driver's seat of the pickup, half of him hanging out the open door as he nudges the Toyota closer to the precipice, centimeter by agonizing centimeter. Hashim's feet scrape the edge, and they start to slip, the gravity pulling his weight from the front of the car until he is left dangling over oblivion, held in check by the ties binding him to the truck, the vultures impatiently circling their impending feast.

Hashim's voice rings out in desperation, "Please! Please, man! Stop! I don't know where he is... I don't know where he is..."

Peter engages the parking brake. The pickup halts, front tires teetering perilously close to the edge. "Come again?"

Hashim shakes his head vigorously. "You've got the wrong information, man. I don't know this guy."

With a nonchalant shrug, Peter slowly eases his foot off

the brake pedal. The vehicle creeps forward, just an inch, but enough to send Hashim's heart pounding against his ribs like a frantic drum.

"Okay! Okay!" Hashim yelps, fear winning over his stoicism. "I lied. I did escort him into Khartoum. I picked him up at Port Sudan. I got him through the front lines, guided him into the city, but after that... He paid me, and I left him."

Peter brings the vehicle to a halt, the tires mere inches from the abyss, Hashim's feet dangling into it. He considers him for a moment before posing his next question. "Where in Khartoum did you leave him?"

Hashim's flippant façade fades. "Abbas Street and Sahafa Avenue. You know it?"

Peter, unamused, retorts, "Don't play games" as he places a hand on the parking brake. Hashim's eyes track the movement over his shoulder, his Adam's apple bobbing anxiously up his long throat.

"It's the truth," he gasps. "That's where I left him."

"He was supposed to be heading for the other side of the city," Peter bawls at him, "to Sahafa Avenue. Why would he get you to take him there?"

"I know nothing of where he was heading. I didn't get involved with his private business. I simply did my job. Got him into the city, collected my pay, left him where I said. With Hemedti's men beginning their assault, it seemed wiser to make a getaway. Better to get out of Dodge, as you Americans are fond of saying."

Peter mulls it over. Then, "You want to know something?"

Hashim says nothing, just stares at him with shimmering eyes.

"I heard another story."

"Really?" Hashim queries, feigning innocence.

"I did. I heard a story about a certain guide who not only failed to get Daniel Burns to his destination, but sold him out to some pals of his."

"Oh?" Hashim says before swallowing.

"Does that sound about right to you?"

The denial is immediate. Hashim shakes his head. "You are wrong. I swear it. On all the prophets and all the gods." He flashes a gold canine in a nervous smile.

Peter, unperturbed, takes in a deep breath, drilling into Hashim's soul with his hard gaze. He doesn't rush to break the silence. Just stares at him.

Eventually, Hashim breaks under the intensity. "What are you going to do to me?" he whimpers.

———

As he drives into the desert city of Al Fashir, the sound of Hashim complaining loudly rings out along the streets as he bumps around in the back of the Toyota.

"You bastard. You bastard," he repeats as he lies on the swelteringly metal bed before breaking into Sudanese Arabic, then a little Swahili, some Somali, a bit of Nigerian, essentially every language he knows—every curse word he knows. All of it reaches Peter in the cab.

Azrael ignores it, of course. Just takes in the surroundings.

Al Fashir is known as the heart of North Darfur, a

mosaic of tradition and time, a city that breathes in the hot, arid air of the desert. Peter drives along a wide boulevard lined with swaying date palms, the tarmac of the road scorched dark by the sun. He is flanked by an array of buildings—some modern structures, standing tall, their glass façades cloaked in desert hues from the constant bombardment of the surrounding sands, while others are humbler, one- or two-story buildings reflecting Sudan's past with their mud-brick walls and thatched roofs.

He enters a labyrinth of side streets, narrower and dustier, Hashim's muttering gaining the attention of the pedestrians they pass. Here, the paths are unpaved, lined with buildings of earth and clay. He drifts past street vendors, the air thick with the aroma of their wares, a fragrant blend of spices from sizzling Sudanese dishes. The sounds of daily life fill the cab: the call to prayer resounding from the minarets bringing to a sudden end the haggling voices at the bustling markets, the laughter of children escaping schoolyards.

Unlike most of the people, Peter ignores the call to prayer. The streets become less dense, and he is able to reach his destination in good time. Perched on the outskirts of al Fashir, a compound of formidable demeanor looms, cutting a stark silhouette against the vast Sudanese sky. Sun-baked earthen walls, sturdy and high, encircle it in an imposing embrace. The walls, thick as the secrets they must surely hide, reach toward the heavens, holding an air of stoic vigilance.

Armed men pace the ramparts. Their outlines, broken only by the glint of their assault rifles, oscillate with the harsh sunlight that bleaches everything into a canvas of white and gold. As they patrol the walls, their keen eyes never stray far from the undulating expanse of sand and scrub beyond the compound.

The den's entrance is no less formidable, with a hefty metal gate standing guard, dusted with the relentless sand of the Sahel. Manned day and night by vigilant guards, the gate serves as the compound's mouth, opening only to swallow or spit out selected individuals. The scrutinizing gazes of the two men keeping watch in front of it stretch out along the street, coming to rest on the beaten-up Toyota trundling toward them: the same Toyota they're waiting for.

Peter glides to a halt beside them.

"Where's the target?" queries one of the guards, an Australian with a robust accent.

Without uttering a word, Peter lazily flicks a thumb over his shoulder, directing attention to the back of the pickup. As the guards approach, a sweat-soaked Hashim squirms to life.

"Get me out of here, you bastards! I'm practically fried to death back here!" he gasps.

Unmoved, the guards signal the gate to open. The bulky metal structure scrapes aside, breaking the street's tranquil silence. Peter steers the Toyota through the yawning mouth into a courtyard teeming with pickups, armored vehicles, and armed men. After parking, he gets out, yanks a struggling Hashim from the back, and drops him on his feet, which like his arms, are bound by thick plastic ties.

"Fetch Frank," orders one of the guards.

Peter snips off the ties on Hashim's legs, keeping a firm hand bunched up in the fabric of Hashim's T-shirt to prevent any rash escape attempts. Even if he did, with the array of firepower around, running would be futile.

As they wait for Frank, Hashim begins to spew threats and curses. "May you be smitten with plagues, infidel," he hisses at Peter. "I curse you with cholera, rabies, AIDS, and the worst cancers. I hope they consume you from within, you fiend." But then, his bravado crumbles, and his voice dwindles to a child-like whimper. "Let me go," he implores Peter in a whisper. "Let me go, and I'll forgive you. There's still time. I can lead you to riches greater than what these savages are offering. Please. You don't understand. I'm unwell. I think I'm about to faint." He stumbles, and Peter has to hold him upright. "You shouldn't have confined me to the back of that truck. I've been burned. I need water."

His plea is interrupted by the arrival of Frank.

Frank is an intimidating figure, a bald, steel-eyed man in his fifties, barrel-chested and fit, with a pistol strapped to his thigh. Spotting Peter, his eyes narrow and his lip curls into an expression of clear distaste.

"Water!" Hashim whines again.

Frank dismissively gestures to one of the guards. "Get him some water. If only to shut him up."

A water bottle is fetched, uncapped, and pressed to Hashim's lips as he holds them open. He fills his entire mouth but then, rather than swallowing, he spins toward Peter and spits the water into his face, buckling over with laughter once he has pulled the prank.

His mirth is short-lived, however. His hair dripping, Peter delivers a punch to Hashim's midriff, forcing a gasp out of him as he falls to his knees. Peter then hauls him back up with a single hand.

"Enough!" Frank intervenes.

Hashim regains his breath. "Who is he?" he queries Peter, nodding toward Frank. "He your boss? Another bastard? One bastard hands me over to another?"

Frank's gaze, like a laser, stays trained on Peter.

"What's this about you abandoning the others in the desert?" Frank inquires gruffly. "I had to send a vehicle to retrieve them. They're lucky to be alive."

"Listen," Peter retorts, his fierce gray eyes meeting Frank's firm stare, "I've had trouble ever since I arrived in Sudan."

At this point, the man from the hangar, his broken arm now in a sling, steps forward from behind Frank. "*You*'ve had trouble!" he snaps. "You broke my bloody arm, you prick!"

Frank gestures with a hand for him to take a step back.

"Like I was saying," Peter goes on, "I've had trouble. But now the job is done. I have your man. Now pay me my dues, and you and your men never have to see me again."

At Frank's nod, one of the guards holsters his weapon, seizes Hashim, and begins to guide him away.

"No. No. Please," Hashim implores. "Who are you handing me over to?"

"Doesn't matter," Frank replies curtly.

"No, please," Hashim pleads as he is ushered away.

Another guard, signaled by Frank, approaches Peter with a small case. Upon opening it, he reveals several bundles of US dollars.

"Whatever your true motive was in coming here," Frank says as Peter inspects the money, "it seems to have worked out for everyone. No hard feelings."

"Sure. I guess," Peter responds nonchalantly as he closes the case and accepts it.

"You enjoy your blood money!" Hashim roars from the other end of the courtyard. "You savor your thirty pieces, Judas. But you listen here, you won't get to spend it. It'll all end up in the hands of the undertakers!"

Peter disregards him. Having secured his payment, he prepares to depart. But as Hashim is being escorted into the compound, he cries out one final revelation: "Without me, you'll never find Kamal Osman!"

Peter whirls around, his eyes widening.

He mentioned Kamal Osman, not Daniel Burns.

"Hold on," he demands, striding toward Hashim. "What did you just say?"

Hashim grins, his gold canine glinting. "Oh, you're interested in a conversation with Hashim now," he teases as Peter reaches him. "Well, I'm afraid I have an appointment with these gentlemen. You'll have to catch me later if you wish to learn who I sold him to and where he might be at this very moment." He executes a mocking bow. "As I said, I have a prior engagement."

Hashim willingly departs with the bounty hunters, leaving Peter to watch the man nicknamed the Rat disappear into the building. As he does, a hand claps down on Peter's shoulder, and he twists around to find Frank.

"I think it's time you left, mate," Frank advises him.

ELEVEN

UM KADADAH REGION, SUDAN - 15TH APRIL, 17:23 (EAT)

Two hours later, under the scorching Sudanese sun, a convoy of three hulking Hummers plows down an isolated desert road, engines growling and kicking up a swirl of dust. Hashim, arms bound behind him, sits in the backseat of the central vehicle. Two men inhabit each of the three vehicles: a driver and a gunner, each one's grip tight around the wheel or the shaft of their assault rifle, which they maintain upright and alert.

The convoy is a moving beast, unstoppable—until an obstacle confronts it. In the middle of the road, an unexpected crater blocks their route, forcing the line to a jolting stop. It's a fresh wound, smoke curling lazily from its epicenter—the aftermath of a mortar shell.

The men pile out of the Hummers, their boots crunching on the gravel as they cautiously inspect the blasted terrain. Lifting radios to their mouths, they report the incident, their voices bouncing back and forth across the silent desert, disturbing the quiet with their growing unease. The barren landscape yields no response, no clue about what's coming. Until it comes.

The crack of a gunshot whips through the air.

One man staggers back, the side of his head blown away at the jaw, a crimson bloom spreading across his uniform from his open neck. He gets a few steps and collapses. The sound of the shot echoes eerily across the desert, followed by another. A second man falls, crumpling to the dusty road. Panic ignites among the remaining men as bullets whizz from the desolate expanse. They scramble for cover, diving behind the bulk of the Hummers, hearts pounding.

A shout breaks out. "There!" One man points to the infinite horizon. About a hundred meters away, a glint of sunlight reflects off something, a silent whisper of danger—a sniper's scope. They unleash a hail of bullets in that direction, maneuvering around the vehicles for better cover. But then a lethal shot suddenly roars from the opposite direction, dropping one of the men who had relocated. "A second sniper!" someone shouts, the terror palpable in his voice. Meanwhile, Hashim watches the scene unfold from his seat, a hint of a sinister smile playing on his lips.

Another glint catches their eyes, far off in the desert: a third sniper. Then a fourth. Until soon, a constellation of twinkling lights peppers the distant, dusty landscape. An encircling formation of what must be at least thirty snipers, all laid out in the desert like a deadly mirage. The men fire at one position after another, but nothing can stop them being picked off one by one, their confusion and fear escalating with each fatal shot. The desert, silent just moments before, now reverberates with the harsh punctuation of gunfire and bodies dropping to the hard ground.

Eventually, only one man remains, zigzagging frantically between the Hummers in a terrified dance of survival. His attention is ensnared by the glinting desert, eyes shooting from one glint to another, firing his weapon randomly into the desolate infinity. Amidst the terror-fueled chaos, he stumbles backward when, abruptly, he collides with a solid object behind him and freezes.

Before he can whirl around, a sharp pain erupts in the back of his head, and he falls to his knees. A second, decisive blow from the rifle's butt seals his fate, and he collapses, unconscious, onto the sun-bleached road.

Peter towers over him, appraising his handiwork. Satisfied with the man's unconscious state, his gaze wanders back toward the shimmering mirage of the desert. Hashim, still captive within the central Hummer, watches Peter walk off, his form merging with the desert's dusty haze, his actions obscured. When he reemerges some time later, he carries with him a bag filled with an odd assortment of small mirrors mounted on sticks. The desert's deceptive glimmers are revealed: a myriad of strategically placed mirrors concealing Peter as he systematically eliminated the men.

Armed with his bag of mirrors and his trusty Desert Tech SRS A2 bolt-action rifle, Peter slides into the driver's seat of the central Hummer and starts the engine.

The first words out of Hashim's lips are, "How much they pay you?"

"Ten thousand," Peter replies, shifting the vehicle into gear and maneuvering out of there.

"Give me half," the Rat bargains, his tone measured, "and I'll tell you what you need to know."

———

IN THE SECLUDED sanctuary of a desert crag, a hidden cave nestles them away from the relentless sun. Here, amidst an outcrop of ancient rocks, Peter and Hashim find a momentary reprieve from the barren expanse outside.

A band of dust-laden light seeps in from the entrance, casting an eerie glow upon the occupants. Peter, his face etched with the harsh lines of a man who's lived too long in a world of shadows, is engaged in an ancient ritual of trust and betrayal—counting out money. His hands, weathered and steady, flip through the stacks of green paper with mechanical precision, the crisp rustle of the bills punctuating the heavy silence.

Across from him, Hashim watches, his dark eyes gleaming in the dim light. Still bound, his wrists chafed raw by the zip ties, his position is no less authoritative. He follows the dance of Peter's fingers over the money with an inscrutable gaze, the traces of a knowing grin playing on his lips. Despite his physical limitations, he is a silent participant in the transaction, the gravity of his information holding its own weight in the makeshift scales of negotiation.

"Really," he says, a smirk curling up his lips, "I ought to demand more than half. After all, I'm the one with the bounty on his head, and you'll be getting your information, too. Isn't that the only thing you care about?"

Peter's gaze remains fixed on the green bills he's counting. "The way I see it," he begins, flipping through the final notes, "I'm gonna need this money to pay more little runts like you for information."

Hashim edges forward, twisting around to him. "At least cut me loose."

Lifting his gaze from the money, Peter scrutinizes Hashim, then bends down to retrieve a knife tucked into his boot. The blade gleams menacingly, catching a sliver of sunlight sneaking in through a crack in the rocky walls of the cave. However, as Hashim awkwardly moves his bound wrists toward Peter, the latter makes no move to free him.

"So," Peter starts, his voice as icy as the desert night, "who did you sell him to?"

Hashim's sharp, rodent-like teeth glint in the dim light as he scowls. "That's your game then, is it?" he grumbles, twisting back around in frustration. "Fine. I sold him to the Janjaweed."

"The RSF?"

Hashim nods curtly.

"And who in the RSF?"

"Colonel Tariq al-Sisi."

"When?"

His gaze magnetically drawn to the money in Peter's hands, Hashim answers, "Not long after we arrived in Khartoum."

"Where?"

"The location I mentioned before."

"On the intersection of Abbas and Sahafa?"

"Yes. There's a mosque there. That's where I handed your man over to them."

"And he confided his real identity to you?"

"No. I figured it out myself. During the drive to Khartoum, I snooped through his belongings while he was paying for gas. Found his real passport. American. He had claimed he was British, but I knew he was bluffing. His accent didn't fit."

"Did he meet anyone while he was in Khartoum?"

"No. He didn't get the chance. Al-Sisi's men collected him not long after we arrived."

"So he made contact with no one, then?"

Hashim shakes his head. "Isn't that what I said?"

"Did al-Sisi tell you his plans for him?"

"He was vague. Something about exploiting him for the benefit of their cause."

"They explain how they would do it?"

"No, but their methods are no secret. Brutal torture, reaching out to his family for ransom—the same old unsavory tactics they always resort to."

"You have any inkling of where they might have taken him?"

"No. The RSF are constantly on the move now. But if I were you, I'd start with the mosque where I left him. Your particular set of persuasive skills might coax something out of the locals."

Peter breathes out. Then, "Is that all you've got?"

"Everything I know. Now will you cut me free?"

Peter contemplates this for a moment. Then says, "No."

He tosses Hashim's share of the money onto the sandy floor between the latter's feet and makes his way toward the warm sunlight of the entrance.

"Wait, what do you mean 'no'?" Hashim sputters, his gaze darting between Peter and the money scattered on the ground.

"I mean"—Peter pauses at the cave's mouth and glances back at him—"no."

Slower this time: "What do you mean no?"

"I mean, it's safer for me if you remain tied up. That way, you won't go stabbing me in the back like you did Kamal."

A frown creases Hashim's brow as Peter steps out of the cave and begins making his way down to the Hummer.

"Hey!" Hashim yells, eyes flicking back to the money he can't bear to abandon. "I can't pick up my money with my hands tied. Hey!"

He stumbles out of the cave, negotiating the rocky terrain as he hops down to the road. He catches up with Peter just as he reaches the vehicle, nudging him in the shoulder with his head. Peter whips around and places a firm hand on Hashim's chest.

"Not so fast," he cautions. "You stay here."

Hashim's frown deepens. "No. This is some joke. You can't..."

"Al Fashir is roughly fifteen miles away," Peter interrupts, "give or take. Conserve your energy, and you just might make it." He gives Hashim a short, sharp shove, causing him to tumble backward onto the dusty ground.

"You beast!" Hashim splutters, struggling to regain his footing.

Peter opens the Hummer door, slides into the driver's seat, and starts up the engine.

"You despicable pig!" Hashim hollers, charging at the vehicle and banging on the door with his shoulder. "You wouldn't dare abandon me if you knew exactly who Hashim Iqbal is," he snarls through the window. "The resources at my disposal. The people I can summon." He tries to laugh it off. "But there's no need for threats. You're not serious about leaving me here—you can't be." He shakes his head, forcing a smile. "This is some silly American joke."

Peter meets his gaze with a chilling stare, shifts the Hummer into gear, and pulls away. Hashim stumbles backward, aghast.

"No, it's just for show. This is still a joke," he mutters to himself as he stands in the road. But when Peter stretches out an arm from the window to give him a nonchalant wave, he realizes that the American isn't joking. He is leaving.

"Wait! Don't leave me!" he pleads desperately.

As the Hummer fades into a swirling cloud of dust and exhaust fumes, Hashim's self-assuredness evaporates. A potent blend of fury and fear seizes him, and his eyes turn a frightening shade of black. "If I ever get my hands on you," he growls, trembling with rage, "I'll tear your heart right out your chest and eat it. I'll scalp you! I'll skin you alive! I'll hang you by a meat hook! You wretched parasite! I'll murder you! I swear on my life, I will hunt you down and end you if it takes the rest of my life."

TWELVE

KHARTOUM, SUDAN - 15TH APRIL, 18:07 (EAT)

THE ROAR OF ITS ENGINES SUBSIDES TO A LOW grumble as the military plane touches down on a private airstrip just outside Khartoum. Nestled amidst the endless sand dunes, the airfield is a rare detail on the ancient desert landscape. As it taxis along, the plane's hulking shape momentarily breaks the merciless afternoon sun, casting long shadows across the dirt runway. Coming to a stop, the rear hatch opens with a hiss of hydraulics, and the second the ramp touches the dirt ground, a man on a KTM 1290 Super Adventure R dirt bike thunders down it from the back of the plane, the tires spitting up a trail of dust behind him.

Cloaked in a hooded jellabiya, the rider's face concealed beneath a black litham veil, only his rabid eyes are exposed— sharp and unflinching like a desert hawk. His metallic left hand, ending in a claw, grips the bike's handle and smoothly pulls in the clutch. The bike roars as he guns the throttle, the sound reverberating through the heat-hazed airfield, and in moments, he is hurtling along the highway toward the city.

Entering Khartoum, he weaves through the crowded streets, the city unfolding around him in all its chaotic vibrancy, underpinned by the palpable tension of war. Makeshift barricades, hastily thrown together from wreckage and rubble, checker the cityscape. The low, flat buildings wear a patchwork of bullet holes, while the intricate minarets of mosques jut defiantly into the sky above.

Khartoum is a city besieged. Soldiers of the RSF patrol with a predatory swagger, their AK-47s slung low and their eyes cold and watchful, a rabid hunger to them. Armored vehicles rumble through the streets, their gun barrels sweeping menacingly over the terrified population.

He observes rebel soldiers yanking civilians from their homes and cars. They line them up against the cracked and worn walls, their weapons trained on the frightened and pleading captives. Then a burst of gunfire, some screams, a shout, and the bodies are left in the street as warnings.

The hooded rider doesn't stop—he can't. His mission is both singular and relentless.

Ahead, a makeshift checkpoint materializes. Menacing figures in ragtag military fatigues and armed with rifles man the blockade. The man on the bike throttles down, his bike growling as he approaches, his hooded figure and masked face a stark silhouette against the shimmering backdrop of Khartoum.

A rebel soldier saunters over, demanding his papers in Sudanese Arabic. He silently complies, offering an assortment of stamped documents he pulls from his jacket. Then, in Arabic so polished it would put a native speaker to shame, his voice as cold as the infinite void of space, he announces, "I'm here to see Colonel Deng."

Rummaging through the paperwork, the soldier fails to find this information. He squints at the man, curiosity piqued. "And your name is?"

"Tell Deng it's the Hunter," he responds, a note of icy finality in his voice.

"The Hunter?" the soldier repeats, his eyes narrowing slightly.

Affirming with a curt nod, the figure on the bike keeps his piercing gaze locked on to the soldier. A chilling silence settles over them until the soldier, apparently unfazed, fishes out a mobile phone from his uniform and dials a number. The conversation is brief and to the point.

"He's expecting you at a nearby café," the soldier tells him at the call's end. "My men will guide you there." He gestures to a pair of soldiers. A few terse words are exchanged, prompting crisp salutes from the soldiers before they scramble into their dust-laden Jeep. With Semyon Mikhailovich tailing on his rugged KTM, the unlikely convoy sets off.

He follows the Jeep to the middle of a marketplace that's been taken over by RSF, the rebel soldiers busy harassing the vendors for 'taxes' when they arrive. They park outside the entrance to the café, a brick and clay three-story building.

Stepping off his KTM, Semyon sweeps his hood back, revealing the litham that veils his features. His piercing gaze undeterred by the veil, he follows his escorts, who have just jumped out of their Jeep, his appearance earning him side-long glances from the milling soldiers and the people of the street. There's an air of intrigue about him, a palpable electricity that seems to disrupt the casual buzz of life outside the café.

As the three men enter the café, the air is pungent with the aroma of strong coffee, broken only by the sweet scent of shisha smoke. The interior is steeped in worn, rustic charm. A hodgepodge of mismatched tables and chairs are scattered around, filled with clusters of rebel soldiers. Some are engaged in hushed conversation while others recline with hookah pipes in hand, their faces bathed in the soft glow of antique lanterns. Each puff of smoke sends swirls toward the weathered rafters, telling a tale of camaraderie amidst conflict.

Navigating through the maze of tables, they arrive at a partitioned section of the café, cordoned off by a beaded curtain that sways gently at their approach. The beads click together softly, their sound somehow harmonizing with the low murmur of the crowded rooms and the clink of tea glasses. Here, away from the soldiers' banter, a hint of secrecy lingers, the beaded curtain serving as a veil, separating this sanctuary from the boisterous world beyond.

One of the soldiers holds the curtain aside, and Semyon the Hunter strides through the beaded threshold into a secluded room, his journey through the heart of the bustling café ending in this private realm.

The room is compact and minimally adorned, boasting only a single table and a smattering of chairs. Seated at the center of this austere setting is a pallid man adorned in the standard beret and uniform of the RSF, his fingers curled around a coffee cup and a hookah pipe, his companions flanking him on either side.

Colonel Deng, once a robust figure of authority, is now

in his late sixties and reduced to a specter of his past, the pallor of his skin accentuating the fatigue etched deep into his features. His eyes, sharp and watchful, are the only remnants of the formidable soldier he once was.

As the Hunter emerges from the curtain, Deng's gaze instantly latches on to him. In an abrupt tone, he dismisses his companions with a single command, "Out!" The order extends to the men who have escorted Semyon. The beaded curtain is drawn closed behind them, leaving the room in a transient state of stillness, its sole occupants locking eyes in a silent contest.

A grin inches its way onto Colonel Deng's face, his eyes sparkling with recognition. His head tilts in a gesture of casual greeting, and he says, "Long time, old friend. I'd stand for the traditional welcome, but I'm afraid that's no longer an option." With a grim sense of exhibition, he lifts the tablecloth to unveil the remnants of his legs, amputated at the knees. "Car bomb," Deng explains. "A little gift from our friends in the government. And what about you?" His gaze becomes contemplative as he scrutinizes the hooded figure. "I heard you should be dead."

Answering in actions rather than words, Semyon claims a seat opposite Deng, his attention shifting to the pot of coffee before him. Deng watches with morbid fascination as the Hunter's left hook—where a hand should be—comes into view, resting atop the table. It gleams ominously under a sliver of light that seeps through a gap in some curtains.

After dispensing some coffee into a glass, the Hunter starts to peel off the litham, revealing his disfigured countenance bit by bit. Deng's eyes track the slow unveiling, his curiosity piqued. Semyon's face, an intricate tapestry of scarring and skin grafts, seems barely human. His ears are reduced to mere indents, his nose burned to the raw cartilage, and his lips pulled back in a permanent snarl. But amidst the ruins of his face, his eyes, sheltered by remaining eyelids, still hold a glimmer of something human. Though only a glimmer.

As Deng's gaze lingers on Semyon's marred features, he thinks to himself that the man is lucky—at least he still has his eyelids.

"Apologies for your plight, Comrade," Colonel Deng murmurs softly once the Hunter's features are completely unveiled.

"Occupational hazards," retorts Semyon, leaning back to sip his coffee. "What intelligence do you have for me?"

"Direct and to the point," Deng acknowledges, bobbing his head. "I always did admire that about you. The individual you're pursuing, Daniel Burns, is under RSF control."

"Good. That means you can lead me to him."

"It's not that straightforward. He's under the custody of a man named Colonel al-Sisi. He's the one holding your man."

"You have a location?"

"On the other side of the city, across the Nile. But unfortunately, that's where the fiercest combat is occurring."

"Then you will guide me to him. It's simpler that way."

"That, I'm afraid, is out of the question. You see, my orders confine me to this area, this section of Khartoum. During times of war, it's safer to obey orders, my friend, lest you become the next casualty. I'm just a half-soldier left to secure the perimeter. My authority doesn't extend beyond this zone. Leaving my post could see me court-martialed. No. I managed to bring you this far; the next steps are on you."

Inhaling deeply, Semyon releases the breath through the remains of his nostrils.

"Al-Sisi, you say?"

"Al-Sisi," Deng confirms.

THIRTEEN

AL FASHIR, SUDAN - 15TH APRIL, 19:09 (EAT)

As dusk unfurls its blanket over the city, a phantom materializes on its desert fringes. Hashim, weaving in exhaustion, ventures deeper into the urban web of clay houses, his dry, gray lips mumbling away a silent prayer, his face heavily burned by the sun, his dark complexion no barrier to extreme sunburn.

On an open street, the growl of an approaching M113 armored personal carrier startles him, and he shrinks back into the shadows of an alleyway, watching the monster roll by before it vanishes. Once safe, he reemerges and resumes his weary journey.

Upon reaching a weather-beaten shack peddling an assortment of goods, he spots the merchant inside, the tall, skinny man engrossed in a crackling radio, an auditory lifeline reporting the war's grim chronicle, evaluating the likelihood of its arrival in al Fashir.

"Help me, brother," Hashim pleads, panting heavily. "Help me."

The shopkeeper ventures out from his hovel, alarmed. "What happened?"

"Desert bandits. Set me free." He twists around, holding out his bound wrists.

Answering the plea, the man produces a penknife, slicing through Hashim's bindings with a swift flick. "By Allah!" Hashim exclaims, wriggling his arms around, their first movement in nearly half a day.

Spying a refrigerator inside the confines of the man's shack, he lunges for it, pulling the door open and seizing a water bottle. Twisting the cap off, he sprinkles the cool liquid over his face, his parched lips, his burning back. He avoids gulping it down, careful not to provoke a choking fit. The shopkeeper protests.

"You intend to pay for that?"

Hashim levels a challenging gaze at him. "I have money."

"Then the bandits didn't rob you?" the shopkeeper puts to him with a dubious look.

"I never said that," Hashim retorts.

His gaze then drifts to the rear of the shack. A curtain conceals a space beyond, but a gust of wind momentarily parts the veil, revealing a sight that grabs Hashim's attention.

"What's this, eh?" he remarks, making his way toward the obscured area.

"No! Stay out of there!" the shopkeeper interjects, but it's too late.

Hashim pushes him aside, taking swigs from his bottle as he strides through the curtain, only to discover a table brimming with weaponry.

The shopkeeper rushes to his side. "You must leave."

Hashim, however, can only beam at the arsenal. "You're storing weapons for the rebels. And there was I thinking this was my *unlucky* day." He chuckles, lifting a Beretta M9 pistol from the table.

"These guns don't belong to you," the shopkeeper snaps. "They belong to the RSF."

"And who did they belong to before that, huh? From whose cold, dead hands were they plucked, and whose stolen money funded them? In the end, these guns belong to whoever has earned them." He pats his own chest. "And that today, my friend, is me."

Eyeing him suspiciously, the shopkeeper queries, "Who was it that tied your hands?"

"Does it matter?"

Hashim tests the heft of the pistol, slips it into his waistband, pushing away the shopkeeper when the man tries to stop him. He then picks up a grenade from a box and rattles it beside his ear before pushing it into a pocket of his fatigues.

"If you take these," the shopkeeper whimpers, "they'll murder me and my family."

"Don't worry," Hashim soothes him. "I have money."

He produces the dirty wad of US dollars he ran back to the cave for, waving it enticingly before the shopkeeper.

"I have enough here," he says, "to buy all of these guns. Your little shack, too."

"It doesn't matter. They'll kill me if I sell them. Even if I bring them the money."

Hashim leans in close. "Then use it to get yourself and your family to safety. Head to Ethiopia or South Sudan.

Eritrea. Any place where you can enjoy your dollars until this storm of a war passes. Now"—he raises the wad of cash high —"what do you say, brother?"

FOURTEEN

OMDURMAN, SUDAN - APRIL 15, 19:58 (EAT)

As the dusky evening approaches, the fiery sun dips below the modest skyline of the city. The streets are now embellished with elongating shadows and swarming with military checkpoints; the city's jurisdiction still under the grip of the regular army, the SAF.

For now, at least.

Peter navigates the Hummer into the cityscape, crossing the al Dabbaseen Bridge over the murky green waters of the White Nile into Omdurman. A checkpoint greets him on the other side. He presents the guards with a press pass belonging to Doug James from CNN, accompanying it with paperwork and a generous tip in US dollars paper-clipped to it. The guard, taking the money and largely ignoring the pass, signals his comrade to open the barrier.

With the Hummer back in gear, Peter is about to drive off when the soldier offers a word of advice in English.

"Consider yourself warned, my American friend," he cautions. "Rebels will be in this part of the city any day now. It's safer to retreat to somewhere under firmer army control if you want to steer clear of danger."

Acknowledging the warning with a curt nod and a half smile, Peter proceeds farther into Omdurman.

He pulls up outside a ramshackle five-story hotel teeming with chaos and frenzied activity. Bags are strewn haphazardly around the lobby as people vacate the premises in droves—journalists, envoys, NGO workers—all eager to escape the impending arrival of Hemedti's rebels.

The hotel counter, weathered by time and marked by countless transactions, is a patchwork of chipped veneer revealing the cheaper wood beneath, bearing testament to its many years of service. International reporters from America crowd around it, rushing to check out, their equipment hastily packed at their feet.

The harried hotel owner, a tall man with worry etched across his face, spots Peter and approaches.

"I called earlier," Peter informs him. "Reserved a room under the name of Doug James."

"Ah, yes. Mr. James. An unusual occurrence at this moment in time, a foreigner checking *in* rather than *out*, given the extreme circumstances we find ourselves currently under. As you can see, all foreigners are deserting this part of Sudan."

"Unlike them," Peter replies dryly, "I need to stay."

"Two rooms, wasn't it?"

"Yes, opposite each other in the hallway. Did you manage to accommodate that?"

"Certainly." The hotel owner retrieves two sets of keys

from a hook behind him and hands them over. "Rooms four and five," he explains. "Directly across from each other."

Once the flurry of journalists abates, Peter is handed the register and begins filling it out.

"When do you expect your companion?" the hotel owner queries.

"Soon, I hope."

"And which room will you, yourself, be occupying?"

"Number four," Peter tells him.

"Noted. I shall remember it if anyone asks for you."

"You do that."

Once done, Peter ascends to the second floor, settling into room five, across from room four, the one he told the owner he'd be in. In the privacy of his quarters, he conducts a thorough check of his weapons. Ensuring they're in prime working condition, he secures an FN509 Tactical to an underarm holster, drapes a sports jacket over it, and double-checks in a cracked mirror to verify the firearm's conceal-ment. Satisfied, he stows a hunting knife into an ankle holster hidden within his tall desert boot, another knife—a bayonet—to his inner thigh under his fatigues, and a garrote within a slender copper bracelet, which he slips onto his wrist.

Then, using the satellite phone, he dials a number, speaking the second it is answered. "Okay. I'm here."

"Omdurman?" a voice on the other end asks.

"Yes. Just arrived."

"There is a café in the Nile Street market. There's a butcher shop nearby, known for its spectacle of a cow's head skewered on a spike, its tongue lolling out. Quite a sight for the children. The café sits opposite this attraction. Meet me there in one hour."

———

PETER WEAVES his way through a pulsating river of humanity, the streets clogged with a hodgepodge of traffic—rickshaws, minivans, and haphazardly loaded pickups. Symbols of military presence are as ubiquitous as the dust—armored vehicles and soldiers, their intimidating AK-47s brandished openly. They sift through papers, berate locals, and claim the backs of trucks as their own. An offbeat attraction captures Peter's attention—the ghoulish display of a decapitated bovine head, its bulbous eyes bulging from the sockets and its cobalt blue tongue lolled out in a gruesome spectacle. The grisly sight, to his surprise, seems to delight a cluster of children and is proving a feast for swirling, insistent flies. Directly across from this morbid spectacle is the café he seeks.

"Doug?" a voice calls, punctuating the din.

Glancing up, Peter spots a small balcony jutting out from the second floor, like an eagle's nest perched over the bustling marketplace. A man is waving to him from it.

Moments later, Peter is comfortably seated across from an elderly Sudanese gentleman, his hair a silver halo, spectacles perched on his nose and an aura of worry etched on his deeply creased face. This man is Hassan Ahmad.

"Time is a luxury, old friend," Hassan says, his tone hurried. "One we do not have. I currently wish to get out of here as quickly as possible. As a former government minister, I don't need to tell you how despised I am by the rebels. Do you have the money you promised? After all, a man in flight can do with all the resources he has available."

Without a word, Peter reveals a thick stack of US dollar bills, placing it deliberately on the table. As Hassan reaches for the money, Peter's hand snaps over it. They lock eyes.

"The intel," Peter grumbles, his voice a low growl.

"Ah, yes," Hassan replies, withdrawing his hand and leaning back in his chair. "You're looking for al-Sisi. Well, you're in luck. He's on his way."

"On his way?"

"Indeed. The belligerent Colonel al-Sisi and his band of RSF savages are set to be Omdurman's first uninvited guests once the western part of Khartoum succumbs to the rebels —and it will."

"And when's his grand arrival?"

"Imminent," Hassan leans in, lowering his voice. "The army is already abandoning many of their posts and falling back. We expect him sometime tomorrow morning. Noon at the latest."

"And he's got my man?"

"Your American? Yes, he does. But not the child."

A frown creases Peter's forehead. "Child?"

Peter hadn't mentioned anything about the girl Leila.

"Indeed, a little girl he was apparently traveling with."

As Hassan goes on, Peter's heart rises in his throat.

"She was with him when they nabbed your man," Hassan says, "but she has since slipped through their fingers somehow. You didn't know he was traveling with a young girl?"

"No," Peter growls, anger bubbling up inside of him. Hashim most definitely lied to him when he said they'd never met anyone. "Do you have any information on where she could be now?"

"No sign of her."

"And Burns? Is he...?"

"He's not dead, that I can tell you," Hassan says with a grim nod. "Though I imagine his current circumstances are less than hospitable. They're extracting money from him—slowly. I hear he's got access to it. So the rebels see him as a veritable golden goose during these times of conflict. Why? Is he worth more?"

"Doesn't matter," Peter says, releasing the money and standing up. "Good luck with your escape."

"Thank you," Hassan murmurs, his eyes already on the cash as Peter leaves the café.

On the street, he calls Knight. "I just got intel that Kamal actually managed to reach the girl."

"Really?" Knight snaps in his ear.

"Yes. But no one knows where she is."

"And Kamal?"

"With this al-Sisi guy."

"Well, they've been taking money out of Kamal's expenses account. Five hundred dollars a day via ATM withdrawals."

"They think he's still a journalist."

"You think you can find him?"

"I think so," Peter replies. "My source told me that al-Sisi is due in this part of the city by tomorrow. So I'm gonna stick around. Wait for him to come to me."

FIFTEEN

ONLY RECENTLY ARRIVED IN OMDURMAN, HASHIM Iqbal sets his sights on the skeletal remnants of an apartment building on the city's outskirts, a naked beast of concrete and bricks—unfinished and forsaken. He knows these types of buildings only too well. They are old acquaintances of his. Places where a man can find a home when no other is available.

Now dressed in newly acquired attire and fortified with a pair of Beretta M9s and a Heckler and Koch G3 battle rifle slung over his shoulder, he cuts an imposing figure in the morning light. In his grasp, he cradles the lifeless form of a white-feathered chicken.

Hashim penetrates the building's perimeter through a breech in the fencing, treading an earthen path, trampled by so many feet before his. He navigates through the haggard remnants of the five-story building, its concrete bones littered with the detritus of transient existence—abandoned food packages, makeshift beds, charred imprints of long-extinguished fires. Though supposedly alone, he feels the presence of human life lurking all around him in the shadows.

Ascending a set of concrete stairs to the third floor, he's greeted by the scent of smoke. In the building's skeletal heart, he finds a fire spitting embers beneath a small, beaten pot suspended over the flames on a rudimentary spit of wire-bound metal scraps.

Steam spirals from the pot, carrying a peculiar odor that prompts Hashim to investigate the contents. Spotting the gray meat boiling inside, he clucks his tongue, gently shaking his head in disbelief.

"Rat," he proclaims loudly, his voice bouncing off the concrete walls. "You have to be real poor to eat rat."

He settles himself on an old car wheel serving as an impromptu stool and starts plucking the chicken with practiced hands. "I've eaten rat myself," he continues, his voice resonating through the desolate structure, "so I know how poor a man has to be to resort to it. But now"—his tone takes a hearty turn—"I'm flush with cash and dine on chicken daily. Only I'm all alone."

His gaze sweeps across the desolate expanse, glancing from one pillar to the next, anticipating the figures lurking behind them.

Returning to his plucking, he resumes his monologue. "Indeed, I could use some companionship. Some pals to partake in my windfall. You see, there's this vile white devil carrying five thousand US dollars around with him." He underscores, "Five thousand US dollars. A fortune, when divided among three, and sufficient to buy all the chicken in this wretched city."

A faint scratching sound draws his attention to a pillar approximately thirty feet away. "And I just happen to know," Hashim adds in an even tone, "precisely where to locate this pink-skinned bastard. But alas, I lack the necessary assistance to confront him. To rob him. To kill him." He hisses these final words into the building's parched air.

Then he waits.

Gradually, faces emerge from the gloom, and five ramshackle men, aged between seventeen and thirty, come shuffling out from behind the pillars and begin edging toward Hashim and the fire.

"Five of you," Hashim addresses them, his voice rippling through the empty expanse, "and only a single, miserable rat. Shameful." He shakes his head solemnly. "Join me. We'll pluck and gut this chicken and feast like kings. Then, once our bellies are full, two of you, which is all I require, will assist me in dispatching this villain and in doing so earn enough money to leave the slums behind forever."

The eldest of the men ventures a question. "You want help in murdering a white man?"

"Indeed. I require two who can handle a gun." Lifting his cloak, he reveals the Berettas hanging from his belt. "Can you shoot?"

The men respond with confident smiles. "Yes," the eldest man confirms as they all inch closer, halting after a few steps. "And we can trust you?"

"Of course you can," Hashim responds, pointing a feather at him. "By the prophet's life. Aid me, and I'll respond in kind. Now, come along. Enjoy the chicken, and soon, you will never have to eat rat again."

SIXTEEN

THE ARMY RETREAT IS IN FULL SWING, A CHORUS OF unrest filling the air. Soldiers move sluggishly along sidewalks. Their presence, like the specter of defeat, casts a dark pall over the city. The streets are churning rivers of metal and manpower—tanks, armored vehicles, and various military apparatus flow steadily in a hasty exodus. Orders are barked, rapidly executed as checkpoints are stripped bare and electrical junction boxes are brutally sabotaged, plunging the city into an uncertain power cut. And it isn't just the army abandoning ship—civilians swarm the boulevards, weighted down with salvaged belongings, a human tide retreating from the city to assume the dreaded title of refugees.

From the edges, the determined few who are staying watch the spectacle. They peer from windows of apartments, from café terraces, and from the doorway of a modest hotel, where the hotel owner and his wife silently witness their city's unraveling.

"Well, it's all over the radio," the hotel owner mutters to his wife, her face flushed from the heat as she fans herself. "Hemedti and his rebels are closing in and will have taken over Omdurman by tomorrow. That's why the regular army are moving out... cowards," he adds under his breath. "They ought to stay and protect us."

"Maybe we should leave too," his wife suggests.

He swivels sharply toward her, aghast. "Abandon our hotel to looters and brutes? No," he insists, gazing back out at the human river coursing along the street. "We'll barricade ourselves. Pray to Allah for protection."

A maimed soldier, arms replaced with bandaged stumps caked in dust and blood, rolls by in a wheelchair. "Poor things," his wife murmurs.

"All this fighting," the hotel owner grumbles, "was meant to end when we got rid of al-Bashir. That was the promise. But here we are, a mere four years later, on the brink of war yet again. As you well remember, my love, my own youth was marred by the second civil war in the 1980s. Back then, forming attachments to people was pointless—you never knew when a friend might..."

The ominous click of a gun interrupts his bitter reminiscing. Turning around with painstaking slowness, the hotel owner finds himself face to face with a man in pristine attire flanked by two raggedly dressed men, each clutching a Beretta in his dirty hand.

His wife gasps as the hotel owner locks eyes with the immaculate stranger, who promptly places a finger to his lips. "We're not here for your valuables," he assures them. "All we want is the owner of *that* vehicle."

He gestures out the door to the dirt-encrusted Hummer parked outside.

The hotel owner's frown deepens. "There's a war about to begin, and you're chasing car owners? What, he's overdue on a parking ticket?"

His wife's chuckle fills the room, only to die abruptly as the stranger responds, his face devoid of humor.

"Amusing," he says. "But consider this: Either you tell me where the owner of that vehicle is, or we shoot you and your wife and find out for ourselves."

His eyes widening in fear, the hotel owner blurts out, "You'd kill us in plain view of an army?"

"A retreating army with its tail between its legs," the stranger corrects. "One devoid of fight. And, anyway, what would you care? You and she will be dead. Whether we are set upon by the army or not, it doesn't mean a damn thing to a dead man and his dead wife."

"Tell him, Ahmed," his wife urges, the joviality drained from her face. "It isn't worth dying for."

"Room four," the hotel owner capitulates.

"Much appreciated." The stranger turns to his accomplices. "You heard him. Room four."

The two tramps dart toward the stairs at the back of the lobby without a word.

———

IN THE DIMLY LIT CONFINES OF his room, Peter perches, rigid, on the edge of a worn armchair, the ancient springs creaking under his weight. The steel grip of his FN509, cool and unyielding, melds with his hand.

A window, neglected and covered in grime, stands ajar behind him. A torn and faded curtain flutters in a rhythm that syncs with the cacophony of chaos rising up from below. The noise of the retreat infiltrates Peter's secluded space, permeating every corner as the silence typical of early morning has been replaced by a relentless march of military machinery and humanity, all of it in disarray.

Unfazed, Peter remains impervious to the surrounding pandemonium. His exterior presents an image of stony stillness, broken only by the subtle rise and fall of his chest with each shallow breath. His gray eyes, piercing and alert, remain riveted to the door, a silent sentinel watching and waiting.

———

THE TWO VAGRANTS MOVE STEALTHILY, their forms slinking like shadows up the creaky wooden stairs, the Berettas heavy on the ends of their skinny arms. Each step is measured, a masterclass in silence and precision, their breaths held in check as if the very air around them could betray their intent.

Emerging into the dimly lit hallway of the second floor, the peeling wallpaper and the worn-out carpet bear silent testimony to the countless stories these walls have seen. A single flickering bulb hanging from the ceiling casts an eerie glow on their surroundings, a slender corridor punctuated by four doors, arranged in an even pair on each side, each facing another.

On the right side, at the far end, their target looms. The door marked number four.

————

PERCHED IN THE MUTED SHADOWS, Peter finds himself in a delicate dance between vigilance and rest. He hasn't slept since he arrived in Sudan three days ago. One eye remains fastened shut, yielding to the fatigue that tugs at the edges of his consciousness, while the other maintains its steady gaze on the door. His fingers, curled tightly around the grip of the FN509, are the only visible evidence of his alertness in the otherwise placid room.

But he's certainly not asleep. Not by a long shot.

This silent, half-conscious vigil is a testament to his training and instincts, allowing him to drift at the fringes of sleep, yet remain tethered to the reality of imminent danger. As his body replenishes itself, drawing from these stolen moments of quiet in the storm, his mind, with an animal-like awareness, roams in and out of wakefulness.

————

THE LEAD TRAMP arrives at his destination, his tattered shoes whispering against the worn-out carpet as he plants himself in front of the worn-out door—number four. His silhouette, mingled with an air of feral readiness, seems to merge into the gloom of the hallway.

The other man, moving with a predatory stealth honed by a lifetime of survival, slinks up to flank him. Each finds a spot to settle, their lean bodies pressing against the faded wallpaper, their faces etched in grim concentration. The door stands as a monolith of wood and peeling paint, its brass number glinting with foreboding in the dim light. From all angles, it is now under a silent siege, the tension humming in the stillness of the corridor.

———

HOVERING at the edge of sleep's embrace, Peter battles against the seductive pull of unconsciousness. His second eyelid, a weary watcher, teeters precariously on the brink of surrender, its fluttering dance threatening to plunge him into oblivion, the tantalizing lull of slumber ebbing and flowing, teasing and testing his steadfast resolve.

Despite the weight of fatigue pushing heavily on his shoulders, he must resist. The training that has honed his skills to a fine point, that has fashioned him into a relentless machine, is slowly becoming helpless against the onslaught of sleep's surrender. The labyrinth of his thoughts starts to blur, the edges of consciousness beginning to fray.

Each heartbeat seems to toll the knell of his waking state, every blink a gamble against the soothing call of the abyss. The lines of reality waver, as if viewed through a dirty puddle, yet he fights it. For in his world, sleep is not a respite —it's a vulnerability. He walks the tightrope between wakefulness and slumber, caught in an ethereal purgatory of his own creation.

His mind's grip on reality slackens, a loosened grip on the precipice, and just as he's about to surrender to the inevitable, to fall into oblivion, an unexpected chaos jerks him back from the edge.

WITH A SHARED NOD, the tramps muster their courage and explode through the door, hitting it with their shoulders and breaking the threshold with reckless haste—only to encounter a chilling void.

The room is empty.

A gunshot shatters their confusion. One man crumples to the ground, a jet of skull and brain hitting the opposite wall. The other, drenched in confusion, fear, and his companion's blood, whirls around, preparing to shoot. But the next gunshot is not his.

He lets out a strangled cry as he drops to the floor and bleeds out quickly, joining his companion in an abrupt demise.

Peter stands in the doorway across the hallway, his form barely discernible in the dim light of room five. He stands there, cautiously listening, until he feels safe enough to return the FN509 to its holster.

Then, just as his senses return to normalcy, a sound prickles at his awareness: a man tutting loudly behind him.

He whips around, adrenaline spiking once again, and, lo and behold, who should be standing in his own room but Hashim Iqbal, his figure framed by the backdrop of the open window, the thin curtains fluttering in the nervous breeze where he had climbed through from outside.

Hashim is holding a Heckler and Koch G3 battle rifle, his eye lined up with the barrel, its end directed at Peter. The soft click of the gun's safety being released resonates ominously in the room, signaling a new wave of confrontation.

"There exist two breeds of killer, my friend," Hashim begins, a tinge of mockery staining his words. "Those who attack from the front, and those who sneak in through a window at the back. You see, I know a little more about you than you think. I know the types of tricks you like to play. Like booking two rooms next to each other and taking the spare. A nice little ruse, *Azrael*." He drops Peter's CIA moniker into the conversation with a pointed undertone. "Now remove your weapons."

With a subdued compliance, Peter unstraps the holster, letting it and the FN509 clatter onto the floor. His heart thumps. He has clearly underestimated this man a second time.

"And the rest," Hashim prompts, a chilling firmness underlining his words.

Peter systematically strips himself of an arsenal—the covert hunting knife tucked into his boot, the compact snub nose hidden in his other boot, the lethal bayonet strapped to his thigh, the SOG Instinct mini knife secured to his upper left arm, the deceptive garrote disguised as a bracelet—all the way until a formidable heap of weaponry lies at his feet.

Hashim tosses him a pair of zip ties, crudely strung together to form impromptu handcuffs. "Secure one around your wrist and turn around."

Peter submits. Hashim sidles up to him, the cold, metal tip of his assault rifle burrowing into Peter's back. "I could shatter your spine into a million splinters with a mere twitch of my finger," he warns. "Now put your hands behind your back."

As Peter complies, Hashim cautiously peels one hand

from the gun, his other hand ensnared around the grip of the battle rifle, a finger hovering precariously over the trigger.

Aware of the fragile equilibrium of the situation, Peter willingly extends his other hand, conscious that any abrupt motion could lead to an inadvertent trigger pull, severing him in two. Hashim snags the free end of the zip tie around Peter's remaining wrist, tugging it taut, binding his hands together behind him.

"All right," Hashim announces, a cruel satisfaction creeping into his tone. "Let's move, bastard. Because you and me are going for a little drive."

SEVENTEEN

SAHARA, SUDAN - 16TH APRIL, 10:11 (EAT)

IN THE HEART OF THE SAHARA, THE UNFORGIVING midday sun reigns supreme. The vast landscape is a relentless stretch of sand dunes, their rippled surfaces shaped by the whims of the wind, stretching out as far as the eye can see like waves in a storm. A road, more a beaten path than anything else, traces a lone, linear scar through the ocean of sun-scorched sand.

Hashim, gripping the steering wheel of the rugged Hummer, steers Peter into the depths of this desolate wilderness. His brow furrowed against the blinding light reflecting off the sand, he scans the surroundings with a calculated gaze. "Right," he declares with an air of finality, his voice unnaturally loud in the stifling silence of the desert. "Here should do."

The Hummer grinds to a halt, its heavy-duty tires sinking slightly into the soft sand. Hashim kills the engine, its rumbled purr ceasing abruptly, leaving only the distant whisper of the wind whistling over the dunes. Removing the keys from the ignition, he opens the driver's side door, the metallic click and creak sounding loud in the hushed desert air.

Circling around the vehicle to the passenger side, he wrenches open the passenger door, the gust of air carrying a cloud of sand into the cabin. His eyes, cold and unwavering, meet Peter's as he points the barrel of his Beretta at him, the cold steel glinting menacingly under the sun. "Out," he orders, the single word resonating with an air of chilling finality.

Peter gazes back at Hashim, his eyes hard and unwavering. He takes a deep, calming breath, the desert air dry and hot in his lungs, and then slowly exhales, his chest sinking. "You're making a big mistake," he says.

"Get out!" Hashim's voice cuts through the silence, a whip-crack command that echoes in the desert.

In response, Peter propels himself out of the vehicle, landing nimbly on the yielding sand. His shadow, elongated and distorted by the stark desert sun, lies before him, a mute accomplice in this deadly game.

Hashim steps back, creating a cautious gap between them, the M9 gripped tightly in his hand, the black barrel aimed unerringly at Peter. "Get to the front of the truck," he orders, his words cold and sharp as shards of glass.

Following the instruction, Peter makes his way around the large front bumper of the Hummer. As he reaches it, Hashim instructs him to turn around. He then cuts Peter's ties and jumps back, the aim of the Beretta never leaving his enemy.

Peter, his hands free, faces him. Hashim tosses him a packet of zip ties, the light, plastic bundle landing at Peter's feet with a soft thump. "Loop one in the grill on that side," Hashim instructs, pointing to the far edge of the gleaming chrome.

Peter bends down to pick up the packet, his gaze never leaving Hashim's. He pulls out one of the ties, its plastic ridges rough against his fingers, and threads it through the Hummer's grill on the indicated side. The clicking sound of the riveted tie against the grill rings out in the silence.

"That's it," Hashim commends, a malicious smile tugging at his lips. "The bastard knows how to do it. Put your hand into it and pull it tight."

Peter complies, his hand slipping into the loop of the zip tie and pulling it taut.

"Now the other side. Put your hand through it."

Again, Peter does as instructed, placing his other hand through a second tie on that side, so that he is stretched out across the grill as though crucified. Hashim shuffles up, presses the gun into the back of Peter's neck, and secures the tie himself.

"Set your feet on the tow," he says next, coming around the front. "Otherwise, you'll be dragged under, and it'll break your legs."

Peter hitches his feet up onto the tow hook, the metal hot under the soles of his boots. He continues to stare at Hashim, his eyes unblinking in the face of the searing desert sun. "Where are we going?"

Hashim taps his chest with a pointed finger, a smug grin playing on his lips. "Not we, friend. But if you want to know where I'm going, it's over that way." He gestures vaguely into the distance, his arm extended toward an endless expanse of undulating sand dunes. "Another hundred miles of beautiful, sunbaked sand." Turning back to Peter, he adds, "You know you left me in the Nubian Desert. Very rocky compared to this part of the Sahara. Plenty of shade to hide in for a while. Not out here, though. This is the vast belly of the Sahara. Only sand dunes out here, not a wedge of shade for many, many miles."

Peter's brow furrows slightly. "What's a hundred miles away?"

"Not that you'll be alive when I get there, but I'm meeting someone. You see, Azrael, I know more about this all than you may think. Only after I'd already handed him over to al-Sisi did I discover that not only was Kamal's name not Daniel Burns, but he wasn't a journalist. He was CIA."

Peter's heart sinks.

"But me and him made a deal," Hashim goes on. "He's going to help me. He's going to get me out of here, away from this life."

"Then you need to get me down," Peter says. "Because that's what I'm here for: to find Kamal. To rescue him."

Hashim leans in, making sure to press the Beretta into the back of Peter's neck just in case. "He told me people would come," he hisses straight into his ear. "Told me they would lie to me, say that they are here to help him, but really they want to harm his mission. He told me not to trust anyone."

"But you *can* trust me. You know me as Azrael. You know I'm CIA."

"But that's where you're wrong. The Azrael I know is

freelance. A mercenary. He used to work for the CIA, but he got burned a long time ago. Now he works for himself."

"Look into my eyes, Hashim," Peter implores. "See that I am telling you the absolute truth. I have been sent to rescue Kamal Osman. I am CIA. I can give you a number to call. Speak with my handler."

Hashim stares into the gray eyes, feeling himself slip.

But he looks away. "I see nothing but hell in your eyes. You are an enemy, nothing else. Kamal promised me American citizenship if I help him against his enemies—and that is what I have done. See, I have many contacts in the RSF. For a price, one of them has agreed to bring me Kamal Osman. And that is where *I* am going: to meet my contact. Where *you* are going, on the other hand, is hell, my American friend."

With a final taunting grin, Hashim goes back to the truck and swings himself into the driver's seat, restarting the engine with a roar that sends a cascade of sand dancing around the Hummer's wheels. He begins to drive, the massive vehicle rolling slowly over the dunes, its path marked by the deep ruts left in the sand.

The air-conditioning purrs as it pumps out cool air into the cab, a clear distinction to the inferno outside where Peter is lashed by the unforgiving rays of the sun. It isn't long before his skin starts to blister under the intense heat, his lips cracking in the dry air. Behind the windshield, Hashim watches him with an amused smile, his eyes gleaming with a vulture's anticipation.

After enduring two relentless hours under the Sahara's punishing sun, the Hummer grinds to a halt. Hashim emerges from the cool, air-conditioned interior, stepping onto the blistering sand. He saunters to the front of the vehicle, his eyes scrutinizing the handiwork of the sun's wrath. Peter's state is already pitiful, his body sagging from the grill of the Hummer. His once vibrant face is now a marred tableau of blistering skin, and stark, pain-filled gray eyes bore into Hashim.

Savoring the moment, Hashim unscrews a water bottle, the audible hiss of escaping air punctuating the desert silence. He declares, "Only another seventy miles to go," his words wafting effortlessly through the arid stillness.

In a cruel taunt, he drenches himself with the water. It cascades over his head, trickling down his face and soaking into his hair in a luxuriant display of hydration.

All the while, Peter languishes under the merciless sun. His parched lips strain, nearly tasting the tantalizing coolness of the water that remains agonizingly out of reach. Hashim's laughter slices through the desert hush, a jarring, harsh melody in the otherwise silent expanse.

Reveling in his triumph, he strides back into the Hummer, the engine revving back to life, and they resume their cruel journey, leaving behind nothing but churned sand and the taunting sound of cruel laughter.

As the miles stretch on, Peter's mind starts to fray at the edges, delirium sinking its claws into him. His voice, raspy and hoarse, repeats hauntingly in the open air as he mumbles a name, the syllables rolling off his cracked lips in a hoarse whisper. "Mikey... Mikey..."

———

As the sun descends, painting the sky in hues of oranges and purples, they finally reach their rendezvous point: an unremarkable expanse of flatland, its sole feature an old stone well, protruding like a lone figure amid the endless sea of sand. Hashim brings the Hummer to a halt, his boots crunching on the coarse ground as he jumps from the cab.

Peter is a pitiful sight. Bound and broken, he hangs limply from the front of the vehicle, his wrists marked by the cruel imprints of the plastic ties. His face, once an impassive mask, is now a grotesque patchwork of raw, weeping blisters, a testament to the Sahara's ruthless onslaught.

Hashim checks Peter's pulse, his fingers soon discovering a stubborn drumming against their tips. "Impressive," he admits. "A heart that withstands hours in the desert is truly a tough one. But it'll do you no good."

With a knife retrieved from his belt, he hacks through the bindings, causing Peter to fall face-first onto the dust-laden ground like a puppet with its strings cut. Holstering the knife, Hashim trades it for his pistol.

"Well, Azrael. Our journey ends here," he says, standing over Peter, the gun cocking with a harsh sound that invades the stillness. "Farewell."

Peter lifts his head, his one open eye meeting the cold glint of the pistol's barrel. With his fate dangling on the precipice, there is, however, a faint respite. The distant growl of an engine pricks Hashim's ears. Turning toward the sound, he spots a pickup in the distance, its form distorted by the shimmering heat waves.

"Ah, my friend is here," Hashim says.

But something feels odd. The pickup is racing toward

them, driving erratically, as though hurried on by a pack of chasing wolves. It skids to a halt nearby, prompting Hashim to wave it over enthusiastically, wondering why it has stopped so far away.

It is then that his excitement withers completely as he takes in the unnerving sight of the bullet holes that riddle the vehicle. He breaks into a run, his boots kicking up clouds of dust.

Hashim finds the pickup in a terrible state. It is filled with the lifeless bodies of rebel soldiers. The driver, barely clinging to life, is desperately clutching a blood-drenched abdomen.

This is his friend.

Hashim reaches him. "Ahmed? What happened?" he gasps, his features paling as he pulls open the door.

His contact, Ahmed, almost falls straight out. Hashim has to push him back in.

The injured man then manages a weak whisper. "Water..."

Frustration creasing his brow, Hashim roughly shakes him. "Never mind water. What happened? Where is Kamal?"

"Taken... in... ambush," Ahmed manages to rasp.

"By who?" Hashim demands, his eyes wide with panic. "Who has him?"

Ahmed only stares at him. "Water?"

Losing his patience, Hashim barks, "Who took him?"

Ahmed furrows his brow. "Would... you let... a brother die?"

"No, of course not," Hashim replies, but his patience is fraying.

"Then fetch... me the water first."

Realizing that cooperation is his only option, Hashim sprints to the Hummer, rummaging through the empty plastic bottles that fill the footwells. When he finally procures one containing water, he rushes back to the pickup, only to find a scene that roots him in place.

Peter, barely more than a living corpse, has managed to crawl or stumble to the open door of the pickup. He sits propped up against it, exchanging whispered words with Ahmed, holding a bottle of water. Then, before Hashim can do anything, he buries a knife into Ahmed's neck, finishing him.

This act completed with the last of his ebbing strength, Peter falls onto his back in the sand, exhausted, a deathly grin etched on his face.

"No, you bastard... No!" Hashim dashes to Ahmed, pulling the dying man into his arms. His hands become slick with blood, his voice hoarse as he accuses, "You killed him."

"Yeah," Peter wheezes, lying on his back in the sun-parched sand, all but dead himself.

Grabbing Peter, Hashim shoves his Beretta into his chin. His words come out in a growl. "I'll make you pay. You think you suffered before..."

Peter, however, interrupts him. "I wouldn't do that if I were you," he manages in a slow drawl. "Or you'll never find out where they've taken Kamal Osman. Then you'll never get out of here."

Turning back to the corpse, Hashim demands, "What did he tell you?"

Peter just smiles, his eyes closed.

"Who has him? Where?"

With the smile tugging at his burned lips, Peter slips into unconsciousness. Hashim, suddenly understanding his situation, stows away his gun. He hoists Peter up, desperation tinging his voice.

"Don't die, Azrael," he blurts out. "I'm your friend, remember? Hashim is your friend. I'll help you, see?" He sprinkles water on Peter's burned chest and face, moistening his lips. "Stay with me, Azrael. Please!"

His eyes sweep over the desert as he mutters to himself, "Where to go from here? North, Khartoum? No. West, RSF? No. East, army? Or... south?" His eyes spark with realization. "South, of course. Yida!"

EIGHTEEN

KHARTOUM - 16TH APRIL, 16:17 (EAT)

ASTRIDE HIS MUSCULAR KTM MOTORCYCLE, THE Hunter arrives at an army barracks located in the heart of the beleaguered city. RSF flags, stark in their vibrant white hues, snap sharply in the hot, turbulent air, mounted atop weathered poles. In the background, the city echoes with the incessant symphony of war, each distant detonation reverberating before being overshadowed by the staccato beat of gunfire.

Semyon dismounts smoothly, his boots crunching on the loose gravel, leaving the bike nestled against a makeshift fortress of sandbags and salvaged metal. A battle-scarred soldier watches his approach, the man's eyes scanning the Russian's hardened features, the mottled skin of his face wrapped in a black litham veil. A terse exchange follows as he hands the soldier a folded sheet of paper.

"You're Colonel Deng's friend, aren't you?" The soldier's eyes flicker with recognition.

Semyon confirms with a nonchalant nod. "Uh-huh."

"This way then." The soldier beckons. "I'll take you to the colonel."

Semyon is led through the heart of the barracks into a somber courtyard that's more of a makeshift cemetery. Fallen warriors, their lives extinguished before they'd even been lived, lay scattered in the dirt, as if tossed aside by the unforgiving hand of conflict. A solitary, skeletal street dog noses through the remnants of food, its tail wagging listlessly amidst the dust and detritus.

He is brought to an infirmary where evidence of a hundred battlefield surgeries lie in gruesome exhibition. Blood-soaked bandages discarded haphazardly are stacked to waist height, surgical tools still smeared with the crimson evidence of life-and-death struggles lay scattered about, the air thick with fat flies.

The room is dense with the labored breaths of the injured, interrupted by the occasional groan of pain. The soldier guides Semyon to the bedside of a particularly pallid man, a river of life-giving blood flowing into him through clear tubes.

Introductions are made in whispers, the soldier murmuring into the older man's ear before gesturing toward the Hunter. "This is Colonel al-Sisi," the soldier then says, stepping back.

"Where's Kamal Osman?" The Hunter's question is direct, his gaze unblinking.

A faint smile creeps onto al-Sisi's face before a hacking cough rattles his frail body, blood tinging his lips. He wipes it away, then meets Semyon's stare with a glint of defiance. "Where's Kamal Osman, you ask." His voice is weak yet undeterred. "Well, where was my backup when the regular army led us into an ambush while my intelligence assured me they were retreating? Where were the reinforcements when al-Burhan's savages tore us apart? Tell me, Russian; when your men—men you love like sons—are being slaughtered all around you, your only instinct is survival. Not to protect your prisoners."

Without a word, Semyon retrieves a thick roll of dollars from his pocket, offering it silently to the colonel. Al-Sisi shares a brief, knowing glance with his subordinate, nodding subtly. The soldier retrieves the money, his fingers quickly counting the bills before giving his superior a confirming nod.

"They took him," al-Sisi reveals, his voice barely above a whisper.

"Alive?"

"Last I saw. Unharmed, too. He spent the entire attack hiding while my men were being slaughtered. I cannot confirm if he's alive this very minute. I was evacuated quickly, with no time for a head count. But if the regular army are smart, they'll keep that one alive till they've gotten what they need from him."

"Do you know where they'd take him if he was still alive?"

Al-Sisi gives one word, saying it like a curse. "Abri."

"What's in Abri?" Semyon inquires.

Al-Sisi manages a weak snort. "Only a place you should pray you never get to see."

NINETEEN

YIDA REFUGEE CAMP, SUDAN - 16TH APRIL, 18:12 (EAT)

WITHIN A STARK DESERT VALLEY, A MISHMASH OF refugee tents unfurls upon the landscape, teetering on the outskirts of an oasis town in the Sahara. The camp is a roiling sea of humanity—of dispossessed souls, torn from their homes and lives. Mothers bathe their children using scant water rationed from bottles and jugs, the droplets precious as diamonds. Others line up at the food counters, aid workers passing out food packages containing staple grains, pulses, fortified cereals, vegetable oil, sugar, and salt. In more open areas, refugees cook over fires, their food strung up on makeshift spits in billy cans. In other places, they sit in the dirt, spooning the food into their mouths and fighting off the flies.

In the center of all this tragedy stands an ancient mosque, its minaret in a state of gradual decay. It rises amidst the sea of canvas tents, standing in the middle like a shepherd surrounded by his flock.

Hashim navigates the Hummer along a dust-blanketed lane that winds its way through the makeshift settlement. Approaching the mosque, he parks the vehicle and leaps out.

"Hey!" he bellows, dashing around to the passenger side.

From the shadows of the mosque, a tall aid worker emerges, his European features sunburned, his eyes an arresting shade of blue, his hair silvered by the unforgiving sun.

"Help me," Hashim implores as he swings the passenger door open. "I have a very sick man here."

The aid worker assesses Peter's condition, eyes widening at the sight of the unconscious man. His skin is a map of pain, raw and blistered, the ruptured bubbles leaking fluids. A pulse check confirms life still flickers within.

"He's still alive, at least," the aid worker mutters. Turning to Hashim, he advises, "You'll have to take him to the hospital in Arras. It's fifteen miles north. Twenty minutes, if you hurry."

"No," Hashim retorts, shaking his head adamantly. "Arras is under military control."

"Then surrender him to the military."

"No! He needs help now."

"We have no room."

Hashim, struggling to hold down his rising anger, pleads, "We can't go to Arras. We can't go anywhere near the army, and I don't have time to explain why. This man has already spent a long time in the desert. He is very sick. He needs medical care. *You* have medical care. Please, I'm begging you. Help him."

Their eyes lock, Hashim's resolve like hardened steel, unyielding. The aid worker's gaze softens first, buckling under the weight of the other man's desperation, and he relents.

"Very well," he sighs in resignation. "We can put him in the nurses' quarters." He turns, calls out in patchy Sudanese Arabic, and moments later, two men emerge, bearing a stretcher. They heave Peter's body out of the Hummer with an effort similar to hoisting a medieval suit of armor.

The two bearers carry the heavy load into the mosque, trailed by the aid worker and Hashim. Their path takes them through the prayer room, which, having surrendered its sacred purpose, now serves as a sanctuary for the innocent casualties of the escalating conflict. The once serene space brims with cots cradling the wounded, each life tethered precariously to the world by the skill of the aid workers fluttering around them.

Every corner of the mosque is claimed by cots, their inhabitants draped in pain, their moans bouncing off the ancient stone walls. The once sacred spaces are now inundated with an army of aid workers, doctors, and nurses, each moving as though guided by a divine force, navigating through the suffering sea with determined purpose.

Peter is carried past a throng of curious faces, each pair of eyes heavy with burden, yet drawn to the spectacle of the foreigner. The wounded warriors, the children orphaned by the war's indiscriminate hand, the widows scarred by the loss —each life is a testament to the war's relentless erosion of hope. They are the human cost of conflict, stripped to their bare existence.

They take Peter into the cool air of a sparse dormitory; a

space furnished with little more than four bunkbeds, a time-worn dresser, a pair of wooden chairs, and two iron-clad footlockers, likely safeguarding the nurses' personal effects.

They carefully deposit Peter onto the lower bunk of one of the beds. The blue-eyed aid worker departs the scene, returning shortly with a man who radiates an aura of medical authority, a towering figure of African descent, possibly native, clad in doctor's whites. A stethoscope, the symbol of his trade, hangs loosely around his neck.

Without missing a beat, the doctor takes stock of the sight before him—a man scorched by the wrath of the desert sun, skin blistered and raw, features distorted from hours of brutal exposure. His trained eyes swiftly evaluate Peter's form before he checks his airways, noting the labored, shallow rhythm of his breathing.

"Get an oxygen mask on him," he instructs the blue-eyed aid worker, who leaps into action, vanishing quickly, only to reappear just as quickly with the necessary equipment before deftly securing an oxygen mask over Peter's sun-ravaged lips. Meanwhile, a second nurse strides into the room, cradling an intravenous drip.

The doctor swiftly checks Peter's pulse at the wrist—it is weak, but thankfully, present. "Start him on isotonic fluids, and I want his vitals monitored closely," he orders, his gaze never leaving the patient.

As a third nurse arrives with monitoring equipment, the doctor conducts a swift neurological examination. His penlight exposes Peter's unresponsive pupils. "Likely heat-stroke," he murmurs, the words aimed as much at himself as his team. "We need to begin cooling measures."

As the team works in orchestrated harmony to stabilize

the patient, the doctor turns his attention to the sunburns mutilating Peter's skin—a grotesque canvas of blistered wounds. He instructs his nurses to carefully undress the patient and commence treating the burns with cool saline compresses and analgesics for pain management.

Throughout the frenzy of organized activity, Hashim watches nervously from the edge of the room. While his team cuts the sun-seared clothing from Peter, the doctor pivots toward him.

"You brought him?" he inquires.

"Yes," Hashim answers. "Will he live?"

"With our care."

"Thanks be to Allah."

"What happened to him?"

Hashim hesitates, then replies with feigned innocence, "I just found him in the desert like that."

"Well, he's fortunate to have you as his guardian angel. Another hour and he might not've made it. It's a miracle he has at all. But he has a strong heart that refuses to give up. Its tenacity is a testament to his will. Once we've stabilized him, we'll continue fluid replacement, round-the-clock monitoring, and if Allah's grace persists, he might yet come through in full health. Now you need to leave myself and my nurses to do our jobs."

His words reverberate in the sterile brightness of the room as he gestures to the exit. Hashim retreats, his gaze lingering on the hive of medical activity all the way to the door, the doctor and nurses focused on their singular goal: to bring this man back from the brink, to pull him from the clutches of the unforgiving desert and the inhuman cruelty he has endured. A cruelty he has endured at the hands of another man.

Something Hashim is all too aware of as he guiltily turns from the unconscious man and heads out the door.

————

A MERE HOUR LATER, Peter's condition has significantly stabilized. Hooked up to a drip line, his blistered and ravaged body is now bound in dressings, lying still in the cool shadows of recovery. The medical team has withdrawn for the time being, only checking on the patient intermittently to ensure that his condition remains stable.

The solitary presence in the room now is Hashim, who occupies a seat by Peter's bedside. A window in the corner is wide open, revealing the sweeping valley, the oasis palm trees standing tall in the distance and silhouetted by the sun. A gentle breeze sighs into the room, carrying with it the fresh scent of the desert.

From the depths of his unconscious state, Peter's parched lips twitch, his voice barely audible as he mutters, "*Mikey... Mikey...*"

"Ssh, take it easy," Hashim soothes, placing a comforting hand on Peter's bandaged shoulder.

He settles down, his body once again sinking into a tranquil state.

"The doctor thinks you'll be back on your feet in a day or two," Hashim continues in a low, comforting tone. "He says you're lucky I was around."

Peter stirs, muttering incomprehensibly, appearing to possess some degree of awareness of his surroundings—one foot in sleep, the other in the here and now. Hashim waits, keeping a cautious watch over his charge until Peter's restless movements come to a halt.

"You know, Azrael," he begins once the room has again sunk into silence, "I'm going to tell you now how I know who you are. You see, we've met before, you and I, although you probably have no memory of it. See, that day I escaped with my life by a hair's breadth." He whistles pointedly. "You remember the compound outside Adado in Somalia, 2012? You rescued the crew and captain of a hijacked oil tanker that day." He pauses a beat, allowing the memory to settle before continuing, "Maybe you remember the nine Somalian pirates you killed better?" His gaze drifts downward, his voice dropping to a mere whisper. "Of course you do. The official report attributed the feat to a four-man Seal team, but I know the truth. They weren't there. *I* was. It wasn't four commandos who stormed our stronghold that night; it was just one man: *you*."

Peter rustles slightly before quickly lapsing back into silence, Hashim's revelation hanging heavy in the air of the dimly lit room.

"Anyway," Hashim resumes, a faint smirk playing on his lips, "when you attacked that day, I was, let's say, indisposed in the restroom, too far from my firearm to offer any resistance. Nevertheless, what I first took for misfortune I quickly realized was its much prettier sister, luck. That night, Allah must have deemed me worthy of his favor—because if I had been with my gun and with the others and not squatting over a hole emptying my bowels, it wouldn't have been nine dead hijackers, but ten. You see, there was a concealed hole nearby where we stashed weapons. Hearing one man after another drop and being unarmed, I scurried there, waited out your deadly assault, and then, as you ushered the hostages away from the compound, slipped out of my hideaway and observed you from an upstairs window. I saw your gray eyes, glinting with the flames of Jahannam beneath a streetlamp. It was like looking into the face of the devil. It wasn't until later that I could match a name to that face: Azrael. The master assassin."

Hashim allows a moment of silence to punctuate his story, letting his gaze linger on the man in front of him before continuing, "In the ensuing years, rumors of your exploits trickled into my ears. Reports that you'd been betrayed by the CIA, then again by your boss at some private security company. Then there were whispers of a son you had, the pair of you adrift in the world, taking on private contracts. Legends of the stir you both caused in Ukraine, Europe, and then Japan. But, most of all, I heard how you were a motherless nomad walking the earth, all alone."

He sighs, his tone softening, "And *that*, Azrael, is where our paths converge. Because, like you, I am a nomad bereft of a mother's love, condemned to a life of solitude. But perhaps now we have found friendship in each other, right?"

One of Peter's eyes cracks open, a spark of cognizance flickering in its gray depth. It appears he's been more attentive than Hashim initially thought.

A touch of satisfaction seeps into Hashim's voice as he notes, "Ah, so you have been listening, after all." He continues, referencing the doctor's earlier diagnosis, "You heard what I said, right, about the doctor? It'll take a few days for you to recover. So"—drawing his chair nearer, he hunches over Peter, his voice dropping to a conspiratorial murmur—

"it's in our best interest that you tell me where Osman is right away and who's holding him captive. This way, while you recuperate, I can go retrieve him. Otherwise, we risk losing him if he's relocated. What do you say, Azrael? You share the information, and I bring Osman back here. I'll stake my life on this promise." He solemnly lays a hand over his heart.

Peter's lone gray eye remains fixated on him, unblinking.

"Come on," Hashim urges, frustration creeping into his voice. "Time isn't our ally here. Share the location, and I swear I'll retrieve him immediately."

Peter, with a barely discernible movement of his finger, beckons him, his voice a mere wheeze. "Come closer," he breathes.

Hashim's eyes light up. Leaning in until his ear is near Peter's parched lips, he listens intently. Peter whispers something, so faint it's practically inaudible, so Hashim prompts him to repeat it louder. Straining his senses to catch the faintest murmur, until he finally deciphers Peter's words. "Back in 2012," he rasps out, "those men I saved told me there were ten of you. That one more was inside the compound." He pauses to swallow. Then, "I should have gone back and made it ten."

And with that, he sinks back into unconsciousness, a small, triumphant grin etched on to his chapped lips.

Surprise flickers across Hashim's face, soon replaced by a scowl, fists curling reflexively, jaw set in a hard line. He mutters under his breath, "Bastard."

TWENTY

ACROSS THE GLOBE - 16TH APRIL

Antione, nondescript in a suit as gray as London's persistent drizzle, glides through the bustle of Heathrow Airport. He moves with a practiced ease, blending seamlessly into the airport's chaotic ballet. He reaches a bathroom, locking himself in a cubicle. From a plain carry-on, he withdraws a vial so tiny it practically disappears in his grip.

He leaves the washroom and reenters the scurrying masses. In a smooth motion, he uncaps the vial and begins releasing its invisible cargo among the unsuspecting crowds of tourists, all of them flying across the world to spread it. The virus, already loosed elsewhere, now finds a new home in London.

In the vibrantly chaotic Chhatrapati Shivaji Maharaj International in Mumbai, Hamid, garbed in a stark white kurta, mirrors Antione's movements halfway across the planet. As he strides through the terminal, a lethal, colorless mist slips into the muggy Mumbai air, seeping into the lungs of unwitting travelers.

In New York's JFK, Jackson follows suit. The already unleashed plague disperses farther, its existence now woven into the very fabric of the international transport system. As he makes his way toward his next flight, the calm flow of the airport routine is broken by a news bulletin that fills a giant telescreen hanging from a wall. An anchor with grave features reports on a strange new virus cropping up globally with people being admitted into hospital with an unknown illness. Her report switches to a World Health Organization official. "There's no cause for panic as of yet," the elderly man claims. "But we are keeping a watchful eye."

As the reports circulate, phones chime and buzz with the news across all three airports as the sleeper agents move through them, unleashing death. The digital murmur swells, the situation's gravity amplifying in every tweet, every news update, every shared post.

Amidst this, Antione disappears into Heathrow's hive of activity.

In Mumbai, Hamid fades into the sea of travelers, leaving an invisible wave of devastation in his wake.

Back in JFK, Jackson stands at passport control, an airport staffer going over his documents.

"Golly. You've been traveling a lot lately, haven't you?" she comments as she looks through it.

"Just trying to rack up the Amex miles," Jackson responds with an easy smile, his deadly mission veiled behind a façade of normalcy.

At Auckland Airport, Liam hands over his own passport, also stamped with numerous recent entries. Like his counterparts, he unleashes his minuscule package of terror into the air of the busy airport.

In Buenos Aires, Helena does the same, each agent originally armed with a total of twenty vials, now down to ten.

The world is on the brink of an invisible war, one it doesn't even know it's fighting. Yet.

———

CIA HEADQUARTERS, Langley, Virginia, USA.
16th April, 13:11 (EAT).

IN THE HEART of the immense conference room, an undercurrent of apprehension swells, a storm brewing in the midst of a hushed sea. Seated at the end of a polished table with the General Council of the CIA, Director Sandy McLean is transfixed, her gaze locked on the towering digital screen casting an eerie glow against the room's shadowy recesses. The spectral reflections of numerous specialists, analysts, and leaders reciprocate her stare, their forms wavering with each flicker of the screen.

From the World Health Organization, a woman's voice illuminates the room's taut silence, her words resonating against the lofty ceiling. "We're standing on the edge of an abyss," she intones, her delivery frigid and heavy with portent. "The global crisis is imminent. Our healthcare infrastructure is standing on the edge."

The crushing weight of her words looms in the room, a suspended hammer on the verge of a devastating drop.

Charts and figures materialize on the screen, painting a chilling picture of the unfolding terror—hospital admissions in a vertical climb, infection rates twisting into an unchecked spiral.

Next in line to address the room is a man bearing the standard of the Department of Justice—impeccably groomed with a meticulously shaven face and hair neatly side-parted. "Examine these visuals," he commands, his words initiating a montage of bone-chilling footage mirroring the chaos unfolding beyond the room's walls. "Since the news started to break, supermarkets have morphed into war zones," he tells them, "aisles turned into fighting rings."

The footage shows two women locked in a bitter struggle over dwindling goods. Another shot is of a man brandishing a pistol in the middle of a Walmart, his shopping cart piled high with toilet paper.

"Panic reigns as resources dwindle to a trickle," Director McLean remarks.

"This can't go on," the DOJ representative relays. "Tonight, the President intends to enforce a nationwide lockdown. However, the news has already leaked, triggering pandemonium in the streets."

With each passing image and chilling account, Sandy senses a lump of unease form within her.

"We're dealing with more than just the virus," the chief of Cybersecurity and Infrastructure from Homeland Security interjects. "The digital landscape is rife with dangerous conspiracy theories and outright lies. It's pushing an already strained society toward hysteria."

The woman brings up a screen capture: Internet billboards crying out 'hoax,' hyperlinks disseminating half-truths, a headline boldly declaring: "The government is setting us up for perpetual lockdown." It's a world teetering on the brink of implosion.

"Much of this can be sourced back to the Russians," Sandy states.

"There's more," the man from DOJ interjects, his voice cutting through the room.

The screen flickers as CCTV footage commandeers her attention. Armed vigilantes are seen storming a hospital.

"These men are from a group called American Patriots," he explains, his voice grave. "They stormed this hospital in Montana, insistent on seeing the infected. We have National Guard units deployed across major cities, struggling to stem the growing unrest. It's as though we're living through a horror movie. Only this is now our reality."

Sandy McLean shakes her head, the lines on her face deepening. "After COVID, the public resilience is worn thin. Another quarantine won't be swallowed easily. We're in for a lot of unrest. Putin must be loving this," she adds, her words a clandestine whisper meant only for the General Council.

"We're ready to offer our full support," declares the woman from WHO, her voice carrying a note of unwavering determination. "This crisis is global and demands a global, unified response."

The meeting barrels on, the virtual space charged with an atmosphere of palpable desperation and fear. They stand at the precipice of catastrophe, staring into an uncertain void. This is the world they now inhabit, their duty clear—to wrest control from the jaws of chaos, whatever the cost.

Finally, the call ends. The screen fades to black, leaving Sandy McLean in a heavy silence, the lingering echo of the crisis haunting the room.

TWENTY-ONE

YIDA REFUGEE CAMP, SOUTH SUDAN - 17TH APRIL, 00:18 (EAT)

THEY DON'T HAVE A DAY OR TWO. THE importance of the mission means that Peter merely spends another six hours recuperating at the camp, instead of the two days the doctor recommended.

Under the cover of night, Hashim hurries through the bustling refugee camp. The influx of displaced peoples, many of them wounded, has escalated, the camp's main thoroughfare illuminated by sporadic headlights and lanterns, choked with a ceaseless stream of incoming vehicles and their human cargo, piled precariously in the back of pickups.

Hashim steps inside the repurposed mosque, the dim interior lit by a few oil lamps. He charts a course through the teeming chaos toward the nurses' dormitory. Upon entering, he finds Peter propped up on his side, the moonlight filtering through the open window casting a silver sheen on him, boots casually resting on the bed's footboard.

"All right, my friend," Hashim begins, "the truck's prepared and ready to roll. And with the way the wounded are pouring into this place, we'd better get the hell out of here before we're caught up in the war."

"You're forgetting," Peter retorts, "you don't know where we're heading yet."

With a smirk, Hashim replies, "For now at least."

As Peter carefully swings his legs off the bed, Hashim assists him by holding up a clear bag of fluid. A thin drip line connected to the bag leads straight to Peter's forearm. The shadows cast by the lamps accentuate Peter's red and blistered skin, which contrasts sharply with the pristine white bandages wrapping his arms and neck. Despite the searing pain, determination is evident in the way he holds himself.

"Here," a voice interrupts, and both men turn to see the blue-eyed aid worker holding out several fluid bags, his face illuminated by the soft glow of a nearby lantern. "You'll need these. Make sure he keeps replacing the fluid, or he won't last long out there."

Hashim nods gratefully. "Thank you."

The duo makes their way out, with Hashim keeping the fluid bag high to ensure a steady flow. They weave through the chaos of the refugee camp, the sights and sounds of despair all around. Children crying, women comforting them, the elderly looking lost, their features etched in the faint glow of campfires. All the while, aid workers, like angels in the midst of hell, try their best to bring order to the chaos.

Their Hummer waits for them. When they reach it,

Hashim loads the additional fluid bags onto the backseat. Peter, still weak and shaky, climbs into the passenger seat.

"You sure about this, Azrael?" Hashim asks. "The doctor said you needed at least another day. The offer is still there. I can go get Kamal by myself. Bring him back."

Peter merely clenches his jaw. "Let's move."

With a nod, Hashim starts the engine, the Hummer rumbling into life, the headlights cutting a path through the darkness. They make their way out of Yida via a worn track, past the fringes of the sprawling camp. Refugees slink about, fear glowing in their eyes. With each passing meter, they bid farewell to the makeshift city of tents, its tattered silhouette shrinking in the rearview mirror, soon lost altogether in the darkness of the desert night.

———

Nubian Desert, Sudan.
17th April, 14:13 (EAT).

The journey is relentless; they drive solidly through the night and well into the next day. Having gone through all the bags of fluid the aid worker provided, Peter feels at least eighty percent fit, the pain in his blistered skin reduced to a mere afterthought. This renewed strength allows him to take the responsibility of driving. With the barren, sun-scorched landscape stretching out before them, he mans the wheel of the Hummer while Hashim stares despondently at his phone, its signal icon relentless in its emptiness.

Disgruntled, the Sudanese pries open the glove compartment, extracts a crumpled map, and lays it out across his knees, his brow furrowing as he tries to make sense of their route.

"Where in the hell are you taking us?" Hashim grumbles, frustration in his voice.

Rather than providing a direct answer, Peter shifts the conversation. "You lied to me when you said Kamal never met anyone."

Hashim remains silent, watching Peter out of the corner of his eye.

Peter adds, "You never mentioned that he picked up a young girl."

Hashim jerks his head Peter's way, a flicker of alarm passing over his features. After a moment's pause, he regains his composure, responding nonchalantly, "Well, you never asked."

"That's beside the point," Peter persists. "Where is she?"

"I left her with Kamal," Hashim tells him, a glum expression on his face.

"And the RSF took her with him?"

"Yes."

"You gonna tell me about it?"

Hashim sighs, resigned. "What's there to tell?"

"You can start," Peter suggests evenly, "with the part between you arriving in Khartoum with Kamal and you handing him and the girl over to the RSF."

Hashim groans out of the side of his mouth. Then, realizing he has no other choice, he begins, "Soon after we got into the city, we found our way to some old couple's place in the rich quarter."

"In Um Dalil?" Peter asks.

"That's right."

"And what happened there?"

"I find out that we're here to pick up a little girl. Leila is her name. The old couple don't like it, though. Don't want the girl to go with us, but Kamal insists. In the end, he convinces them, and they give in. We leave. That's when I tell him I'm no babysitter. I agreed to get one man into Khartoum, that was all, but now he wants me to smuggle him and this kid out of the country. He practically begged me, and in the end, I agreed when he offered me another ten thousand to get them both out."

"Why didn't he call it in?" Peter inquires.

"There was no power in the entire city. None of the cell towers were working. Even the satellite phone he had wouldn't work. We had to leave the city. That was when I called my friend in the RSF. I needed his help to get us out of Khartoum."

"Help?" Peter questions skeptically, narrowing his eyes.

"Yes."

"So it wasn't to sell them out, then?"

"No, not at first," Hashim admits, his voice dropping to a hushed murmur. His face clouds over with regret. "I agreed to help, lured by the prospect of the twenty thousand dollars Kamal promised if I could get him and the girl out of Sudan. But for this, we needed papers to get Leila out of the city, because by that point, the RSF had the place on lockdown. The only way out was with their permission. That was where my contact came in."

"But something went wrong, didn't it?" Peter asks as he gazes across the cab of the Hummer, reading the guilt on the other man's face.

"Yeah," Hashim murmurs, a little light leaving his eyes. "Just like something always does."

"What?"

"You can probably guess."

"Your RSF contact?"

"Correct," Hashim sighs. "Kamal said he could travel out of Sudan so long as I could get him away from the no-fly zone."

"He was trying to set up an extraction point," Peter comments to himself.

"To get there, though, meant having to travel through rebel territory," Hashim continues, "which had become covered with their checkpoints. Anyone traveling without their permission risked being shot. I needed my RSF friend to obtain the necessary permits and to get my name across to the relevant people so we could safely travel out of the no-fly zone, and Kamal and Leila could be picked up."

"But that's not what happened?"

"No," Hashim confirms, shaking his head. "Right from the beginning, things seemed off. I was used to dealing with my friend alone, but when he showed up for the meeting, he had a second man with him—some sergeant with an attitude. Turns out, my friend has got a big mouth, and word had spread about his profitable side-deal, catching the attention of his superior. This superior was intrigued by the idea of someone paying a thousand dollars just for some papers and a few phone calls."

"You should have offered less," Peter interjects. "It would have drawn less attention."

Hashim sighs. "I know that now, but at the time, I was desperate. I thought if I offered five times the going rate, it would be done more urgently. Instead, it caught the sergeant's attention, and he decided to muscle in on my friend's operation."

"What happened when they showed up?"

"The second he sees Kamal Osman, this *ghabi* sergeant straight away spots him for what he is: an American. He hears the twang in his Arabic, spots the quality of his clothing, sees the girl."

"What happened next?" Peter prompts.

"The sergeant starts ordering Kamal and Leila into their truck. Right away, I knew what was happening, but before I could do anything, another two pickups filled with RSF come around the corner, and there was nothing I could do. The sergeant warned me that all future operations were to go through him. Then he tossed me fifty dollars in crumpled, dirty bills and climbed into the truck. That's when Kamal called out to me. He poked his head from the truck's window to catch my eye, and when I came to him, he whispered in my ear."

Hashim falls silent.

"That's when he told you he could get you into America, wasn't it?" Peter asks, raising an eyebrow.

Hashim nods. "Yes. He whispered to me that he was CIA. Said that if I could save him and the girl, he would make sure that I got clemency from the American government and a new life in the USA."

"So that's why you're so eager to reach him," Peter surmises.

"Yes," Hashim confirms. "If I save him, I can have a better life. I suppose it hasn't escaped your attention, but I am getting old for an outlaw in this part of the world. Men like me don't usually make it past thirty. I am now thirty-seven. I have no home, no savings, no pension, and no children to look after me. Like an old street dog, I will one day have nothing more to do than to crawl somewhere to die alone. I don't want to end up like that."

A tense silence ensues. After a moment, Peter asks, "Why didn't you tell me all this from the start, when I picked you up out in the desert?"

Hashim scoffs, a humorless grin playing on his face. "You think you're the first person to ask about Kamal Osman since I lost him? You think I should have trusted you, after you literally tied me to the front of a car and threatened to it drive off a cliff, then left me in the middle of the desert to die?"

He directs a disbelieving look toward Peter across the Hummer's cab.

"I didn't think so," he remarks, turning back to the desolate expanse of sand dunes and the barely discernible path cutting through them. His voice lowers, laden with suspicion as he adds, "To be honest, I'm not even sure I can trust you now. For all I know, you could be planning to abandon me in the middle of *this* desert."

Peter doesn't answer right away, allowing the thought to build some momentum inside of Hashim. Then he says, "Perhaps. It doesn't sound like such a terrible idea."

Hashim looks at him sharply, his eyes narrowing. "And you still expect me to trust you?"

Peter opens his mouth to answer, but his words are drowned out by the sharp crack of a gunshot reverberating through the valley. The front tire of the Hummer bursts instantly. A second gunshot rings out, puncturing the other front tire, causing the vehicle to buckle and career out of control. The truck skids to a stop, and they scramble out before more bullets come, the two men getting into cover behind the enormous bulk of the Hummer.

Opposite them, a towering sand dune stretches along the edge of the road. They scan its crest, quickly spotting the glint of a sniper's scope, then another. Soon, figures rise into view, lining the dune—these aren't mirrors on sticks—and within moments, at least thirty armed men are glaring down at them.

Squinting, Hashim recognizes their uniforms. "Regular army," he states. "SAF."

"Then we should surrender," Peter suggests.

Hashim looks at him, his brow furrowed. "Why?"

"Because we're not too far from our destination, and I have a feeling that if these men take us prisoner, they might just deliver us to exactly where we need to go."

"Hands up!" a voice commands in Arabic as several soldiers start rushing down the dune toward them. In the meantime, four pickup trucks equipped with mounted M4 machine guns appear from the towering sand mound.

"And where do you think it is they'll take us?" Hashim inquires, raising his hands along with Peter and cautiously emerging from their hiding spot.

"Abri," Peter tells him.

"Abri?" Hashim repeats, his frown deepening. "But there's nothing in Abri except..." A wave of dread washes over him as he reaches a chilling realization. "Oh no."

TWENTY-TWO

ABRI POW CAMP, SUDAN - 17TH APRIL, 16:03 (EAT)

THE SUN STANDS UNBEARABLY HIGH IN THE VAST cerulean sky, its heat hammering down on the seemingly infinite stretch of undulating desert. Amidst this arid sweep, an imposing structure of stone and concrete breaks the monotony of the sandy sea—a formidable compound standing in stark relief to the surrounding emptiness. This structure is called Abri Prisoner of War Camp. Its sprawling architecture, a mix of enclosed courtyards and stern two-story buildings, radiates a harsh authority, its intimidating mud-brown structure stark against the brilliant blue sky.

The army stronghold is girded by an impenetrable barrier: a massive concrete wall, relentless and unforgiving in its purpose, its stark gray surface threaded with menacing strands of concertina wire. Dotting its height at calculated intervals, severe guard towers jut out like skeletal fingers, the men occupying them sweeping stern gazes across the desolate landscape that surrounds the prison.

A pickup truck, kicking up swirls of dust in its wake, barrels toward the compound. Peter and Hashim sit in the back of it, the air ruffling their hair, their clothing and faces caked in desert dust. Opposite them sit two soldiers, AKs grasped in their hands. As the vehicle approaches, the colossal metal gate set into the compound's wall grinds open, a yawning mouth revealing a hive of army activity within. The air bristles with tension as countless soldiers, like worker bees, buzz around, their green uniforms practically glowing against the drab surroundings.

The pickup is taxied into a central courtyard. Orders are barked, ricocheting around the barren space, and the passengers are roughly prodded from the back of the truck. Peter and Hashim stumble out, their bodies stiff and weary from the journey. The two of them line up as directed. Hands shackled behind their backs, they stand there while a three-soldier team forms an arc around the rear of them, their AKs held in the low-ready position.

Abri is a grim sight for sore eyes, a dystopian vision etched in stone, sand and rusted metal, held captive under a relentless sun. With the prison so full with rebels, they've had to erect temporary holding cells outside in the courtyard. Two rusted metal cages hold sway at the other end of the yard. They hold at least fifty people each. Which isn't good when you consider that each cage is designed for ten. The men are pressed together. Some of them have climbed up on the bars to escape the press, nothing to protect them from the scorching sun except the rags of their uniforms.

With an air of resignation and not a little sarcasm, Peter remarks out the side of his mouth, "Nice place."

"Maybe our cell will have a ceiling," Hashim whispers back.

"Shut up!" the closest soldier snaps before ramming Hashim in the thigh with the butt of his AK.

The force of the blow nearly sends Hashim sprawling. He careens sideways, his momentum halted only by Peter, who stands as rigid and immovable as a statue. Grasping his solidity, Hashim wrenches himself back to a vertical position, a pained grimace contorting his face. Muttering low curses, he steadies his trembling legs, steeling himself for whatever might come next.

Abri is their reality now, one they must adapt to, endure, and ultimately survive. And quickly, too.

"What are we waiting for, anyway?" Peter asks.

The man closest to him leans in. "Colonel," he hisses.

"Oh, he can talk, but I can't?" Hashim complains.

Another blow, this one in the small of his back, sends him tumbling forward. He barely stays on his feet before being hauled back in line, grumbling incessantly under his breath.

Around them, the courtyard hums with a unique life of its own. Soldiers, already hardened by the recent fighting, are scattered across the open spaces between the holding cells. Among them, in a secluded corner close to the mesh wall of a cage, a hulking figure holds court with two corporals. His broad back is turned to the new arrivals, and he is wearing a hood, hiding his features. A metal pincer gleams in the sunlight on the end of his left arm.

A silent observer, he seems disinterested, and yet he is

listening. The twitch of his disfigured face betrays his alertness—each conversation, each sound, each nuance is registered and logged as he speaks with the corporals.

On the other side, one of the soldiers at the edge of the yard comes forward and breaks the uneasy quietude, his accusatory finger stabbing the air before Hashim. "Hey, don't I recognize you?" he demands, his gaze invasive. "What's your name?"

"Azam," Hashim responds, his voice a quiet rumble as his eyes avoid contact.

Suspicion narrows the soldier's gaze into a sharp, piercing line. "No, it's not. I've seen your face on the news. You're Hashim Iqbal, the terrorist."

The accusation resounds in the courtyard. The hooded figure in the corner, seemingly uninvolved until now, reacts. He stops talking to the corporals and swivels around, steely eyes locking on to the commotion.

"That's it. Hashim Iqbal," the soldier chimes in.

Another soldier comes forward.

"Can't be," he muses with disbelief.

"Sure it is," the first soldier says as the team of three men move around to the front of the prisoners, all attention on Hashim. "See the beady little eyes, the rat face? It's him," the first soldier insists, turning the men's doubt into certainty.

Other soldiers join in until there is a veritable crowd gathered around them. The courtyard then erupts into a chorus of amazement. "Wow. We got the Rat."

The first soldier tells Hashim, "You know there was a guy in here, American I think. Said he came to Khartoum with you."

The news makes both Peter and Hashim turn.

"Is he still here?" Hashim counters greedily.

The soldier simply shrugs in reply.

A stern voice suddenly slices through the clamor. "Privates?!" The courtyard falls silent, all attention pulled to the white-haired old colonel walking up on them.

Colonel Abubakar stands as a stark relic from Sudan's tumultuous past. A veteran of the Second Sudanese Civil War and a soldier of its first, age has weathered his once formidable frame, yet his eyes retain a steel-hard intensity that has not dulled with the passage of years as he stares fiercely at his soldiers. His uniform, fitting a bit loosely on his shrunken form, is meticulously pressed, displaying the pride he still carries, and his grizzled face is etched with the hardships of a soldier's life. This man has clearly come out of retirement to run this camp.

"Step away from the prisoners," he orders with an authority that belies his age. The soldiers hurriedly step back, their swagger replaced by an almost sheepish stance as the old man takes control.

"Who are these men?" he demands.

One of the soldiers explains, "They were traveling along a restricted road that we were told the rebels were using to transport weapons. This one"—his eyes narrow at Hashim —"has been identified. He is a well-known scoundrel. Piracy, terrorism, arms trafficking, people smuggling, stealing. Any way to get at money, this one."

The colonel leans toward Hashim, bringing his scowling face close. Then his attention is on Peter. "And the white one?"

"He was with him. Driving the vehicle."

Looking at Peter, the colonel grunts, "Mercenaries. They

flock to war like vultures to a dying man. Get them processed and inside."

"Yes, sir."

As the colonel retreats from the yard, the first soldier commands them to undress before ordering another soldier to fetch them prison uniforms. One of the soldiers steps forward and unlocks their shackles. The whole time, the three men keep their guns trained on them.

While they undress, Hashim's eyes skitter across the courtyard until they latch on to an arresting sight—the hooded figure who earlier seemed only passively interested. "Whoa," Hashim murmurs, nudging Peter. "You see that guy in the corner? The really ugly one in the hood?"

Peter follows Hashim's gaze and immediately stiffens as he locks on to the figure. Those eyes, those merciless, predatory eyes staring right at them. There's no forgetting those eyes, not even a chance. He swears involuntarily under his breath, his body taut as a bowstring.

Hashim arches a brow at his reaction. "You look like you know the guy," he probes, intrigued.

"I do," Peter admits tersely, unable to peel his gaze away from the figure.

"Really?" Hashim is more than just curious now. There's a note of alarm in his voice.

"Yes. We go way back," Peter responds, his words heavy with unspoken history. "I thought I'd killed him. Twice."

Their conversation draws the hooded figure's attention. The man they call the Hunter sends a penetrating glare their way, his gaze slicing through the distance between them.

"He looks like he crawled all the way out of hell,"

Hashim quips, trying to lighten the tense moment. "Who is he?"

"He's earned many names over the years, but most know him simply as the Hunter. He's tied to Russian GRU, FSB, SVR. An assassin," Peter explains, his voice as grim as a tombstone.

Hashim's eyes widen, a spark of fascinated horror igniting within them. "What do you think he's doing here?"

"I can't say for certain," Peter admits. "But I know this much: His presence can't possibly bode well for us."

As if on cue, the colonel, in his departure from the courtyard, pauses by Semyon Mikhailovich. "Could I have a word in my office?" he asks, his voice filled with an unspoken tension.

The Hunter inclines his head in a silent assent, rises from his seat, and follows him from the courtyard, leaving behind an atmosphere heavy with dread and unanswered questions.

———

INSIDE THE COLONEL'S OFFICE, the Hunter's presence fills the compact space. He settles himself down on a threadbare couch, beneath an old, worn-out fan that groans and creaks with each rotation, barely stirring the stagnant air.

Settling his old bones behind a desk, the colonel starts, his voice like gravel, "I understand that as you are paying me a heavy sum to watch over these prisoners, you have certain *rights*, should we say, but I must insist that you keep the torture down to a minimum. The screaming unsettles my men."

"I'm afraid it's necessary to extract the information I need," Semyon rebuts, his tone bordering on defensive.

"Yes. But not when it is taken too far," the colonel declares, his voice flat and eyes sharp. "What information is it you're after, anyway?"

"That's none of your business, Colonel."

Colonel Abubaka slams a frail fist on his desk. "This camp *is* my business!"

Semyon studies the old man for a second. "What is it?" he asks, an edge creeping into his voice. "You want more money?"

"That would be a start. Another thing would be to make sure whatever happens in those quarters of yours stays away from my men," the colonel adds.

"My place is secluded. They don't see anything, only hear it."

"But it's not just the screaming. It's what you've done to that... thing. The way you treat him, make him do things. Like he is your slave. No, worse. Like he is your dog," the Colonel accuses, disgust in his voice.

"Well," Semyon starts, glancing out of the window at the sight of Hashim and Peter being escorted out of the courtyard with the rest, both now dressed in the striped uniforms of prisoners, "you won't have to worry much longer. I'll be moving on soon enough."

The colonel raises an eyebrow. "Oh?"

"Yes. You see," the Russian agent hisses as Peter and Hashim pass by underneath, "the man I've been waiting for has just conveniently landed in my grasp." His lips curl into a predatory smile, his eyes fixed on the courtyard below. The chess pieces are all falling into place.

As PETER and Hashim tread the grounds below the colonel's office, they cast their eyes upwards, catching a glimpse of Semyon's silhouette framed in the dusty window. There's an unspoken tension between them as they continue onward, stepping into the hub of the prison.

The sight that greets them is heart-wrenching. Rebel soldiers, once oozing with fight, are now reduced to gaunt shadows of their former selves. They loiter behind bars, stacked together in cramped cells made for a tenth of their number. Forced to stand, their vacant eyes follow Peter and Hashim as they're marched along a damp corridor. Hunger and suffering is etched into their hollowed cheeks and sunken eyes, and it's clear they're being slowly starved, their strength whittled away with every passing day.

The air within the prison is heavy with an acrid stench of despair, the walls reverberating with low murmurs. They're walked through another courtyard. Cages litter the area, packed with men crammed together like cattle. They huddle in the corners, their faces haunted by the horrors they've experienced, bodies marred by brutal beatings and untreated injuries. Each one is a living testament to the atrocities committed within these walls.

Peter and Hashim navigate through the labyrinth of suffering, their eyes scanning the prison's population, searching for one face among the sea of many, a needle in this horrific haystack—Kamal Osman.

Finally, they reach their cell. They are thankful it is indoors, under a ceiling. Nevertheless, it is filled with sweating, coughing men, all dressed in the tatty remains of their

RSF uniforms. They are ordered back from the rusted door, an order they comply with immediately, and Peter and Hashim are pushed inside.

Hashim turns instantly to the bars as they close them in. "Our shackles?" he asks one of the guards in Arabic, twisting around to show his secured hands.

"We have orders that you're both to stay that way."

The two escorts begin walking away. Pressing himself to the bars, Hashim calls out to them, but they ignore him, the sound of their retreating boots taunting him.

"Bastards," he hisses under his breath before turning to the room. It is no bigger than a two-man prison cell and yet there are ten men in there. Half stand, while the other half squat with their backs to the walls. They soon learn that the prisoners take it in turns, swapping over every so often from standing to squatting, squatting to standing.

Leaning in to Hashim, Peter says, "Ask them about Kamal and the girl."

Inquiring among their fellow prisoners, Hashim describes Kamal and Leila, hoping for a lead. A prisoner, his face lined with the burden of war, shakes his head slowly. "No girl, as far as I know. But the American was here."

The hope within Peter and Hashim flares. "When?" they ask, urgency underlining their words.

"The last time I saw him was about two days ago. That was when the Russian took him to his place, and... well..." The prisoner trails off, leaving the implication hanging heavy in the air. "People don't normally come back from there. If they do, then they're usually broken."

TWENTY-THREE

In the scarcely furnished room that makes up the main part of his quarters, lit by a single dangling bulb, sits Semyon Mikhailovich the Hunter. His boots resting up on an oak table with a casual air of authority, he leans back as though upon a throne. His unfathomable eyes glint with cold, dark amusement as his mind works away behind them. The man they call the Hunter is not like other men; the rules of human empathy, dignity, and decency do not apply to him.

Flanking him along the table are two corporals, his selected accomplices, their main qualifications being their brutality. They sit there eating, basking in their borrowed authority. The table before them is a decadent display of food, a clear contrast to the destitution just beyond the door of their little hovel. As they eat, their laughter echoes off the stark concrete walls, a grotesque soundtrack to their revelry.

They are not alone. Shuffling about the room is the figure of a man, or what used to be one. His once proud stature has been reduced to a stoop, his eyes hollow from enduring the unendurable within this place. His feet shackled, chains clank with his every movement, a constant reminder of his imprisoned state.

The corporals, gorged on power and the bounty before them, turn their twisted humor onto the chained man. A smirk etched on their faces, one of them hooks a foot through his chains, sending him sprawling across the cold stone floor. The men laugh, Semyon merely smiling as the prisoner pulls himself upright. Food is then tossed deliberately onto the ground, the mirth in the corporals' eyes shining brighter as the beaten man stoops to pick up the scraps.

Through it all, he endures, his spirit flickering like an undying flame within his weary eyes.

As the revelry continues within the room, the world outside seems to shudder and quake. The distant thud of an explosion serves as a haunting warning, the blast vibrating through the walls, the floor, and into their bones.

The men pause to listen, looking up from the food and the chained man.

"Eat," Semyon tells them. "It's still far away."

The men look at him, then turn back to their meals. Despite the bleakness that surrounds them, the feast continues. Semyon, immovable in his seat of power, looks on with his steel-cold gaze.

"Mutt?" His voice cuts through the room.

The beaten man turns, his chains jangling, his eyes meeting the icy stare of the Hunter. There is a tension between the two men, a twisted bond formed in the crucible of torture.

"We're about to have a visitor." Semyon's voice hangs heavy in the air. "Now is the time to see how truthful you were being."

"Mutt" nods, a meek acknowledgement of some unspoken pact.

"Okay," Semyon grunts, turning his attention to one of his henchmen. "Go fetch Iqbal."

The man leaves, and moments later, the door creaks open, and Hashim is thrust inside. The sudden transition from bright daylight to the gloom of the room makes him squint, but as his eyes adjust, he catches sight of the hooded figure seated at the end of the table.

He doesn't, however, look at him for long. Instead, his eyes gravitate to the food, widening as he takes in the spread laid out before him. A feast in the midst of hell.

"Your name is Hashim Iqbal, is it not?" Semyon's voice is a grating whisper, hissing through the room.

"Uh-huh," Hashim replies, his own voice barely audible.

As he stares at the food, an empty growl resonates from his stomach.

"Have they fed you yet?" Semyon inquires, a wolfish grin playing on his lips.

Hashim shakes his head, the silence saying more than words ever could.

"That's a shame."

"I haven't eaten a full meal in three days," Hashim admits, the hunger making him bold.

"Then come, take a seat. Don't be frightened. Eat," the Hunter invites, his voice unnervingly friendly.

"You mean it?" Hashim asks, his hope desperate and brittle.

"I do." Semyon's affirmation rings out through the room, a chilling promise in the midst of a nightmare.

Hashim doesn't need a second invitation. He rushes to the table, taking a seat at the farthest end from the Hunter. His hands shake as he serves himself the array of food before him—warm bread, aromatic tagine, fluffy couscous, succulent chicken legs, tender lamb. He starts eating greedily, stuffing his face as though it's the last meal he'll ever have.

It could well be.

"The friend you're with," Semyon starts, his gaze never leaving Hashim.

Hashim looks up, his mouth full of bread. "Not friend," he corrects after swallowing, a bit of color returning to his gaunt face. "Acquaintance."

"But how did you end up with him?" Semyon asks.

"He was with some bounty hunters I bumped into in al Fashir. He took me as his prisoner," Hashim explains, tearing into the meat with more vigor.

"Then what?"

"He bundled me into that Jeep your people found me in and drove me into the desert. Now I'm here."

"So he never hired you, then?" Semyon asks, a hint of curiosity breaking through his icy demeanor.

"No," Hashim says vehemently.

"Then what was he bringing you here for?"

"I don't know." Hashim tries to hold Semyon's gaze, but there's a chilling intensity in those eyes that forces him to look away.

"Well, he had to be coming here," Semyon insists. "The

road you were on only has one destination your friend could have wanted: Abri prisoner of war camp." He states it matter-of-factly.

Hashim frowns, feigning confusion. "What could he possibly want that's here?"

"That's what I'd like to know. Did he mention anything while he had you captive?" Semyon inquires, leaning back in his chair.

"No," Hashim says, struggling to keep his voice steady.

The Hunter gives him a sinister smile, his rattlesnake eyes holding a terrible coldness. "A drink?" he asks.

"Yes. Thank you," Hashim responds, feeling the dryness of his throat.

"Mutt!" Semyon calls, tapping the table twice with his pincer.

Something shuffles out of the beaded curtains separating the room from a small bedroom. A figure, bent and broken, carrying a tray with a water jug on it. When Hashim turns to see who it is, the blood drains from his face, and for a moment, it feels like he might pass out.

"Oh no," Hashim mutters, his appetite suddenly vanishing.

"You recognize him, then," Semyon purrs, a trace of satisfaction creeping into his voice. "Even after my... changes."

The man standing there none other than Kamal Osman. Hashim had last seen him in Khartoum, a man in full command of his faculties. Now his face is a horrid map of torment—a patchwork of raw scars, bruises, and burns. His cheeks are sunken, suggesting the loss of most of his teeth, and one of his legs seems to have been shattered and

crudely reset, the ankle grotesquely swollen. He is a carica-
ture of human suffering, a grotesque testament to the
Hunter's brutal methods.

Kamal shuffles over, serving Hashim a glass of water. His
movements are mechanical, as if he's been reduced to an
automaton. Hashim finds that he can't take his eyes off the
specter of the man he left in Khartoum, no more now than a
hollow shell.

"You see," Semyon says, breaking Hashim's horrified
reverie, "I know who you are, Hashim Iqbal, A.K.A. the
Rat. I know what you've done, and I know why you're here.
Now tell me the one thing I really want to know." He levels a
hard, icy stare at Hashim. "Where's the girl Leila?"

Hashim visibly shudders and swallows hard. His throat
feels like sandpaper. He goes to speak but can't. He sips
some water from a metal cup. Then he says, "I don't know
anything about any girl."

Semyon's voice is dangerously soft, his patience clearly
thinning. "She was with you when you handed him over to
the rebels, but she didn't come with. They left her with you.
Now I'm going to ask you again: Where is the girl Leila?"

"I... I left her on that street corner... That's the truth,"
Hashim stammers, his eyes flitting between Semyon and
Kamal, a gnawing dread growing in his gut.

The world flips upside down in a heartbeat. With a curt
nod from Semyon, the two corporals seize Hashim. A
moment of violent disorientation and he's flung face-first
onto the table, his body slamming down onto the rough
wooden surface. One of the men manages to hold his left
hand to the table. Before Hashim can react, the bone-
chilling sensation of cold steel pierces the back of it. He

screams out in agony as a knife skewers his flesh, pinning the hand to the table. The pain is a white-hot flash, blinding and absolute. Another knife follows suit, impaling his other hand, and in less than ten seconds, he's trapped to the table. His body writhes in torment. Words tumble out of him in a frantic, incoherent stream.

Rough fingers grip his hair, yanking his head up, forcing him to look at Semyon. The Hunter's eyes bore into him, twin glacial pools of menace that glow from his scar-mottled face.

"Your friend may have told you about me," he growls, "or he may not have. I don't give a damn either way. Because soon enough, he'll be dead, and you'll know exactly the type of man I am." Semyon's words are a chilling promise, a foreboding prophecy.

With another cold nod, one of the corporals steps forward. The sudden, terrible sensation of a cattle prod jamming into Hashim's ribs overwhelms him. The electric shock convulses through him, making him jerk violently, straining against the knives pinning his hands.

Off to the side, a broken figure watches the macabre scene unfold. Kamal Osman, already stripped of so much, is now a helpless bystander, unable to intervene as the horrors escalate. His eyes, wide with terror, mirror the gut-wrenching helplessness that engulfs him.

———

AT THE SAME time as Hashim finds himself being tortured in Semyon's quarters, Peter is confined to a tiny cell, the cold, indifferent gaze of a guard fixed to him as the man sits beside the door of the confined space holding his AK firmly. A fact that Peter has to grin about. After all, if that man fires that AK in this closet of a room, it'll deafen them both.

Other than the danger of losing his sense of hearing, the cell stinks of sweat and blood. When they brought him here, he'd actually stepped on a discarded tooth as he'd made his way to the chair bolted to the middle of the floor. The one he sits in now. Or, more precisely, the one he's strapped to now like some psychopath in a mental ward.

The cold metal clasps bite into his shins, chest, and arms, securing him in place with relentless, impersonal precision, trapping him like this, marooned in this claustrophobic space.

The silence of his confinement is disrupted by distant cries of anguish. Hashim's faint screams, carried to him through the prison walls. Peter listens. But then, another sound punctures the auditory landscape. The sudden, reverberating force of an explosion, significantly closer than the others, rattles through the prison, the dust vibrating in the air. The suspended particles are thrown into frenzied motion by the shockwave, heralding a change, a disturbance in their bleak circumstances.

———

HASHIM HANGS FROM THE TABLE, his strength depleted, the edges of broken words spilling from his cracked, bloodied lips. Rough hands hoist his head up, forcing him to face his tormentors.

"Does Azrael have the girl somewhere?" The words resonate in the cold, sterile room.

Hashim manages to swallow, his head swaying from side to side in a weak denial. Retribution is swift and brutal, a vicious strike shattering his legs, collapsing them under his weight. The painful jolt ripples through him, straining his impaled hands and exacerbating the already agonizing wounds.

"What does Azrael know about Symbio-B?" The question hangs in the air, a sinister melody in the symphony of torment.

All Hashim can do is groan.

A tacit signal from Semyon, and the larger of the two corporals steps forward. His hands, weathered and scarred, take hold of Hashim's throat with a frightening intensity, the vise-like pressure slowly strangling the life out of him.

"Do the Americans have the research data?" Semyon's question pierces through the haze of pain.

"I-I-I don't know what you're talking about," Hashim manages to gasp, struggling against the hands crushing his windpipe.

"Where is the girl?"

"I... left... her!"

A second nod from Semyon. The other corporal steps forward. He wields a metal bar, a gleaming instrument of pain. With a brutal swing, it slams into Hashim's hip, a jarring strike that sends waves of pain coursing through him. A scream rips from his throat, choked and distorted by the hands relentlessly squeezing his life away.

————

IN PETER'S CLAUSTROPHOBIC CELL, the guard decides to break the silence. He leans closer, his cold eyes reflecting the dim light, his voice a coarse whisper.

"You should count yourself luckier than your friend," he murmurs, a sinister grin playing on his lips. "The Russian? He'll have him beaten until he's almost unconscious. But don't think that's the end; they'll never let him have the luxury of sleep." His gaze hardens, and he leans closer still. "They'll pump him full of drugs, keep him awake through every moment of it. I've seen men, strong men, hauled into that room... and they all emerged broken. More shattered than any man should ever be."

His words hang heavily in the cell when, without warning, another nearby explosion ruptures the tense atmosphere. The guard, momentarily thrown off balance, surges to his feet, the grating sound of his chair against the rough concrete floor slicing through the aftershock's gentle rumble. Panic flickers in his eyes as his hand instinctively darts toward his AK, bracing for an unknown threat amidst the dust and turmoil.

As the grumble of the explosion gradually recedes, a chilling realization begins to set in: Peter may not make it as far as Semyon's quarters. He might be crushed under a ton of concrete and bricks before then.

———

THEY'VE MOVED AWAY from choking and returned to the cattle prods. The room is filled with the stench of sweat and blood, punctuated by the crackle of electricity and the muffled screams of a man on the edge. Hashim is strung out on the table, the red slick of his blood painting the aged wood, forming slow rivers that follow the grain and dribble onto the already stained floor below.

The two corporals, their faces obscured by the dim light, force their cattle prods into his flesh, sending violent jolts of electricity coursing through his body.

At the table's other end, Semyon reclines, his feet propped up on the surface, unfazed by the grotesque spectacle before him. "Where is the girl?" His voice cuts through Hashim's ragged gasps, filling the cold stone room. "Where is she?"

Through gritted teeth and trembling lips, Hashim barely gets out, "I-I have nothing to tell you." His defiance is met with another jab of the prod—this time to his neck. His scream is guttural, an animalistic howl of pain that shreds through the air.

With sudden force, however, the torture is eclipsed by another explosion, sending tremors through the ground, rattling the room and the smashed crockery covering the floor around them. Dust rains from the ceiling, churning in the sickly yellow glow of the lone, dim lightbulb. The corporals pause, their attention momentarily torn between their task and the looming threat outside.

"That one was really close," murmurs one of them.

Unperturbed, Semyon rises from his chair at the end of the table and makes his way around to Hashim. With his metal pincer-hand, he cruelly tightens his grip on the little beard hanging from Hashim's chin, lifting his barely conscious face up. "You felt that one, didn't you?" His words are a venomous hiss. "We're running out of time. The rebels are almost here. Tell me where the girl is. He told you to look after her." His eyes look over at Kamal, who hovers at the edge of the room. "I know because he told me," Semyon goes on, his gaze back on Hashim. "As you can see, I have a way with people. They tell me things. He told me he offered you a way out of Sudan, a way to lose your wanted status, a new life in America. He told me that he would do these things for you if you looked after the girl and helped rescue him. That is why you are here in Abri. So tell me: Where is the girl?"

Hashim's lips part, dry and cracked, each word an effort. "She's... she's dead."

Semyon narrows his eyes. "Dead?"

"I left her in the desert."

The Hunter's eyes are piercing, the scar tissue gathering atop of the stunted, burned remains of his nose. "You left her in the desert?"

"Y-yes."

"Why?"

"Because I never intended to look after her. I just drove to the desert... and left her there."

"Then why are you here?"

"The other guy... He took me... Made me come."

Semyon's stare is penetrating, his mottled face drawing tight. "You know," he starts, dropping Hashim's head with a callous disregard. "After years of interrogating men, I have developed an uncanny ability to see through them. I can't read their thoughts, but I can tell when they're lying."

A signal, a nod to the corporals. They grasp Hashim's feet, lift them up, then, without warning, they begin to pull him, his hands caught on the knives, the blades slicing through them. Pain, sharp and intense, engulfs him.

"Where is she?!" the Hunter roars, the question resounding off the stone walls.

Hashim's scream is raw, agonized. "I left her in the desert!"

———

EACH RESONATING boom of distant artillery sends tremors through the spartan cell. The grim-faced guard, his knuckles whitening around the grip of his AK-47, grows visibly more agitated with each impending shockwave. His eyes, once focused solely on the captive, dart anxiously to the prison door behind him.

"The rebels are closer than you think," Peter says, his voice a low, steady rasp that resonates in the confining space. His eyes, cold and unyielding, never stray from the guard. "Sounds like they'll breach the camp perimeter pretty soon. I wouldn't want to be a soldier here when they release those prisoners. Let them do whatever they want to you. Get their revenge on you all."

The guard bristles at the captive's audacity, his facial muscles contorting into a scowl. He rises fully, the barrel of the AK-47 angling toward Peter's face in a silent threat of violence. Flipping it around, he rears back, going to hit Peter in the face with the butt. But he is interrupted by the cell door creaking open, the rusty lock grinding.

Semyon Mikhailovich's imposing form fills the doorway, the sparse light outlining his sinister silhouette. The guard steps back, making way. He strides in, the room growing colder with his presence. The Hunter and Peter lock eyes, the electricity of their shared history igniting the air between them. But there's something else, too. Peter's eyes take in the mottled face.

Semyon's visage tells a haunting story. The burns have claimed most of his skin, twisting and warping it into a landscape of scar tissue. Where once there were gentle curves and edges, there now lie jagged peaks and valleys, distorted almost beyond recognition.

The skin itself is a patchwork of discolored hues, shades of shiny reds, pinks, and purples, mottled with patches of disconcerting white where the heat had been most intense. His eyes, thankfully spared from the devastation, peer out from his marred countenance. They are clear and bright, contrasting sharply with the ravaged terrain around them, and carry a potent depth that seems to defy the horrors his face has endured.

His nose is merely a vague suggestion, the shape twisted and shrunken by the flames, while his lips, or what were once his lips, are a thin, distorted line that only gives a hint of the mouth that used to be. But despite the severity of his scars, there's a stoicism etched deep into the lines of his face, a defiance that the inferno could not consume.

"You're admiring your handiwork up close, Pete," Semyon suggests. "Does it make you proud?"

Peter's response comes without hesitation. "Leaving you alive on that submarine was a mistake."

"And in those dark woods back in Alaska all those years ago," Semyon adds, his cold smile a bare show of teeth. "Survival's always been second nature to us both, though, hasn't it, old friend?"

Immovable in his restraints, Peter meets Semyon's

chilling gaze with unwavering defiance, a silent declaration of his own survival instinct.

The air grows heavy as the Hunter exhales, a sound brimming with decades of unspoken animosity. "Even now," he murmurs, a dangerous growl woven through the rasp of his voice, "I should end you." In a fluid movement, he unhooks the lethal Sig Sauer P226 from its snug home at his hip, the gleam of deadly steel catching the dim light. "A bullet to the brain," he muses, racking the slide with a chilling click, the hollow gaze of the barrel aimed directly at Peter's unwavering eyes.

Yet he hesitates. "But I find that I can't," Semyon admits, his voice softening into a low, grating whisper. "Our pasts are too entwined, our futures also, I feel. After all, you are the last vestige of a family I once knew." A twisted smile dances on his lips as he eases the Sig Sauer's hammer down, sliding the weapon back into its holster. "Life would lose its purpose without you, Peter Black."

Peter meets his declaration with unbroken resolve, his gaze hardened. "Tommy," he says, his voice barely above a whisper.

A flash of rage sparks in Semyon's eyes. "That's not my name," he snaps, his voice stealing the air of the cell. "Not anymore."

"Tommy," Peter repeats, his tone softening, a trace of their shared Alaskan childhood simmering beneath the words. "You know what you're defending, don't you? The mass extermination of millions. All to support a dying tyrant's final, destructive stand. This could throw the world into chaos."

Semyon, his stare unyielding, matches Peter's intensity.

"Perhaps that's exactly what this world needs, Peter," he says, a cruel edge slicing through his voice. "Look around. You can't deny the decay, the creeping rot. Everyone clings to hope for a better tomorrow, yet the ground beneath them crumbles. Pitiful. Your so-called civilization is a festering sore of corruption. Wealth and power have obliterated humanity's worth. The strong prey on the weak, the innocent suffer, and all the while, they chant the anthem of progress. Is that the civilization you so desperately cling to?"

His damning question lingers, his scornful rebuke painting an unsavory portrait of a world on the brink of destruction.

Semyon issues a sharp, mirthless laugh, his penetrating gaze seeming to delve into the deepest recesses of Peter's being. "You believe in man's inherent goodness," he sneers, "yet every glance you cast upon this world shows you a spectacle of decay. You bear witness to a civilization dangling on the precipice of self-destruction, choking on the fumes of its own hubris."

His tirade is interrupted by the violent tremor of another explosion, the prison walls shuddering in response as more dust cascades from the ceiling.

"You can't deny the truth of my words," Semyon continues relentlessly. "Regardless of the underlying motives for the President's orders, it represents a path to salvation for all humankind. The impending storm will cleanse this world of the rotten, the diseased. It will herald the birth of a new era. An era devoid of the corruption that has plagued our past. I don't dread pushing this world over the precipice. I welcome it. Only in the crucible of chaos can purity take form. Only once we've razed the remnants of this decrepit world to the ground can we dream of erecting a superior one." He inclines toward Peter, bringing his scarred face mere inches from Peter's own. "Can you envision it, Pete? A world phoenixing from the ashes. A world that values the sanctity of life over the trappings of wealth. But for such a world to ascend, this one must plummet. X-9 is the flood, the necessary conclusion. It is the cleansing flame. The tempest that will dismantle the old world to construct a new one."

His monologue reverberates in the confines of the dank cell, lingering as an ominous echo.

"Is that all?" Peter finally quips.

Semyon offers no response.

"If only my hands weren't bound," Peter adds with biting sarcasm, "I'd clap."

Semyon holds Peter's gaze for a moment, one that feels like a lifetime. Then, with a grim finality, he declares, "It's time, Peter."

He steps away from the door, revealing the two hulking corporals who step inside the cell. With practiced efficiency, they unlatch Peter from the chair, securing his hands in front of him with rugged shackles. They flank him, their rigid stances an unspoken threat as they escort him outside.

They emerge into the blazing sunlight of a courtyard, and Peter's eyes rest for the first time upon Semyon's quarters: a solid barracks building constructed of raw concrete, topped with a rusted, tin roof.

Semyon, a cruel glint in his eyes, turns to face Peter. "Welcome to my humble abode," he jeers. "I trust you will find your—"

BOOM!

His taunting words are abruptly silenced by a massive explosion, this one practically on top of them. The neighboring wall, along with a substantial portion of the prison, is obliterated in an instant. Tons of rubble rain down upon the unsuspecting corporals, mercilessly crushing them beneath a wave of concrete and debris as Peter dives out of the way.

Semyon sprints for cover as the remnants of the wall crumble, creating a deadly shower of shrapnel. The air is thick with dust and the deafening cacophony of gunfire bursting through the complex.

Then, as if that wasn't enough, another explosion rocks a different part of the prison, ripping another gaping hole in its formidable structure. Many of the prisoners, suddenly unfettered, seize the opportunity for escape. They surge through the breach, launching themselves at the bewildered guards with a desperate fury. Bedlam erupts, consuming the prison.

Semyon emerges from a makeshift shelter created by a toppled slab of wall that leans against a neighboring structure. He fights his way through the dust-choked air to the carnage where the corporals lie. Their faces are frozen in death masks, blood matting their lips, their lower bodies hidden under a pile of rubble, the dust forming a grim shroud over their bodies. He searches the ground around them for Peter but finds nothing.

Unflinching amidst the relentless crackle of gunfire all around him, Semyon staggers toward the ruined shell of his quarters. Inside, he is greeted by the jarring sight of emptiness. Hashim and Kamal are nowhere to be found; the bloodied knives have been pulled from the table. Just as the prison descends into full-scale pandemonium, he finds himself all alone. His prisoners have escaped.

———

THE CHAOS of the encroaching fighting rattles all around them. Amid a mass of explosions, Peter navigates his way through the maelstrom, half-dragging, half-guiding Kamal and Hashim across a road dangerously close to the prison. Dirt and debris kicks up around them. Stray bullets strike the parched earth with deadly intent as they move as fast as they can, their hearts pounding in their chests, the terror of their situation mixing with the heady rush of freedom.

They duck into an alleyway, a shadowy fissure separating a jumble of one-story mud-brick houses. The walls, baked hard under the relentless Sudanese sun, tower above them in a rendition of their recent imprisonment. Kamal's pace is torturously slow, his swollen ankle hindering him and the iron chains around his feet clanging with each agonizing step. Hashim, the trembling shadow of a man with wounds on his hands hastily bandaged with torn cloth, hobbles painfully behind.

Suddenly, a rebel soldier materializes from the smoke and dust. His rifle swings toward them, the threat of death glinting in his eyes. Peter avoids the lunge, swoops down low, and gets ahold of him, maneuvering behind him, the chain between his hands wrapping around the soldier's neck in a lethal embrace. As the man gasps for breath, Kamal thrusts himself forward, snatching the rifle from the rebel's faltering grip.

Peter drags him into a nook, out of the way, and finishes

the job, strangling him with the chain. Once the RSF soldier's struggles cease, Peter takes his AK from Kamal with a grim determination. Laying Kamal's and his own chains out flat on the fractured pavement, he waits. The battlefield offers a unique advantage—the noise. The atmosphere pulses with the thunder of heavy artillery, of mortar shells landing and buildings collapsing. In the next rumbling crescendo, Peter pulls the trigger, the roar of rapid gunfire hidden beneath the tumult. The bullet shatters the chains, the sharp, metallic ping swallowed by the overwhelming noise.

Freed, they make their way along until a few blocks away, they come across a battered building, a desolate mud-brick structure pockmarked by bullet holes but recently abandoned. They slip inside, their battered bodies sagging with relief as the thick walls offer a fragile protection from the raging chaos outside. In the dim light filtering through the bullet-riddled shutters adorning the windows, their eyes meet—three men tied by circumstance, bound by their desperate bid for survival.

As they explore the rooms, they discover that the place hides a basement, an underground cavern tucked away from the ferocious fighting taking place all around them.

Their ragged breaths are drawn in rhythm with the cadence of the violent eruptions as they descend a set of worn steps. The room itself is stark and utilitarian, its domestic life marked by a washbasin stained with the patina of time and a sturdy but well-worn workbench shoved against a wall. Rusty stains adorn the stone floor, and the men quickly realize that they are standing in the center of a butcher's shop. The air is heavy with a sickly-sweet odor of decay that seems to seep from the very stones, an unpleasant reminder of the mortal danger lurking outside as the fighting continues.

In a corner, Hashim huddles, his face a grim palette of pain and exhaustion. Peter, hardened by years of clandestine operations, moves to examine his injured hands. "Fetch me some water," he instructs Kamal, his voice a rough whisper against the thuds of warfare.

Obediently, Kamal hobbles over to the basin, his movements stiff. Water gurgles from the rusted tap, filling a tarnished metal cup with a clarity that stands in stark contrast to the grime and gore of their surroundings.

Meanwhile, Peter probes the question that lingers in the air, his gaze never leaving Hashim's shredded hands. "What did you tell him?" he inquires of the Sudanese.

In response, Hashim turns his gaze past Peter, focusing instead on the approaching figure of Kamal, his hands carefully cradling the precious cup of water. It is Kamal who speaks, his voice filling the silence. "He told him nothing."

For now, Peter leaves it, continuing to attend to the wounded hands as Hashim's face contorts, a vision of pain playing across his marred features.

"Looks like they avoided the bones," Peter says, checking them over. "So long as we clean the wounds, you should be able to use them. Which is good, because you may need to fire a gun at some point."

Peter carefully pours water over them. The liquid trickles down, taking with it the grime and dried blood of their daring escape. The sight is grotesque yet oddly cathartic, an outward symbol of their struggle and survival. The water, clear and pure, reveals a startling contrast against the harsh reality of their situation.

Peter looks up from the brutalized hands, his eyes locking on to Hashim's swollen, bloodied face. Now he decides to ask. "What did he want to know?" The question hangs heavy between them.

Again Hashim's gaze flits to Kamal, and again it is the CIA operative that answers.

"He wanted to know where the girl is," Kamal says, "but Hashim did well. He didn't tell him. Did you, Hashim?"

Peter pivots, his eyes boring into Hashim. The Sudanese can only offer a weak shake of his head, his denial seeming to hang in the chilled, stale air.

The water momentarily forgotten, Peter poses the question haunting them all. "And where is she?"

Kamal's gaze doesn't waver from Hashim. "I left her with him," he finally answers.

All attention in the dimly lit room shifts toward the hunched figure of Hashim, a spotlight under the swinging bulb.

"You gotta be joking me," Peter grumbles, incredulity lacing his tone. The quiet rustle of his annoyance dances with the distant din of battle. "You've had her all this time?"

"I told you," Hashim responds, defiance simmering in his low voice. "How can I trust you? I thought you were working for the others. Only now do I realize that you are with him."

"So where is she then? Where is Leila?" Peter's question ricochets off the stone walls, a plea hidden within the interrogation.

Hashim's reply is simple, delivered with an unshakeable conviction, "With friends of mine."

"Who?" Peter demands.

"Good people. Not bandits. Farmers."

"Where?"

"North of Khartoum is a set of low mountains in the Green Valley. They have a farm. She is safe there. Just like I promised she would be." The statement resonates in the quiet room, proof of his unwavering resolve amidst the raging storm of war.

Turning to Kamal, Peter says, "We need to get to a telephone the moment we can get out of here. Contact base. Get an extraction team out to her. But for now," he adds as another distant explosion shakes the air of the basement, "we should rest. Wait this out." And as if to punctuate this statement, another explosion rocks their sanctuary.

TWENTY-FOUR

WITH THE RUCKUS ABOVE THEM SLOWLY diminishing, the trio decides to hunker down for the night. Their strategy is to ride out the storm, strike out at first light with the nascent hope of a new day. After all, they have the pieces of the puzzle now—Hashim will lead them to the whereabouts of Leila. Their task, while daunting, has a direction—to reach her. The sting of regret, however, is that their journey is about to be curtailed before they even get a fair start.

Peter is the first to stir from an uneasy sleep, roused by the foreign sounds infiltrating their hideout. He senses them, the intruders, their stealth insufficient to escape his honed instincts. Yet, his anticipation plummets as he comprehends his limited resources—just three bullets left in the magazine of the AK they stole from the soldier, his only defense against the first figure who emerges from the stairwell, a man heavily drenched in body armor and holding an M4 Carbine that he points right at Peter's chest.

"Drop the weapon," the lead man commands in clipped English.

Slowly, Peter complies, laying the AK down, the weapon rattling softly against the stone floor. His hands then ascend in a gesture of surrender. Three more figures emerge from the stairs, forming an intimidating barrier, their military precision evident. As Hashim and Kamal rouse, a realization crashes upon Peter like a wave; the uniforms don't fit the mold of any regular army or RSF—these men aren't even Sudanese, their pink skin evidence of that.

The last figure makes his appearance at the foot of the stairs. As he unwraps the litham from around his face and neck, his identity is revealed—Frank, the formidable leader of the bounty hunters.

"Don't you boys move a single muscle," he growls in a thick cockney accent.

"Good. You're here," Peter retorts, attempting to rise. His movements, however, incite a frenzy among the intruders. He's forcefully pushed back down, landing hard on the cold floor. Kamal and Hashim, in the meantime, watch the scene unfold with muted trepidation.

"Look," Peter starts, his tone straining to remain calm, "I know we got off on a bad note, but it's good that you're here now."

"Oh, it's good, all right," Frank replies, a smirk playing on his lips. "This bounty is gonna make us rich, mate."

Peter's heart clenches. "What bounty?"

Frank's smirk broadens, revealing a chilling amusement. "Why, yours, of course."

"Mine?"

"Yes. I have bounties for you and both your pals here."

"Well, prepare to be disappointed."

"Why?"

"Because we just so happen to be CIA operatives on an extremely important mission. You don't get bounties on American agents. Not unless you wanna lose your license and/or your life."

Peter anticipates a reaction—for Frank to understand and give his assistance. Yet Frank's smirk only amplifies, and Peter is left with a bad feeling.

"He said you'd say that," the bounty hunter tells him dryly.

Peter's brow furrows. "Who said I'd say that?"

"The bloke with his face frazzled. The CIA agent who's paying us three hundred grand to haul your asses back to him. And thank God we put that tracker on your pal here when we had him." He glances sideways at Hashim. "Otherwise we wouldn't have found you all so easily."

"You're making a big mistake, Frank," Peter growls. "The man you're working for isn't CIA; he's Russian SVP."

"Sounded like a Yank to me. And he paid us twenty percent in advance."

"He used to be American, but he isn't now. He's Russian. You're working for a sanctioned government against the interests of American agents. You do this, Frank, and there's no going back."

Frank takes a moment, his deep inhale resonating in the room. Then, staring right into Peter's eyes, he retorts, "Then I'll just have to be in serious trouble then."

"Frank, you're going to—"

"Shut it!" Frank's voice crackles like thunder around them. "I've had about enough of you. Two of my guys are dead and four more are in hospital because of you. I've already wasted enough time. Take 'em away, boys."

Their hands are bound tightly behind their backs with zip ties, and the trio is marched out of the safe confines of the basement into the night. The darkness of the hour is punctuated by the eerie dance of fires, a testament to the battle they're leaving behind. In the distance, an inferno engulfs the prison, its fiery profile etched against the dark sky. Only the sporadic symphony of gunfire still peppers the relative quiet, a jarring reminder of the turmoil that continues to rage on.

Peter and Kamal are roughly escorted into the back of a military-grade Hummer, the vehicle's metal interior a cold, imposing reality. As Hashim is directed toward a separate vehicle, Peter's voice cleaves through the night air.

"Hey, where are you taking him?"

"He's comin' separately. Ain't enough room for everyone in the Hummer."

Powerless, Peter is forced to watch as Hashim is hustled into a battered Toyota pickup, his eyes locked with Peter's in a silent goodbye.

"Come on," one of the men grunts, jabbing the barrel of his M4 Carbine into the small of Peter's back. "Get in."

With no other choice, Peter complies, feeling Kamal take a seat beside him in the unyielding back of the Hummer. With the slam of the door, they are taken away, swallowed up by the chaos of the night.

TWENTY-FIVE

ACROSS THE GLOBE - 18TH APRIL

Two of the sleepers find themselves in trouble.

In the sprawling network of Bangkok's Suvarnabhumi Airport, Hamed, now dressed in a sharply tailored suit, silently navigates the swarm of people.

But something's amiss.

An uncanny uniformity in the crowd ahead catches his attention. The slight ripple of disturbance in the sea of faces. A seemingly normal group of workmen in reflective vests to his left, all looking in his direction, communicating subtly through wireless earpieces.

Too late, he realizes he's walking into a trap.

Thousands of miles away in O.R. Tambo International Airport, Johannesburg, another sleeper agent, Liam, comfortable in a pair of jeans and a loose shirt, experiences a similar chill. His practiced eye picks out airport security closing in like wolves circling their prey.

Back in Bangkok, Hamed's instincts kick in. As the group of disguised officers close in, he grabs a young woman near him, his arm snaking around her neck, his other hand revealing a concealed knife.

"Stay back!" he shouts, his voice reverberating in the sudden silence.

In Johannesburg, Liam reacts differently. He knows he cannot escape. The encroaching security, their hardened gazes, leave no room for doubt. His hand drifts to his collar, fingering the stitching of his shirt. With a sharp tug, he frees a tiny capsule—cyanide, hidden for such an eventuality.

While Hamed's hostage situation escalates into a tense standoff in Bangkok, Liam swallows the pill in Johannesburg. Even as the security team pounces, his eyes glaze over, his body going limp before they can reach him.

Inside the bustling departure hall of Suvarnabhumi Airport, Hamed moves himself and his hostage through the thrumming crowd as the officers follow, the blade of the small knife pressed against the trembling neck of the woman—a flight attendant with an acetate badge on her uniform stating *Marisa*.

"Don't move!" Hamed warns the surrounding security personnel, his voice brittle but steady, fear and fever coursing through him.

Terror seethes in Marisa's eyes, her chest heaving with frantic breaths. In a swift, desperate move, she stomps hard on Hamed's foot. He yelps in surprise, and his grip around her slackens just enough for her to wrench free.

Hamed's eyes flash with something like admiration, even

respect, for Marisa's brave act. But then his gaze hardens, and without a moment's hesitation, he takes a step back from the gasping crowd.

His actions swift and resolute, he draws the blade across his own throat. The crowd screams, recoiling as Hamed's knees buckle, and he crumples to the shiny airport floor, a pool of crimson swiftly spreading beneath him.

The crowd is a frenzy of screams and panic. People rush in all directions, fleeing the sight. Amidst the chaos, Marisa, gasping and trembling, is quickly pulled to safety by security personnel, her eyes wide and haunted. The sleeper agent, determined to die rather than be captured, lies still, his act of final defiance etched forever in the minds of those who witnessed it.

———

CIA HEADQUARTERS, Langley, Virginia, USA.
18th April, 09:11 (EDT).

AT THE NERVE center of the CIA, the news of the men's deaths cascades through the system like a shockwave. Inside her austere office, Director Sandy McLean, her face hardened by the weight of the crisis, watches the footage from Bangkok and Johannesburg. A chill courses through her veins as she beholds the chaotic scenes playing out across the world.

Opposite her on the screen of her laptop is Ben Knight. The lines of his face are taut with concern, his eyes red from lack of sleep, the consequences of their race against time.

"Interpol ran their recent travel history," Director McLean says, her voice a low rumble. "It was a good enough pattern to try and pull them. But as you can see from the footage I just sent you, they weren't willing to come alive."

"That's a level of dedication you have to admire, I guess," Ben Knight comments.

McLean nods, her jaw set. "We wouldn't have gotten anything from them, anyway. Even if they did speak, none of the agents would know about the others."

"Were they carrying the virus?"

"Yes. Both had two vials left. They were also suffering from X-9. Both would have been dead within a week."

"And what about the others?"

"We're trying to track them down, but we're losing precious time," McLean warns, tension lining her voice. "Every minute we're here, that virus is spreading—and the President seems more worried about spooking the markets than shutting the airports down. I mean, it's madness. Some states are locking down while others are open. At least the EU has called a state of emergency. They've shut all their air space. Complete lockdown."

"I saw footage earlier," Knight says, his voice heavy with dread. "It was a hospital in Brooklyn. People in hazmats were loading a truck with bodybags. It's started."

Director McLean braces herself. With steel in her voice, she says, "So that makes my next question an extremely urgent one, Knight. What's the status of your agent in Sudan?"

Knight's body language betrays his discomfort. Even through the video call, Director McLean spots it.

"Knight?" Sandy's voice hardens with growing impatience.

"We still haven't heard anything, ma'am."

The color leaves Director McLean's cheeks. "Oh God," she mutters.

"He was en route to Abri prison camp in search of the operative Kamal Osman when we lost all communication," Knight explains.

McLean's expression furrows. "But I read an intelligence report this morning," she states. "According to it, the Abri POW camp was attacked yesterday by the RSF, and all its inmates are either dead or set free."

"Yes, that's correct."

"Then let's hope your agents are the latter, Knight."

"Yes, ma'am."

TWENTY-SIX

WAD HAMID, SUDAN - 18TH APRIL, 11:10 (EAT)

As daylight seizes the sky, Hashim finds himself sandwiched within the confines of the bounty hunters' Toyota pickup, positioned tightly between two muscle-bound and hardened men. The driver is a beefy guy with a clear South African accent, his words twanged with a unique rhythm that Hashim identifies instantly. His companion, an Australian, judging by the laid-back lilt in his voice, lounges in the passenger seat, casually resting his Beretta M9 in the at-ease position—the barrel's cold steel disconcertingly close to Hashim's thigh, close enough to obliterate his leg if the trigger were to be pulled.

Every rough bump they go over, the Sudanese steels himself.

Ahead of them, they've lost sight of the Hummer carrying Peter, Kamal, and the others, the vehicle swallowed up by the endless desert not long after leaving Abri.

About an hour into the journey, the driver decides to talk. "Do you know what they got planned for you later on, boy?" the South African queries, his voice a gravelly murmur that resonates in the confines of the truck.

Hashim, resolute in his silence, offers no response, his back arching a little from being called "boy."

"He don't appear to care," the Australian drawls, gesturing toward Hashim with the business end of his gun, his tone threaded with dry amusement.

Unperturbed, the driver presses on, a morbid twinkle in his eyes. "Don't matter to me if he wants to know or not. I'll enjoy the look on his face when I tell him." Turning to Hashim, he adds in a glum tone, "You, my mate, have got a date with none other than Boko Harem."

Hashim goes cold, his nerves standing on end. He can't help twisting sideways to the driver, the man smiling back all smug.

"You see," the driver says to his mate. "I told you the look would be priceless." He bursts into chuckling, his Ozzy mate joining in. "Frank heard you pissed Boko Harem off real bad. So after the CIA have finished with you, he's gonna hand you over to them. Let them do what they want."

"Hoo-wee," the Australian whistles the other side of Hashim. "I wouldn't wanna be in your shoes. Why don't you tell him, Kieth, about the last bloke we took to Boko Harem?"

"Oh yeah," the driver, Kieth, chuckles. "What a day that was. It took me a week to get the smell out of my nose." He lets out a laugh, then turns to Hashim. "You wanna hear my story, boy?"

Hashim does nothing but stare at him.

"Well, I don't care if you do or not," the driver grumbles. "I'm gonna tell it. You see, after those jihadis took the fella off us and paid us our money, they invited us to stick around and watch the, eh... festivities."

He leaves the sentence dangling, a mirthless grin splitting his face as he shares a complicit glance with his Australian counterpart. Throughout it all, Hashim maintains an icy composure, his gaze steadfastly focused on the endless expanse of desert track unrolling before them.

"So they take the guy out into the middle of the desert," the South African drives on with his macabre narrative, "and tie him to a metal post sticking up out of the ground, the earth scorched all black around it. Then, as they drench him in petrol, one of the fellas reads out a short statement in Arabic. All the time the guy's begging them not to do it, but you can see it in their eyes. These boys want blood. So after the little speech, they toss a match on him. Woof! He goes up, the flames crawling all over him. Now I'll tell you this for nothing, it's the screaming that gets you. It starts off normal —just a guy screaming. But then, about twenty seconds in, as the flames engulf him completely, the screaming turns into a sound you'll never hear unless you watch a fella being burned alive. The screaming, it changes, distorting into a sound that defies description—it is the purest sound of agony I've ever heard. Then it suddenly stops, replaced by an unsettling silence, and you realize he's gone. After that, it's just the popping sounds as the body fat boils." He finishes at this, his words hanging heavy in the air, laden with an unsettling blend of dread and fascination.

"Reckon he'll go up the same way?" the passenger inquires, his stare fixed on Hashim.

The driver's eyes flicker toward Hashim, sizing him up with a callous glance. "Can't be sure. He's leaner than the fella we dropped off. He was a great big, fat bloke. But it'll hardly make a difference once he's soaked in gas."

They explode into laughter.

The desert rushes by outside the dusty window of the Toyota pickup, the harsh, arid landscape as indifferent to his captivity as the two armed men flanking him. Hashim, his hands zip tied behind him, gazes at the vast expanse of nothingness, his mind whirling. He knows he needs to act, and fast.

With a sudden forceful move, he shoves a foot into the driver's footwell, stamping down hard on the brake pedal. The truck bucks violently, hurling the men against their seatbelts. Quick as a snake, Hashim uses his shoulder to ram into the man on his left, the passenger, knocking the wind out of him and sending his Beretta clattering to the floor of the truck. The surprise on the man's face is priceless but short-lived.

As the driver, dazed but recovering, reaches for the wheel and struggles to control the vehicle, Hashim throws his weight into the passenger. It's a risky move. He has to throw his body around like a weapon, given that his hands are tied.

He thrusts a knee up into the man's gut, doubling him over. The pickup veers off the road, plowing into the sand, throwing a cloud of dust around them. For a fleeting moment, they're engulfed in a gritty, blinding haze that pours in through the open windows. Hashim seizes the opportunity and rams his head into the driver's face.

There's a sickening crunch, and the driver slumps in his seat, unconscious. But the passenger is tougher. He recovers and lunges for his gun, but Hashim is faster. He swings his body, aiming a powerful kick that sends the weapon flying under the seat, out of reach.

Desperate, the passenger reaches for Hashim's throat. Hashim jerks back, avoiding the choking grasp, and, using the momentum, delivers a swift, hard headbutt that leaves the man crumpled in his seat.

Struggling, Hashim manages to kick open the door and rolls out of the vehicle. The coarse sand scrapes his skin as he tumbles onto the desert floor. He can't afford a moment of rest; the passenger, though disoriented, is beginning to stir.

Hashim pulls himself to his feet and starts to run, away from the truck and its occupants, his heart pounding in his chest as he dashes across the merciless desert toward a large group of boulders about a hundred meters away, his hands dangling behind him. It's a sprint, the escape desperate, daring, but he's free, at least for now.

Hashim bursts into the rocky gorge. His heart pounding, he makes a dash through the maze of man-sized boulders, hearing the crunch of gravel under the passenger's boots as the man follows in quick pursuit.

The Australian charges in after him, struggling to squeeze through the narrow fissures that split the jumbled rocks, his path leading him farther into the jagged labyrinth. Hashim, light and nimble, scales a boulder with practiced ease, even bound, and crouches atop it. From there, he observes the man in secret as he passes by underneath him, oblivious to his presence.

Seizing the moment, Hashim pounces down from his

perch and sprints out of the rocks toward the pickup. Opening the driver's door, he discovers a hunting knife sheathed to the unconscious driver's thigh. He hauls the South African out, dumping him in the dirt, takes the knife, and wedges its handle into the crevice between the driver's seat cushion and the seat frame, clamping it in place so that it pokes horizontally out from the seat. Twisting around, he places his bound wrists against the blade and starts to saw the plastic ties against the edge of the positioned knife.

His moment of triumph is short-lived; about sixty meters away, the Australian re-emerges from the rocks, having realized his mistake. Panic surges in Hashim as he lifts his pistol.

Bullets whiz past, missing by mere inches. The pickup truck pings and sparks as the bullets ricochet off its metal surface. Ignoring the deafening reports, Hashim strains against the ties. More shots ring out, metal reverberating against metal, as he saws faster. The plastic finally yields, and his hands are free.

Heart thumping, Hashim whirls around and leaps into the pickup as the passenger closes in. More bullets slash through the air, the driver's window erupting into a shower of glass as Hashim slams the gear into drive. With a deafening roar, the pickup lunges forward, leaving the men behind in a cloud of dust. The last few shots split apart the desert air, shattering the rear windshield as Hashim makes his desperate escape.

———

NYALA, Sudan.

18th April, 13:21 (EAT).

THE DAWN IS LONG GONE, swallowed by the fiery strokes of the midday sun as Frank's Hummer rumbles its way into the fringes of Nyala. Peter and Kamal are locked in the confines of the back seat, hemmed in by two stern-faced men, their callused hands firmly gripping pistols. Frank lounges in the leather passenger seat, his gaze fixed on the scorched landscape ahead, leaving the task of maneuvering the heavy vehicle to another of his henchmen.

Nyala, once a thriving town, is now a macabre shadow of its former self. Wisps of smoke curl upward from smoldering ruins, like ghosts dancing amid the wreckage. A carpet of shattered glass adorns the ground, shimmering fragments that catch the sun's glare, a cruelly beautiful testament to the ravages of war. There is no pane of glass that has survived the onslaught, and the window frames stare blankly, their eyes gouged out.

Hemedti's rebels have taken control of this part of the city, and Frank's Hummer soon reaches an RSF checkpoint, a raw and unforgiving symbol of the new authority. Battle-scarred soldiers, their eyes reflecting the weariness of their souls, inspect their papers with an air of vexation. Their glares are intrusive, dissecting Peter and Kamal through the tinted windows. Finally, after a tense pause, they wave the Hummer through.

As they drive deeper into the city's wounded heart, their destination finally looms before them, a compound fringed with foreboding. "This is the place." Frank's voice slices through the uneasy silence.

The symbol of the RSF is painted on a wall, and Peter spots several rebel soldiers patrolling the streets outside. As the metallic grind of the gate signals their entry, Peter's voice resonates with a trace of desperation, "You're making a terrible mistake, Frank."

Frank swivels in his seat, his icy gaze pinning Peter. "So you keep saying," he retorts in his thick English accent before facing forward once more.

As the RSF compound swallows the Hummer, an uncertain fate awaits Peter and Kamal in its steel-clad belly.

———

As HE DRIVES, Hashim sits tensely in the pickup, listening. The bounty hunters are in radio communication. Therefore, the gruff voice of Frank and his men fill the cab, crackling through the radio speakers and sketching a perilous scenario for him, letting him know their destination and the ominous fate that awaits Peter and Kamal there.

Approaching the battered edges of Nyala, Hashim's heart hammers a cautionary rhythm. In the distance, an army checkpoint squats like a menacing spider in its web, a dangerous hurdle in his path. He makes a snap decision, veering the Toyota off the road, its wheels crunching on the remnants of a bombed-out building. The mound of crumbled stone and twisted metal acts as a discreet camouflage.

His former guardians' weapons, a clunky M4 Carbine and a Beretta M9, are now his trusted companions. Securing the M4 to his back via a strap and gripping the Beretta in his hand, he quietly exits the pickup, a phantom blending into the somber hues of the war-ravaged city.

With a strong wind whipping up the dust, Hashim creeps with measured steps down a desolate stretch of alleyway. In the chaos that has swept up Sudan, each shadow is a potential threat, his senses honed to every minuscule detail, his fingers tracing the textured grip of the Beretta's grip, its cold assurance a stark contrast to the burning determination running through him. Exiting the alley, a ruined street stretches before him, a formidable battlefield under the indifferent sun.

———

Unbeknownst to Hashim, a ghost from his past tracks him with hawk-like precision, the man's arm encased in a medical cast. As a rather recognizable Toyota pickup passed him several minutes earlier, the man's gaze had narrowed. The bounty hunter, by an unfortunate circumstance, had spotted Hashim just as he was entering the husk of the city and followed him in his own vehicle. Witnessing Hashim park the Toyota, he'd maneuvered his own pickup into a discreet spot, vaulted out with an agility that belied his broken arm, and followed.

Now as Hashim slips away into the ruins, the man keeps himself hidden, following from a distance. Staying back, the bounty hunter watches as Hashim leaves the alley, crosses a street, and vanishes into the skeletal remains of a once-bustling hotel.

———

HASHIM'S MIND is already buzzing with plans. The hotel, despite its damaged exterior, offers enough cover and a vantage point that he so desperately needs.

Through the crackling radio, he absorbs the grim details of the compound's defense as Frank checks in with the men guarding it. The place is brimming with them, which means Hashim can't just turn up. He has to plot, to observe before he can make his move. Currently alone in this game of deadly chess, he is a single king cornered by an army of rooks and knights. But little does he know, however, that yet another player is about to join the game, trailing his footsteps with the patience of a stalking predator.

Leaving the shattered wreck of the hotel's foyer behind, Hashim carefully navigates the detritus of fire-scorched furniture. His heavy steps then drum up the charred staircase as he ascends to the upper floors.

———

THE MAN with the broken arm enters the foyer, his fingers flexing against the cool grip of his pistol, eyes scanning the debris for any sign of danger.

A creak above his head draws his attention upward.

———

UPSTAIRS, Hashim discovers a suite that has miraculously escaped the worst of the shelling and the fire. A layer of ash and shards from shattered chandeliers and windows blanket the ruby-red carpet, turning it into a glimmering field of crushed diamonds. Despite the devastation, the place holds a certain charm, whispers of a grandeur that once was.

Pushing open a set of swing doors into the bathroom, he is met with the surprising sight of intact plumbing. He twists a faucet, and his face brightens as water—warm, no less—gushes out. A simple joy amid all this disorder.

Stripping off his dust-covered shirt, Hashim leaves it hanging on the swing doors. His boots are kicked off onto the floor, and as he prepares for a long-awaited bath, the soft hum of a forgotten tune escapes his lips.

———

THE BOUNTY HUNTER, lurking right outside the room, absorbs the sounds of the running water, the soft murmur of Hashim's tune. It's a soundtrack to a scene he can almost picture. He enters the suite, his pulse quickening as he edges closer to the swing doors. The sight of the discarded shirt and boots confirms his prey's location.

With a deep breath, he inches the door open, using the cast on his left forearm to push it, his right hand steadying the pointed pistol. His heart thuds in anticipation of the kill as he swings his aim toward the bathtub. But, to his astonishment, it's empty. The bathwater undulates gently, bearing no trace of Hashim.

Something flickers in the bounty hunter's peripheral vision to his left. His instincts kick in, adrenaline spurring him to pivot on his heel. But it's too late—the sharp crack of a firing Beretta M9 cuts through the watery hiss filling the room, an abrupt punctuation to the tense silence.

Before he can fully comprehend what's happening, a

hot, searing pain blossoms in his chest. He topples backward, crashing into the bathtub, sending splashes of water down onto the tiled floor.

From his sprawled position, he makes a desperate attempt to raise his gun, but it's a futile gesture. Another gunshot rings out, exploding in the compact room. The bullet finds its mark, and everything goes black. His body collapses into the tub, a puppet severed from its strings.

TWENTY-SEVEN

NYALA, SUDAN - 18TH APRIL, 19:44 (EAT)

ACROSS THE CITY, IN A BLEAK, DISTANT CORNER, Peter and Kamal find themselves in a grim predicament. Both of them are bound securely to rigid metal chairs by thick leather straps. Their sole guardian for the past six hours has been one of Frank's stern-faced bounty hunters. He stands nonchalantly beside the room's only door, his assault rifle resting casually at the low-ready position.

The place they're being held in is a study in oppositions: The stark, unrelenting glare of a solitary overhead lamp battles the all-consuming darkness of the windowless, basement cell, the battle between light and dark adding to the tension.

Kamal squirms, his nerves manifesting in every futile tug against the unforgiving straps, legs and arms restless. "How can you remain so calm?" he implores, turning his gaze toward Peter.

"Let's just say this isn't my first rodeo," Peter retorts, an element of dry humor ringing in his voice.

The abrasive creak of the door cuts through the tense atmosphere. Peter's senses, honed by years of fieldwork, sharpen instinctively. Two shadowy figures materialize in the opening and step into the room. They tell the guard he can leave, and the man duly obliges, shutting the door behind himself.

A familiar voice, dripping with smug satisfaction, then greets them. "Gentlemen," it says, "we meet again." Semyon Mikhailovich emerges from the shadows flanked by another man. "Allow me to introduce," he adds, "Doctor Arkady Leonid. Russia's foremost mastermind in the craft of information extraction."

Dr. Leonid presents a harrowing sight—a gaunt man, clad in sterile doctor's whites, his grayed hair slicked back, revealing a face etched with the cruel knowledge of pain inflicted and secrets gleaned over countless ruthless sessions.

He carries a leather medical bag, placing it on top of a stainless steel table, the room's only other occupant except for their chairs. The doctor unzips the bag, tugs it open, and begins unloading it. Methodically, Dr. Leonid begins to arrange the tools of his trade on the table. Vials of varied sizes, each filled with a unique liquid—some clear as water, others stained with hues—form a chilling lineup. As the Russian takes inventory, Peter's hawk-eyes focus on their labels. He recognizes names—sodium pentothal, scopolamine, an assortment of potent benzodiazepines.

In an atmosphere of disquieting serenity, Dr. Leonid selects a vial of crystalline liquid—sodium pentothal. His motions are meticulous, bearing an almost ceremonial exactness. He comes to Peter, the icy depths of his blue eyes clashing with the gray of Peter's own, and administers the injection. The needle bites into Peter's skin, a stark intrusion against the frigid sterility of the room.

The first wave of sensation is subtle, a gentle tide engulfing Peter's senses, as if his consciousness is being swaddled in layers of gossamer. He feels his inhibitions ebbing away, dissolving like mist under a hot sun. Vulnerability seeps into him. He feels exposed. Yet his fear kindles a steadfast resolve to resist.

Emerging from the room's shadowy recesses, Semyon strides into the pool of dim light. His face, a grisly tapestry of old burn scars, possesses a dreadful allure under the feeble illumination. As the drugs commence their insidious dance within Peter's system, Semyon's marred visage appears to shimmer, transforming into a youthful countenance from a bygone era—Tommy, the boy that Peter grew up with all those years ago on that unforgiving farm in the wilds of Alaska.

A wave of sadness washes over Peter's features as his entire physique slackens. "I'm sorry, Tommy," he murmurs, looking visibly uncomfortable.

"I told you," retorts the Hunter, "that's not my name anymore."

"I should've run away with you that day," Peter continues, his voice laced with regret. "Shouldn't have turned on you."

"That's not why we're here," Semyon responds dismissively, launching his line of questioning. His voice resonates through the drug-induced illusion, an eerie refrain to the surreal images unfolding around Peter—his words sounding elongated, as if filtered through a pool of water. He wants to know where the fourth host is—where Leila is, her status with the Americans. His words coil around Peter's drug-saturated mind, exploratory tendrils of sound navigating the altered landscape.

In the meantime, Dr. Leonid sits on a chair beside him, holding a stethoscope to Peter's sweat-laced chest and observing the proceedings with the detached curiosity of a scholar witnessing a lab experiment.

"Do the Americans have the girl?" The question seeps into Peter's consciousness through the mists of his altered state, Tommy's youthful face shape-shifting into a kaleidoscope of familiar figures; Mother, Magda, Michael, Kate. Unbeknownst to him, the denial "no" slips past his lips, the sound of his own voice sounding alien, as if originating from another person's throat.

Semyon continues probing. "Where is she?"

Amid the encroaching fog of his cognition, Peter grasps on to a single lucid thought: resist. He must not allow them to triumph. He cannot disappoint Tommy. Regardless of the chilling charade in progress, despite the intoxicants invading his bloodstream, he fights back, clutching at the fraying edges of his rapidly distorting reality.

"I don't know about any girl," he murmurs. "My mission was... nothing more than the rescue... of a fellow operative."

"You mean this fellow operative?" Semyon queries, gesturing toward Kamal.

With effort, Peter turns to him, the drugs obfuscating his ability to discern the identity of his neighboring captive. In the meantime, Kamal sits strapped to the chair eyeing

Semyon with supreme caution as the Hunter takes his pistol from his belt.

"Yes," Peter wheezes.

A sudden blast jerks him out of his stupor. Kamal Osman convulses in his chair, exhales a heavy sigh, and then, abruptly lifeless, slumps over, a gaping cavity marking the location of his heart.

"Why'd you do that, Tommy?" Peter demands, returning his glazed eyes to Semyon, his words a slurred murmur.

In lieu of a response, the Hunter merely signals Dr. Leonid. Another vial of liquid is drawn into a syringe, primed for administration into Peter.

———

NIGHT IS GRADUALLY FALLING like a cloak over Nyala, transforming the desolate city into a playground of shadow and silence. Hashim, clad in a black litham he borrowed from an abandoned washing line, keeps to the alleys and shadows, his silent approach broken only by the soft crunch of glass shards beneath his boots. The RSF compound looms ahead, a foreboding silhouette against the indigo sky.

Reaching the same block, he enters an abandoned mosque that overlooks the compound, climbing its minaret to see down into it. From his vantage point, he observes the rebel soldiers patrolling the perimeter, occupying the street outside, and walking the top of the wall. There are six in total, all heavily armed with AK-47s.

Hashim's fingers brush over the cold grip of the M4 slung across his back, and he feels a surge of adrenaline course through his veins. But he knows better than to rush into a guarded fortress, especially one manned not only by soldiers but also by Frank's goons. Using his prior experience in tactical assault from his days as a hijacker, he devises a plan, opting to strike at the right moment rather than charging headlong into a deathtrap.

Leaving the mosque via a back alley, he maneuvers around the crumbled structures that surround the compound, meticulously closing the distance with it, little by little, one building at a time.

As he moves down a road that runs along the eastern wall of the compound, Hashim tracks the patrol of the closest guard, waiting for the opportune moment, the soft glow of the man's cigarette creating a lazy trail in the dark. As the rebel soldier passes a narrow alleyway, Hashim bursts out at him.

Using the man's own momentum, he slams him into the weathered bricks of a fallen wall. A swift, decisive punch, followed by a bone-jarring chokehold renders the guard unconscious.

Quickly, he disarms him, dragging him into the shadows, and sets his sights on the compound once more. The assault has begun, but the real challenge is just ahead—infiltrating the heart of the lair under the vigilant watch of the remaining guards. His fingers tightened around the M4, his heart pounds in his chest—this is just the beginning.

———

THE ROOM—ONCE stark and oppressively concrete—now morphs around Peter like a sickly fever dream, its sharp edges warping, bleeding into one another in a phantasmal display. The second injection, scopolamine, infiltrates his system, twisting his perception further into a labyrinth of the surreal. Its effects strike him with the brutality of a hammer blow, his consciousness spiraling, thoughts unmooring from the anchoring shores of reality, fracturing into a nebulous haze of fragmented memories and disorienting sensations.

In the maelstrom of chaos, Dr. Leonid maintains an unsettling constancy. A ghastly half-man, his clinical detachment is a stark counterpoint to the disordered kaleidoscope that Peter's world has twisted into. His gaze, steely and analytical, never leaves Peter, noting the dilation of his pupils as they bloom like dark chasms, the sheen of perspiration glistening his forehead, the staccato rhythm of his pulse as it races like a wild drum.

"Where is the girl, Mr. Black?" Dr. Leonid asks in a repressive monotone.

The question pierces the pandemonium, but the words dissolve before Peter can grasp them. He's caught in the cruel circus of his own mind, where Semyon's visage continues to undergo a horrific metamorphosis. The leathery burn scars undulate like living entities, the familiar contours of his face shifting, warping into an unending slideshow of grotesque distortions.

Tommy's face, youthful and innocent, appears and recedes into the shadowy cavalcade, morphing and duplicating in a grotesque symphony of doppelgängers. An avalanche of faces, known and unknown, flood Peter's senses, each one morphing into the next in a tortuous loop, reality and hallucination dancing in an unholy waltz.

Peter's consciousness is adrift on the tumultuous waves

of his own mind, buffeted and tossed by the stormy sea of images surging before his eyes. A disjointed chronology of his life unfolds in a phantasmal parade—his lonely childhood in the isolated confines of Alaska, the youthful exuberance of Tommy's laughter resonating through the dense forest, the adrenaline of his first covert mission in the twisting streets of Greece, and Kate... sweet, ephemeral Kate, her haunting death shattering his reality. This dizzying carousel of past and present is all punctuated by the insistent drumbeat of the relentless interrogation.

"Please, I don't understand what's happening." Peter's voice sounds far away, as if pulled from him by an unseen force.

"Where is the girl?"

Every question lands like a sucker punch, turbocharging the onslaught of hallucinations. The room disintegrates and reassembles in a pulsating whirl of warped imagery, each shift in perspective catapulting him into a maelstrom of fragmented memories and distorted fantasies. His world becomes a prismatic nightmare, each blink a switch-flip to another jarring scene.

But amidst the tumultuous sea of chaos, a core of steel within Peter roars to life. It rails against the psychedelic onslaught, a solitary lighthouse amidst the storm. The words *resist* and *endure* resonate within his splintered psyche like a sacred mantra. The raspy timbre of Mother's voice cries out from the abyss of his mind, goading him on, stoking the fires of his defiance. "Fight it, Peter!" she bawls at him. "Fight it!" He grits his teeth, refusing to buckle under the pressure, to surrender the information they hungrily seek.

"Where is the girl?"

"I don't know!" His scream cleaves through the distorted serenade as a kaleidoscope of Kates, their faces smiling in a haunting mirage, spiral endlessly into the depths of his drug-addled reality.

Dr. Leonid, the puppeteer, introduces the final player to this theater of the macabre: a powerful benzodiazepine. As the drug infiltrates Peter's system, it engenders an eerie tranquility, a surreal lullaby amidst the tempest of hallucinations. Yet this sedative calm does nothing to quell the vivid illusions; instead, it crystallizes them, amplifying their intensity, their lifelike vividness.

Amid the maelstrom, Peter is a tiny vessel cast adrift, his silent cries for sanity swallowed by the rampant chaos. Yet he endures, a lone navigator battling the capricious whims of the drug-induced tempest, his grip on his secrets firm and unyielding.

Peter's voice, hushed and repetitive, cuts through the silence, mumbling something almost rhythmically. Intrigued, Semyon leans in, his ear hovering close to Peter's lips. "One hundred and one, Al Abdi, Um Dalil. One hundred and one, Al Abdi, Um Dalil. One hundred and one..."

"Is that where she's hidden?" Semyon's voice ripples with sudden anticipation as he steps back, considering the revelation.

Peter, lost in his own repetition, babbles the address incessantly, the sequence of words embedded in his drug-induced delirium.

Semyon takes his chin in his claw. Peter's swiveling eyes settle and fix to him.

"Is that where she is?"

"He left her there... with people."

"Who? Iqbal the Rat?"

Peter nods before sinking back into his feverish tumult.

The Hunter lets go. Fixing his gaze on Dr. Leonid, he gives the order: "Check it."

Dr. Leonid pulls a tablet device from his medical bag. His fingers flick across it, the screen illuminating his face in a sickly glow.

He looks up from the image of a map. "It's real. About fifteen miles."

The Hunter thinks about it. Breathes out. "Okay. Stay here, continue with the interrogation. I'll go see."

"Can't you send one of the others?" the doctor inquires.

"No. They don't know about the girl. I need to go myself."

With that, Semyon Mikhailovich strides out of the room, leaving Peter behind, his muttering continuing like a broken record, the single sentence hanging in the air: "He left her there."

———

THE WORLD outside the compound hushes, seeming to hold its breath as Hashim edges out from his hiding place, darts across the road, and vaults up the wall using the hood of a parked car as leverage.

Keeping low, he scans the yard of the compound from the top. A blur of movement draws his gaze to the other end of the courtyard. It's the Hunter, unmistakable even in the low light. He is mounting a snarling KTM motocross bike, the guttural growl of its engine slicing the stillness of the night.

The compound gate, a rusty beast of metal and wire, grates against the loose gravel as two rebel soldiers pull it to the side, its cacophonous grumble a discordant fanfare heralding Semyon Mikhailovich's departure. Once the men have pulled it out of the way, a plume of dust kicks up in the bike's wake, fragments of debris glinting like diamond dust in the floodlights of the yard.

As the sounds of the departing bike fade, Hashim takes a measured breath and moves onward along the wall, an invisible wraith swallowed up by the enveloping darkness.

He comes over a lone soldier, hunched in the gloom, the man tapping idly on a mobile screen, a soft neon glow illuminating his face. Unseen, unheard, Hashim closes in, sets himself, and takes in a breath before dropping down on top of him. There's a muffled grunt, the soft thud of a body meeting the ground, then silence.

One down.

Moving like a specter through the blackness, Hashim spots his next target. The man stands guard at a corner of the wall, eyes transfixed on the distance as he smokes a cigarette, his assault rifle slung over his shoulder, his pistol holstered, his focus elsewhere, blinding him to the true threat creeping up behind him.

Choosing his moment, Hashim glides forward, as silent as the desert wind. In one fluid motion, he neutralizes the second guard, his surprised gasp swallowed up by the vast night as Hashim holds his mouth with one hand while plunging a knife into his side and twisting with the other.

Two down.

Methodically, Hashim navigates the compound, a ghost in the machine, each downed soldier a testament to his skill and determination. As he moves deeper into the heart of the place, a trail of fallen guards marks his deadly passage.

———

With Semyon gone, Peter is left alone with the cold, calculating gaze of Dr. Leonid. The Russian torturer continues with the interrogation, his tone clinical, unyielding, bouncing off the sterile walls of the room.

Nevertheless, he gets very little by way of a reply.

The repetitive sentence still lingers, Peter whispering it, "He left her there," its haunting rhythm ricocheting around the stark chamber.

"Have you told the truth?" the doctor insists, his cold eyes seeking answers in Peter's drug-ravaged gaze. "Is the girl really at the place you said?" The question hangs in the air, piercing through the hallucinatory haze.

Peter begins to repeat the address like a mantra. "One hundred and one, Al Abdi, Um Dalil. One hundred and one..."

Dr. Leonid's icy gaze narrows, a predatory intuition prickling at his senses. Throughout his career training GRU, FSB, and SVR, he has taught agents how to defy the most determined interrogator, even when drenched in the disorienting cocktail of mind-altering drugs. A sliver of suspicion begins to snake its way into the doctor's mind, a chill of doubt creeping along his spine. He observes Peter, scrutinizing his foggy gaze and the barely perceptible twitch at the corners of his lips. Could Peter be dancing to a tune of his own, playing a game of cat and mouse, all in spite of the potent chemical concoction coursing through his veins? The thought latches on to Dr. Leonid, persistently gnawing at his conviction.

"The address you gave—" the doctor says.

A grin starts to work its way up Peter's face.

"It was false information, wasn't it?"

The smile increases, making him appear deranged.

"Well?"

"Uh huh," Peter drawls.

"Then where is the girl really?" the doctor asks bitterly.

Peter's response comes in a soft, knowing whisper, "The real address wouldn't be any good even if I told you."

"Why not?"

"Only he knows how to reach her."

The doctor stiffens at the unexpected revelation, his face hardening. "*Who?*" he demands, his voice threaded with palpable desperation. "*Who* knows how to reach her?"

Peter doesn't respond immediately. His glazed eyes shift past the doctor's shoulder. Then, with a pointed nod of the head, he murmurs, "Him."

Dr. Leonid, alarmed, whirls around, following Peter's gaze.

His heart lurches into his throat.

There, in the doorway, stands Hashim, his tall shadow outlined by the dim light behind him. A chilling calm radiates from him, his figure almost spectral, and in his hand gleams the deadly promise of a Beretta M9.

Time freezes for a split second, long enough for the gravity of the situation to sink in.

Dr. Leonid lurches for his bag, the desperate scramble of

a cornered animal. But it's too late. The bark of a gunshot bounces off the bare walls, and the doctor crumples mid-reach, his body hitting the ground with a dull thud.

Hashim strides into the room, his dark gaze sweeping over Peter, the twitch of his mouth indicating a brief flicker of relief. But there is no time for celebrations. Time is a cruel taskmaster, and there is none to waste.

In smooth, practiced movements, he unfastens the straps binding Peter to the chair. Peter, dazed, stumbles slightly, his weakened legs struggling to support him. Hashim steadies him, offering support.

It is in that moment that his eyes catch sight of Kamal's lifeless form, and his jaw tightens. "I'm sorry, brother," he murmurs, a whisper of regret carried away on the frigid air. Then, as though time suddenly speeds up, the urgency of the situation comes crashing down.

"We have to leave," he urges Peter, his voice breaking through the drug-induced haze clouding Peter's mind. Nodding, Peter leans heavily on Hashim, their escape only just beginning.

They slip out of the room, leaving behind the chilling remains of Leonid's failed interrogation. In the yard, Peter winces from the floodlights. With sweat beading on his forehead, Hashim maneuvers his languid form into the backseat of Frank's imposing Hummer. He slams the door shut, casting a last glance at the compound, then leaps into the driver's seat. Hashim guns the engine, the Hummer's roar filling the entire courtyard.

As they rumble away, Hashim risks a glance at Peter. "Where was the other one going?" he asks, referring to Semyon.

Peter, despite his disoriented state, smirks. "Sent him on a wild goose chase."

"A wild goose chase?" Hashim says, his forehead wrinkling.

"Yeah. A fake address I memorized on the drive over."

———

SEMYON'S KTM roars down the desolate highway, its piercing headlight cleaving through the darkness. He is a silhouette against the fleeting backdrop, wind tugging at his clothes as he pushes the bike to its limit. Suddenly, the quiet hum in his earpiece is replaced by a grating buzz. Frank.

With a flick of his finger, he accepts the call. Frank's voice comes through, tinny and distant. "The bastard's gone, and your doctor friend is dead."

A cold anger sweeps over the Hunter. He throttles harder, his mind churning.

"How?" he growls.

"The Rat showed up. Beat or killed most of the soldiers at the compound. Took a vehicle. I reckon the address he gave you is bollocks."

Rage bubbles in the Hunter's veins.

"But he won't get far." Frank's voice snakes through the earpiece, holding a promise of impending violence. "I got friends all over this city. He'll be spotted soon enough. That Hummer he stole sticks out like a sore thumb."

The statement hangs in the night air, a threat masked as reassurance. Semyon's grip tightens on the handles, resolve hardening as he swings the bike around in the middle of the road and turns back.

The hunt is far from over.

TWENTY-EIGHT

NYALA, SUDAN - 18TH APRIL, 20:17 (EAT)

HASHIM GRIPS THE WHEEL OF FRANK'S commandeered Hummer tightly, its burly engine rumbling as they carve a path through the wreckage-strewn streets. With the power out in this part, there are no streetlights. The city's skeletal remains loom around them. Shadows dance in the flicker of sporadic fires. Peter, barely coherent due to the cocktail of drugs still raging through his system, hangs on to consciousness with grim determination.

Suddenly, the night erupts in a storm of gunfire. The unmistakable chatter of machine guns punctures the eerie quiet, and bullets ping off the Hummer's heavy-duty frame. A back window shatters, showering them with glass. In the distance, the asterisks of muzzle flash light up the darkness. A pickup truck, men standing in the back with their assault rifles leaned on the cab, comes steaming toward them.

"Hold on!" Hashim barks, wrenching the wheel to the

left. The Hummer swerves, fishtailing across the broken tarmac as he zigzags to evade their pursuers. One of the front tires bursts, Hashim almost losing control, just barely keeping to the road.

Glancing in the side mirror, he watches as they quickly turn around and resume the chase. Hashim presses the pedal to the floor, the Hummer growling in response, but he knows they can't outrun them. Not with a tire out.

He swerves into a narrow alley, the Hummer scraping against the rubble-laden walls. The thunderous din of pursuit fades momentarily, replaced by the clamor of metal against stone. He veers suddenly into the shell of a half-collapsed building, the Hummer's headlights illuminating a teetering mess of steel and concrete.

"Get out," Hashim commands Peter, already unstrapping his seatbelt.

They tumble from the Hummer into a shadowy landscape of ruin. Peter stumbles, and Hashim hauls him to his feet, his eyes scanning the gloom. The sounds of their pursuers grow louder again: the rumble of their pickup's engine, the harsh barking of orders. He hoists an arm around the much larger Peter, taking part of his weight, his knees and back suffering under it, and the two slip deeper into the wreckage.

Behind them, the alleyway fills with light. Hashim glances back to see the pickup skidding to a halt, its headlights glaring off the crumbled masonry. Doors slam, boots crunch on rubble, and six armed men start pouring into the ruins, their assault rifles swaying side to side as they move with menace.

"We have to split up," Hashim grunts at Peter, setting him against a lump of wall for support.

Peter tries to focus, his eyes coming in and out. He nods. "You're right," he slurs. "I'm no good like this. I'll hide."

"Yes," Hashim agrees. "Find somewhere safe, stay there, stay quiet. I'll circle back for you."

As he stumbles away, the shadows swallow Peter. Hashim waits until he's sure Peter is completely out of sight before he turns to face the oncoming threat.

The six men coming after them are well known. They are Frank and his bounty hunters. They move like shadows, communicating in rapid hand signals, splitting up and spreading out, encircling their prey. But Hashim is a master of stealth—the maze of rubble and ruin is his domain. He slips into the darkness, a phantom among the remnants of the city.

Listening for the movement of the men, the M4 Carbine gripped in his hands, he works his way through the ruins. His mind ticks through the possible outcomes. He knows he needs to find Peter and get them both out of the city, away from the Hunter, away from Frank, and to Leila. But the noises of pursuit are growing louder, the bounty hunters drawing nearer, and the night is full of menace.

Blended into the shadows, silent and unseen, he finds one isolated from the rest, a burly man with a scarred face. He rounds a corner just as Hashim steps out from behind a slab of broken wall. The bounty hunter's surprise barely registers before Hashim drives the butt of the M4 into his throat, collapsing his windpipe. As the man falls down, Hashim hits him a second time right in the face, knocking him out.

As he drags the body into the shadows, a tall, skinny bounty hunter nearly catches him off guard. Hashim spots the glint of his rifle just in time to drop the body, lurch out a second time, and grab the guy's AK, ripping it from his hands. But he loses his grip, and the gun falls to the ground. Whipping back around to face his foe, he finds the bounty hunter armed with a combat knife. The man lunges. Hashim parries, the blade narrowly missing his throat. The air crackles with tension as their bodies clash, Hashim getting ahold of the wrist controlling the knife, the two pressed together, each one battling fiercely for the upper hand. A cruel smile tugs at the corner of the bounty hunter's lips, his eyes reflecting a savage kind of joy as he pushes his advantage.

Dangerously close, the blade glimmers ominously under the sparse glow of the moonlight flooding into the roofless wreck of a building, the knife mere inches away from Hashim's chest. The cold steel, sharp and threatening, holds the promise of a grim finale, hovering like a grim reaper over Hashim's beating heart.

Just as the air seems to thicken with the scent of impending doom, something changes. The predatory advance of the bounty hunter comes to an abrupt halt. His body freezes, every muscle going rigid, as if locked in place by some unseen force. Then, with the surreal slowness of a dream, the man falls away from Hashim, crumpling to the ground, his life force extinguished as quickly as a candle in a storm.

Standing behind the fallen mercenary is Peter. His expression is grim, his eyes holding a mix of relief and regret. His hands clutch a piece of rebar, broken and jagged. Its rusted steel is stained with blood. The silence that follows is deafening, punctured only by the distant thud of the bombs beyond their alley.

"I told you to stay hidden," Hashim tells him.

"And you'd be dead if I had," Peter retorts, panting slightly.

There's a hard truth in his voice that Hashim can't argue with.

With a nod, they shift gears. Peter picks up a fallen Beretta M9 from the corpse, checks the magazine, and looks to Hashim. "Four of them left."

"That's right."

"Then let's finish this and get out of here."

Working their way through the rubble, they play off each other's movements. Compared to the bounty hunters, they are quieter, stealthier, luring soldiers into traps by using sounds.

Peter throws a piece of masonry, making a clattering din that reverberates throughout the skeletal building. Alerted, one of the bounty hunters heads straight for it, breaking into a run. He passes Hashim, moving by below him as the Sudanese stands out of sight upon the remains of the collapsed second floor. Hashim lands a burst of suppressed fire right on top of him, and the bounty hunter falls.

They continue to use the craggy environment to their advantage, tricking another bounty hunter into a crossfire. As the man dives for cover to escape Peter's shots, he lands right in Hashim's sights, and the crack of the M4 bounces off the ruined masonry.

One of the last bounty hunters rushes Peter, confident in his brute strength. He comes out of nowhere, trying to take Peter's head off with his pistol as Azrael spots it in time and palms the man's hand, knocking away the gun. The bounty hunter, at least six and a half feet, manages to get ahold of Peter's throat, his huge hand enclosing around his neck. But Hashim, unseen in the chaos, lands a clean shot to his head. The man's fingers let go, and he falls away, a momentary silence passing over the derelict city.

Five men down. Peter and Hashim stand among the debris, panting, their ears ringing from the gunfire. Peter drops the now empty Beretta, the metallic clatter very loud in the sudden silence.

"Let's get out of here," he rasps. Hashim merely nods, looking over the destruction.

In the ruined cityscape, among the fallen bodies of their enemies, they've found a moment of respite. But they both know it's temporary. The night is still young, and the city is filled with many more enemies.

———

EMERGING from the remnants of the bombed structure, Hashim and Peter tread a path of dust and shattered masonry, their eyes firmly set on the bounty hunters' deserted pickup truck. Yet before they can bridge the distance, a subtle disturbance in the shadows of the alleyway catches Peter's attention.

"Get down!" he bellows. With a sudden, forceful shove, he sends Hashim sprawling sideways, an ungainly tumble that saves his life. With the grace of a panther, Peter follows, diving into the grimy alley just as the night air ignites with the lethal chatter of a machine gun.

Bullets rain down, striking the concrete with venomous

intent, sending chips of stone flying like deadly confetti. Their flight is arrested by a small alcove in the broken remains of the buildings, a tiny sanctuary in their hellish surroundings, shielded by a jagged hunk of masonry. There, they take an inventory count and discover that not only is Peter's Beretta empty, so too is Hashim's M4. Gunfire continues to pummel their makeshift cover, brick fragments peppering them like a violent hailstorm, the shooter relentless in his pursuit.

However, even this ferocious barrage has a limit. The sound of bullets fizzles out, replaced by an empty click and the harsh swear of a curse, muffled and frustrated. "Bloody 'ell." A distinctly cockney accent resounds through the alley as the shooter wrestles with the jammed magazine of his weapon, the rhythm of his onslaught interrupted.

Seizing this opportunity, Hashim and Peter exchange a glance, their decision made in the silent conversation of warriors. With a battle cry, they charge.

Their opponent is Frank. When his attempts to dislodge the stubborn magazine fail, he discards the carbine with a grunt, his body transitioning into a defensive stance as Hashim and Peter close in on him.

Unfortunately for Hashim, the art of stealth and hand-to-hand combat are vastly different realms. His haymaker cuts through the air, missing its target by a mile. Frank counters with a swift, brutal punch, an attack so powerful that it catapults Hashim out of the fight, sending him sprawling to the ground, unconscious.

Now it is only Peter and Frank, the next chapter of the confrontation set, the stakes higher than ever.

Frank is armed. His hand flickers, and a wickedly sharp

knife materializes. "I've been wantin' to smack you one ever since you arrived," he growls as they circle each other.

Frank charges. Peter is forced back, stumbling through the debris. He deflects the first slash, barely, the blade singing past his face. The second catches his arm, a quick slice that stings as much as it pours with blood. Frank is relentless, his movements smooth and deadly.

Peter is reeling. The drugs still pulse in his system, making his opponent's face morph into others—a cruel kaleidoscope of enemies and allies. Frank's face distorts into Semyon's, then Dr. Leonid's, even Kamal's and Hashim's.

Drawing on every bit of training, Peter defends himself. He deflects a lunging strike with a swift Wing Chun *pak sao*, then blocks another with a quick *jut sao*. He dances around Frank's thrusts, implementing his knowledge of Capoeira and Jeet Kune Do to remain elusive, to buy time.

Each move drains him more, and the wounds he's sustained, minor as they are, wear him down. Frank, still relentless, continues his assault. The knife swipes again, drawing a line of fire across Peter's ribs. He stumbles, dazed and disoriented, each blow sending ripples of pain that jostle his precarious, drug-addled focus.

Frank presses the attack. His face morphs into Kate's, and Peter's heart lurches. His defenses falter. He diverts the knife but receives a punch that rocks him back on his heels, followed by a swift kick to the gut that sends him sprawling. The world spins, and he sees stars.

Peter can feel the end creeping closer, the knife's gleaming edge promising a swift resolution. But somewhere deep inside him, a stubborn spark of resistance flickers. He remembers the lessons Mother drilled into him—to resist, to endure.

So he fights.

Hauling himself up, he deflects Frank's charge with a Muay Thai elbow strike, following up with a swift knee to Frank's midsection. This opens up a gap. With a Taekwondo front kick, he flicks a foot that strikes Frank's wrist with enough force to make him drop the knife. It also buys Peter a precious moment, enough time to slip behind Frank as he tries to recover the knife, locking him in a Judo chokehold.

Frank struggles, gasping, but Peter holds on, lowering them both to the ground, so that he cradles Frank, the bounty hunter's legs kicking out, scraping in the dirt and detritus as he chokes. Peter's world narrows down to this—the strained gasps of his opponent, the steady pulse of his own heart. His hand reaches out and he grabs the knife.

With a final surge of energy, Peter breaks the hold, spinning to drive the knife into Frank's chest. Frank's eyes widen in surprise as it passes through his heart, his breath coming in short gasps before he lets out his final wheezing breath.

The world sways, and Peter stumbles, the adrenaline rush subsiding, leaving him shivering with exhaustion and pain. He casts a last look at Frank's lifeless body, then turns back to where Hashim lies unconscious.

Gathering his remaining strength, Peter hoists Hashim over his shoulder in a fireman's lift. His vision tunnels, black spots dancing at the corners. His heart hammers in his chest, but he refuses to falter. One step, then another, each movement an act of sheer will.

Against all odds, Peter has won.

Nyala, once vibrant with life and sound, is now a mute canvas of silence and darkness. Amid the ruins and remnants of the recent battles, Semyon Mikhailovich's KTM cuts a swift path through the desolation, a lone specter in the night.

As he draws closer to the compound, he senses the discord. Lights flicker erratically, casting a surreal glow across the pockmarked buildings. The walls surrounding it stand eerily vacant. His instincts scream at him, alarm bells resonating in the pit of his stomach.

Cautiously, he cuts the engine and proceeds on foot, his boots crunching on the gravel as he enters the compound, gripping a pistol. He sees bodies strewn around, their still forms a stark testament to the violence that has unfolded. His gaze hardens, his heart pumping liquid ice through his veins.

He walks into the main building, the harsh fluorescent lights casting a ghostly pallor over the scene. In the far corner, he sees the figure of a man sprawled on the ground. As he approaches, the cruelly familiar features of Dr. Leonid become apparent. His wide eyes stare blankly at the ceiling, a bullet hole in his chest. Semyon's breath catches in his throat, the rage building inside of him.

Looking around, he takes in the scene: the contorted bodies of the rebel soldiers, the stillness of the compound, the inescapable stench of death. It's clear that he's returned to a graveyard.

His fists clench at his sides, the metal of his own weapon

biting into his skin. He's been played for a fool. They've escaped, they've won. But this isn't the end. Far from it.

With renewed determination burning in his eyes, he turns on his heel, leaving the haunting scene behind. The night is deep, and the world is his hunting ground. He knows they're still out there. He will find them, no matter what.

Back at the KTM, he retrieves a satellite phone from his pocket, flipping it open with an air of determination.

His fingers deftly dial a secured line. The static-filled silence that follows is broken by a deep, gravelly voice. "This is Echo," a man says in Russian.

"I need a four-man team." Semyon's voice cuts through the line, steel wrapped in velvet. "Standard SVR commandos, armed and ready."

The voice on the other end acknowledges, a brief confirmation underpinned by years of trust and unspoken understanding.

"And another thing," Semyon adds, his gaze sweeping across the sprawling cityscape of Nyala, a landscape teeming with danger and uncertainty. "Utilize every satellite camera at our disposal. Find me Azrael and his rat."

The satellite phone clicks shut, the Hunter's order resonating with unspoken threats in the quiet that follows.

TWENTY-NINE

USS RAMAGE (US NAVAL DESTROYER), RED SEA, JUST OFF THE COAST OF SUDAN - 18TH APRIL, 20:51 (EAT)

In the silent tranquility of his office onboard the USS Ramage, Ben Knight sits stiffly in a well-worn leather chair, his eyes glued to the flat-screen TV on the wall. The relentless drone of the news reporter bounces off the room's bare metal walls, painting a bleak picture of a world teetering on the edge. X-9 is clawing its way across the globe, leaving pandemonium in its wake.

Knight runs a hand over his weary face, his steel-gray eyes a mirror to the turmoil unfolding worldwide. He feels the familiar cold dread creeping up his spine. This isn't just another crisis to be managed; this is something much more sinister.

His focus is interrupted by the trilling of his burner phone. He doesn't recognize the number, answering it cautiously.

"I'm en route to Leila's location, Ben," comes Peter's voice.

The relief is instant. "Whose phone is this?" he asks.

"Frank's."

"And where's Frank?"

"Dead."

It's the obvious answer, Knight thinks. "Man, am I glad to hear your voice," he tells Peter.

"Well, it's not over yet." Peter's tone is grave, a reflection of the dire circumstances. "I need you to send an extraction team to the location I'm about to give you."

As Peter relays coordinates to him, Knight quickly punches them into his computer, his fingers a blur over the keyboard. His brow furrows as he watches the digital map zoom into an area north of Khartoum. As their bad luck would have it, the area is currently embroiled in the bloodiest clashes of the burgeoning civil war. Both the regular army and the RSF rebels are heavily armed with anti-aircraft missiles in those regions, making it a veritable no-fly zone.

Knight chews the inside of his cheek, his mind already spinning. "Peter, it's suicide to send any aircraft in there directly," he says, his voice grim. "You'll have to find Leila and get her out to a safer location first. There's a stretch of desert about ten miles east of that position that's relatively untouched by the conflict."

"Okay. I'll call you when I'm there. When I need the extraction."

"ETA?"

"I'm not sure," Peter replies. "It should take another hour, but with all the fighting, it could be longer."

"Well, the team are just across the border in Egypt.

Ready for rapid deployment. Contact me the second you have her. And Peter?"

"What?"

"Good luck and God bless."

Peter acknowledges the command, and Knight promptly disconnects the call. He can't afford to waste any more time. He swiftly dials another number, waiting impatiently as the call connects.

"Ma'am, it's Ben. Peter's alive, and he's on the move," he says, a note of urgency seeping into his voice.

"Does he have her?" Director McLean snaps down the phone.

"Not yet, but he knows where she is and is en route."

Director Sandy McLean's voice sounds tinny through the phone speaker, but her authority resonates clear as day. "Okay. I'll let the virologist team know. Get them set up. Anything else?"

Knight pauses, the weight of their predicament pressing heavily on his chest. He gazes at the TV, the chilling news report still playing. "Yes," he murmurs. "Pray. Because if we can pull this off, the world might just have a fighting chance."

THIRTY

BAYUDA DESERT, SOUTHERN EDGE OF KHARTOUM, SUDAN - 19TH APRIL, 05:11 (EAT)

As the dawn's blush attempts to penetrate the thick curtain of night, Peter navigates their stolen pickup through a labyrinth of desert trails. He purposefully avoids the main highway, a death trap riddled with the explosive punctuations of the ongoing conflict between the Sudanese Armed Forces and the RSF.

Stirred from slumber, Hashim instinctively lifts his mangled hands toward his face, his fingers brushing against the coarse bandages that swathe his wounds. Recognition flickers in his eyes as he takes in the clean, efficient dressing.

"You've redressed them," he murmurs, his voice roughened by sleep.

Peter glances at him, a hint of a smile on his lips. "Found a first-aid kit in the back," he explains, steering the truck deftly through a narrow stretch of track that passes between rocks and boulders.

"I take it Frank's no longer with us?" Hashim puts to him.

"No, he's not."

"And how's your head?" Hashim asks next, referring to Peter's intoxication.

"Better" is the reply. "The outlines of everything are still a little loose," he goes on, "and the colors are in sharp focus, but the world's slowly settling down."

"Good," Hashim says. "We're definitely not out of the dark yet. We'll need you in good condition."

As they skirt the jagged crest of a stone-strewn ridge, the images of a huge battle unfolding on the outskirts of Khartoum unfurls below them. Tanks and other armored war machines stand guard on either bank of the wide Blue Nile, their grim outlines stark against the liquid expanse. Arcs of tracer fire slash through the twilight gloom, their incandescent trajectories distorting the tranquility of the morning with their violent intrusions. Rocket-propelled grenades arc across the sky, leaving streaks of fire that briefly illuminate the ferocity of the face-off. The explosive impacts throw dust and debris into the air, obscuring the beleaguered cityscape and transforming the riverbank into a haunting image as the Nile, bathed in dim light, meanders placidly between the embattled city halves.

The dull thuds of the explosions resonate in the cab of the pickup as they drive toward it, punctuating the ambient noise with their terrifying authority. The blasts light up the historic architecture of Khartoum—its proud minarets and distinctive buildings. They stand as stark, silent witnesses to this latest carnage to befall the city, their surfaces intermittently lit by the harsh, unnatural light of gun and cannon fire.

In the river, the reflections of the battle create a strange, disturbing tapestry, a chaotic dance of light and shadow. Gunboats patrol the water, their wakes disrupting the otherwise placid surface of the Nile. Machine gun chatter ripples the air, disturbing the night with its staccato beat of warfare.

"I take it we're supposed to be crossing that river," Peter says glumly.

Hashim nods as his wide eyes take in the devastation in the distance.

"Any other way?" Peter asks.

"It will take two days" is Hashim's cold answer. "And we cannot guarantee that way will be any clearer than this one."

"That's great," Peter breathes. "Just great."

———

BAYUDA DESERT, Sudan.

WITH THE SUN peeking from the horizon, the desert landscape hardens, its edges becoming harsh in the jarring brightness of the African sun. Amid this, the growl of a lone KTM motorcycle cuts through the stillness, a fiery comet blazing a trail across the arid expanse.

Reaching the rendezvous, Semyon halts the motorcycle, dust swirling around him, casting a spectral aura in the growing light. His eyes remain fixated on a single speck in the sky as the whir of rotor blades grows louder. The roar of a powerful engine gradually fills the air as a large military helicopter descends, dwarfing the solitary figure and his motorcycle. It is a Mil Mi-24, a formidable Russian machine renowned for its deadly efficiency. A pair of lethal mounted miniguns flank either side, their menacing shapes stark against the twilight sky as they gleam with a deadly promise, their barrels still cold, yet hungry for the upcoming fray.

The rotor wash sweeps across the desert, the air vibrating as the chopper touches down. The side door slides open, and four formidable men step out, their boots sinking slightly into the sand.

The first man, a towering figure, radiates authority. Scars map his weathered face, each telling their tale of a battle survived. His ice-blue eyes meet Semyon the Hunter's in silent acknowledgement.

"I am Andrei," says the Siberian bear of a man.

He introduces his team. Next to him is Dimitri, a sharp-shooter who hails from Moscow's bleak urban jungles. He is lean and wiry, with a sniper's patience lurking behind his dark, calculating gaze.

Next comes Vladimir, the team's demolitions expert, as volatile as the explosives he masterfully handles. His shaved head gleams under the growing sunlight, his grin as unpredictable as a lit fuse.

Lastly, Ivan, the medic, is introduced. His demeanor is serene, his movements unhurried. Yet his steady hands hide a capability to wreak havoc as much as they heal.

Semyon greets them, each man earning a curt nod. He wastes no time on pleasantries, his voice resounding over the desert, a war drum in the stillness.

"Today," he declares, his gaze sweeping over the commandos, "we hunt a legend. Azrael, the master assassin."

The men look at each other, and some hushed words are exchanged. There is a change in their body language. They have become more upright, rigid, charged, as though primed for battle.

"So," Semyon adds in a roar, "let us send his soul to hell!"

The men cheer. Then Semyon casts one final glance at his KTM before boarding the helicopter, joining the Russian commandos. With a thunderous rumble, the chopper lifts off, bearing them toward the heart of the storm currently brewing in Khartoum.

THIRTY-ONE

KHARTOUM, SUDAN - 19TH APRIL, 06:01 (EAT)

THE STOLEN PICKUP SITS ABANDONED ON THE fringe of the city, about four blocks from where the army's battalions line the riverbank. It's much more inconspicuous to go from here by foot.

Hashim and Peter move swiftly through the shadowy urban expanse of Khartoum. The sprawling vista of sandstone and glass is an alien landscape under the fire-riddled dawn, its usual bustle swallowed by the deafening orchestra of war.

They enter a part where the fires burn bright. Ashen dust falls from the sky like gray lumps of snow, coating their lips and tongues and suffocating the air like a fog. Heat radiates from the broken concrete, making both men sweat profusely. Above them, the purple sky lights up with fiery arcs as flak cannons and anti-aircraft guns paint the heavens with lethal pyrotechnics.

A tank rumbles in the distance, its mechanical growl echoing between the raw-boned structures of what were once bustling marketplaces and office blocks. Hashim, armed with a British SA80 battle rifle he snatched off of Frank, and Peter, carrying a Glock-17 he found on one of the dead bounty hunters, both hurry through the dust in low positions, marching to the frantic tempo of the besieged city's heartbeats.

The scent of cordite and spent rounds is thick and cloying, a toxic perfume that crawls up their nostrils and a potent reminder of the life and death stakes in this perilous game they are playing. Every lungful of the ashy air is a grim toast to survival, to the specter of death that pursues them with every step.

Soldiers stalk the streets, their outlines sharpened by the harsh, flickering light caused by the fires. The sky above them is black with smoke. The soldiers are noisy, their movements easy to predict as their silhouettes amble through the smoke. Hashim and Peter are ghosts in comparison, slipping in and out of the shadows, their presence as fleeting and uncertain as the wind-blown desert sand.

At times, the way to the river is blocked by huge piles of rubble, the results of missile strikes on the surrounding buildings, pulling them down into the streets. Peter and Hashim cautiously maneuver their way out of an alleyway. As they clamber over a massive crater gouged into a boulevard, they come across a city bus. Now reduced to an eerie steel skeleton, it lies askew, forming a precarious bridge over the abyss.

Without a choice, they ascend into the vehicle, their hands slick with cold sweat as they tread carefully over fragments of shattered glass and twisted metal. Inside, a macabre sight greets them. Dead passengers, slumped in torn clothing, their once vibrant lives extinguished by the violent roar of a rebel soldier's AK, lie strewn across the floor and seats, their bodies covered in bullet holes. Peter's voice breaks the stifling silence, a soft whisper tinged with horror. "The innocent are always first to suffer."

Hashim is about to reply something when the morbid scene is broken by an agonized moan that reverberates through the bus. Startled, they turn to find an elderly woman beginning to move. Covered in ash, she looks like a corpse come back to life. A crimson stain blossoms on her dust-covered dress from a shoulder wound, having been caught along with all the other passengers when RSF soldiers stormed on board and began spraying them indiscriminately with bullets.

Consciousness flickers as her eyes open, stark white against the gray of the dust. She reaches out to them, her voice weak yet filled with desperate pleading.

As Hashim kneels beside her, offering her water from a bottle, the woman moans in Arabic about the pain. Peter, ever alert, gazes through the shattered back window of the bus, the woman's voice loud enough to pique his vigilance. As he does, he spots four figures in the dust: rebel soldiers advancing on their position.

"Hashim," he whispers urgently, "you need to keep her quiet."

Hashim begins whispering to the woman softly, asking her her name. But it appears she is in shock. The old woman begins trying to get up when the pain in her shoulder erupts. She screams.

"You must be quiet," Hashim whispers in Arabic.

But it's too late. The soldiers, drawn by the woman's cries, spot the odd duo inside the bus. Harsh shouts burst from their mouths as they call out to their comrades, the calls bouncing off the desolate cityscape.

Peter's response is immediate. His Glock barks, the snap of the gunshot momentarily drowning out the chaotic thuds and crackles of the raging battle. The legs of one soldier cave in, a crimson splash staining the sooty ground beneath him. The surviving soldiers respond with a wild volley from their AK-47s, bullets ripping through the bus, the sharp ping of them ricocheting off metal filling the air as Peter and Hashim dive for the cover of the seating. The dead passengers take the brunt of the shots, their flesh rippling with bullets as the soldiers spray into the bus, blowing out the remaining shards of the windows.

The AKs begin to click, their magazines empty.

Hashim explodes from cover, and another rebel falls to a precise burst of his SA80 battle rifle. Two soldiers remain, and before his aim can reach them, one of the soldiers lobs a grenade into the tilted bus.

In the split second before their surroundings turn into a deadly trap, Peter and Hashim lock eyes, a silent exchange passing between them in the chaotic dirge of imminent death.

"Go!" Peter roars as the grenade skittles into the bus, shoving Hashim toward a broken window. The Sudanese needs no further urging. He propels himself through the shattered pane even as the bus erupts in a fireball behind him, the grenade detonating with deafening finality.

Fire and shrapnel cut a swathe of destruction through

the bus, consuming the old woman's final cries. Peter's world narrows to a sliver of time. The blast wave smashes him like a sledgehammer, throwing him out the window. He hits the broken concrete ground hard, the breath smashed from his lungs as he rolls away from the exploding bus, debris raining down around him along with body parts and blood.

As the dust settles, the surviving rebel soldiers stagger out of their cover, their eyes narrowed on the smoke that rises out of the bus.

Aided by the cover of the smoke and the soldiers' confusion, Peter and Hashim react. Peter's Glock barks twice, quick, controlled shots finding their marks with deadly accuracy. A rebel's knee shatters, forcing him to the ground as he screams in pain and exposing his upper body from its cover. The second bullet is to the chest, ending the scream.

With a war cry, Hashim charges the remaining soldier, the SA80 battle rifle roaring in his hands. But the soldier, quick on his feet, dives for cover behind the wreck of a burned-out car, barely escaping the hail of bullets. Hashim hurriedly follows him around the car, and it is then that the man catches him unaware, clambering over the top of the black remains of the vehicle and lunging at Hashim with a wickedly sharp hunting knife. Caught off guard, Hashim stumbles backwards, his SA80 skittering away on the cracked asphalt. Muscle memory takes over, and he grapples with his assailant, the soldier's sharp blade glinting perilously close to his jugular. Back against the charred metal of the car, Hashim's breath comes in ragged gasps as he wrestles for control.

Just as the blade inches closer, a thunderous shot echoes

through the mayhem. The soldier's eyes widen before he slumps lifelessly off of Hashim. Peter stands a few meters away, smoke wafting from the barrel of his Glock, his face grim with determination.

"Come on," he says. "It's not far to the river."

Hashim picks the SA80 up, and the two move on.

Gasping for breath and smeared with dust and blood, Peter and Hashim hurry through the ruins. The whip-crack of bullets split the air, the staccato reports of distant gunfire, followed by the cacophonous roar of explosions—the sound-track of devastation, of shattered lives and ruined homes.

They slink through deserted alleyways, their figures hunched and silent. They are spirits in a city of phantoms, their quiet passage only marked by the gentle sound of their boots crunching on the crumbling debris. Their journey is marked by more close calls, breath-held moments where the sight of a passing patrol comes too close for comfort, where the thunderous, mechanical footfall of tanks shakes the ground beneath them, and they are forced to hide. The city, once so familiar to Hashim, has become a gauntlet of danger and uncertainty. They move with a constant sense of dread of the unseen enemy, of the next corner that could hide a patrol or a sniper's nest.

Yet amid the tumult, they endure. Fear has become an old companion to the two seasoned warriors, a whispering shadow that nudges at their minds but never quite takes hold.

———

With Khartoum heaving in the throes of war, they arrive at the riverbank, staying hidden in an alley as they survey the way. Not far, only about two hundred meters to the east, are the rebel tanks that are firing across at the army battalions on the other side.

The coast relatively clear, the two men slip across a street bordering the river, vault an iron-railing fence, and descend the dirt bank of the Blue Nile. Bodies float on top of the water, which is stained with blood and oil. Hashim and Peter lower themselves into the murky water, preparing to swim across, a desperate gambit against the backdrop of war.

The smoky air stings their eyes but should give them enough cover to avoid the boat patrols. Gunfire crackles nearby, sporadic at first, then quickly escalating.

As they begin swimming, the coolness of the water is a sharp contrast to the searing heat of the battle. The current tugs at them, a powerful, unseen adversary trying to drag them off course. Above the waterline, tracers fly back and forth, beautiful, like shooting stars, yet deadly, like falling comets. As they kick and struggle against the current, the water muffles the sounds of raging battle, distorting it into an otherworldly hum that buzzes in their ears.

A sudden explosion nearby sends a shockwave through the water. The force propels them forward, disorienting them. Surfacing for air, Peter catches a fleeting glimpse of a gunboat, its machine gun chattering away, spitting fire at the army vehicles lining the opposite bank. He ducks under the water as a patrol boat comes speeding toward them, forcing him deeper into the river. His lungs soon burn with the need for air, the taste of the Nile bitter in his mouth as he chokes on it.

He swims harder, his muscles screaming in protest. The water around him lights up with the reflections of nearby explosions, casting ghastly, flickering shadows. Suddenly, the surface above them explodes in fire, keeping them pinned under the water. Peter's heart pounds in his chest. They're dangerously exposed, but they're so close. Just a few more strokes...

They breach the surface, gasping for air, the world around them a burning cacophony of sound. A high-pitched whistle breaks through the noise, followed by a deafening explosion. A shell lands too close, showering them with water and debris. The shockwave flings them apart, each man lost in a whirlpool of disorientation and fear. Debris grazes Peter's arm, a sharp, slicing pain that briefly takes his breath away.

For a heart-stopping moment, he loses sight of Hashim in the roiling water, his shouts drowned out by the cacophony of battle. But then Hashim surfaces close to him, gasping and sputtering, their eyes meeting in silent relief.

Shaken but undeterred, they forge on, their desperate resolve heightened by the proximity of their goal until finally, their hands scrape against the riverbank.

They crawl out of the water, their bodies shaking from exertion and the lingering chill of the Nile. The day is a blur of sound and color around them, the ringing in their ears muffled, as if they're hearing the world through a layer of cotton.

But they've made it. In the heart of this city under siege, against all odds, Hashim and Peter survive. For now, they are alive, and that is enough.

THIRTY-TWO

KHARTOUM, SUDAN - 19TH APRIL, 07:32 (EAT)

WEAVING THEIR WAY THROUGH THE CHAOTIC wreckage that is strewn across Khartoum, Peter and Hashim glance from one abandoned car to the next, searching for a suitable vehicle to take them the rest of the way.

"We need something sturdy and quick," Hashim grumbles, eyeing a battered sedan doubtfully.

Peter nods, barely registering the words. Scanning the desolate rows of cars, his experienced gaze narrows down their options. Eventually, his eyes land on a hulking Toyota Hilux, weather-beaten but structurally sound. It stands out from the crowd, a rugged testament to the durability of the make.

"There." He points, drawing Hashim's attention.

The latter appraises the vehicle with a professional eye, and a slow nod shows his approval.

Approaching the car, Peter pulls out a small, inconspicuous kit from his pocket—a lockpick set he found in the glovebox of Frank's pickup. He crouches beside the driver's door, inserting the thin piece of metal into the lock. As he works, the tension in the air is palpable, both men straining to hear any sounds over the distant wails of missiles and gunfire.

Hashim, never one to keep still, keeps a constant vigil, the SA80 an extension of his arm, ready to spit death at a moment's notice. He knows better than anyone how quickly a situation can devolve into madness.

Meanwhile, Peter's experienced hands work their magic. The lock is an old one, its insides rusted and eroded by time. But he is no stranger to the craft. The tiny gears and tumblers inside the lock yield to his practiced touch, clicking into place one by one.

With one last, decisive turn of his wrist, he feels the lock give way. A moment of silence hangs between them before the door creaks open, a gratifying sound that signals their minor victory.

Immediately, Peter slides into the driver's seat and yanks off the paneling around the ignition, exposing the wires before skillfully manipulating the mechanism within.

Hashim, meanwhile, has already clambered into the passenger seat, his gaze glued to their surroundings, to the haphazard market stalls laying abandoned, sand-stained apartment blocks, their windows out, the outlines of people in some of them. He holds his breath as Peter works, the seconds stretching out interminably.

The silence is broken by a sudden, satisfying click, and

the dashboard springs to life. As the engine fires, both men let out a sigh of relief. For the moment, they are safe, ensconced in the metal shell of the Hilux. Nevertheless, neither of them is under any illusions. The real battle is yet to come. Their journey has only just begun.

THE BRIGHT MORNING sun swallows up Khartoum as Peter steers the stolen pickup through the winding streets, his focus laser-sharp despite the fighting erupting all around them. Hashim, ever vigilant, scans their surroundings, his experienced eyes picking out potential threats. The rumble of distant artillery fire and the occasional rat-a-tat-tat of assault rifles close at hand provide a grim soundtrack.

Suddenly, the roar of a powerful engine swallows all other sound. A shadow blots out the low sun, a gargantuan bird of prey that plunges from the sky, miniguns blazing, tracers streaking through the twilight. The onslaught of bullets shatters the relative peace, hitting the road right in front of them, shards of concrete flying, as lethal as shrapnel. Peter swerves the pickup, the powerful vehicle skidding across the asphalt as more bullets hammer the street around them, leaving a trail of destruction in their wake. He zigzags through the city, weaving a path of evasion, the scream of the Mil Mi-24 helicopter a constant specter at their back.

A nearby explosion rocks the world, the pickup lurching into a frenzied spin. Peter fights to control it, but it's too late; they careen into the construction site of a half-finished skyscraper, the vehicle crumpling against a steel girder. The harsh metallic crunch resounds in the morning quiet, a death knell for their escape vehicle.

Coughing from the dust, Peter and Hashim clamber out of the wreckage, plunging into the structure. As they run through the construction site, the incomplete tower looms over them, a monolith of steel and concrete, a testament to a brighter future now stuck on pause by the civil war, the eighteen-story building waiting for the interiors and outer walls to be built.

The thumping rotors of the Mil Mi-24 grow louder as the two of them ascend the unfinished staircases, the staccato beat of their boots resounding in the cavernous skeleton of the building. Their pursuers are relentless; two men clamber down ropes into the street, ready to follow them into the construction site from the ground. Once they've dropped and are running into the structure, the helicopter sweeps up over them, rising to the top of the building and landing on the roof with a gust of rotor wash that sends loose debris swirling around it.

Three more figures disembark from the helicopter, spreading out across the rooftop with predatory efficiency. Semyon Mikhailovich the Hunter leads them down a staircase into the building itself, his icy gaze scanning the half-built structure. They move in unison, a deadly ballet of precision and ruthlessness, their footsteps the only sound in the tension-filled silence.

As the commandos advance from above and below in a pincer move, Peter and Hashim duck deeper into the labyrinth, each level a tangle of steel girders and half-completed walls. The sunlight seeps through the partial structure, casting an eerie pallor over everything, turning the building into a ghostly maze.

Peter and Hashim don't falter. They weave through the construction site, always a step ahead, listening out for their pursuers as they lead them deeper into the building. The commandos press on, their tactical expertise pitted against the seasoned instincts of two men who refuse to become prey.

Hashim and Peter split, the decision clear in a single, shared glance. They each dash down separate passageways in the skeletal skyscraper, making sure that their footsteps land loudly through the towering structure, giving their rapidly diverging locations away.

Semyon and his commandos take the bait.

"Andrei, Dimitri," he whispers into his comms mic to the two men coming from below.

"Come in."

"One man is heading for the eastern corner of the building while the other is heading west. Split up and cut them off."

"Copy that."

"You two," he says to the men with him. "Do the same."

The men immediately nod and separate, one heading west and one heading east.

Hashim moves through the bones of the skyscraper with the precision of a man who knows the stakes of the deadly game they are all playing. He finds a good spot, launching himself up onto a small scaffold tower, where he waits. The two commandos pursuing him meet at the stairwell of the floor he's on, silently acknowledging with hand signals that their prey is on this level. With cautious movements, they begin to bear down on his position. A fleeting shadow on the periphery of Hashim's vision signals their location, so he readies Frank's SA80.

Peter, on a lower floor, is currently luring one commando into a trap. He is no longer the hunted; he is the hunter. Moving silently, he sidesteps a shaft of sunlight filtering through the structure then hides, whipping his body into a gap between two partial block walls. He holds his breath as the commando's boots crunch on loose debris close by. The man passes his position entirely, unaware of his presence. Peter waits till he has his back to him, then slips from his hiding place and attacks, striking with ruthless efficiency. His arm snakes around the commando's throat, pulling him into a lethal chokehold as he drags him back into the shadows of the gap. The Russian struggles, but it is over in seconds, Peter breaking his neck with a quick twist.

A moment later, the second commando appears. Before he can cry out, Peter explodes from his spot. But this commando is quicker than his pal.

At the last possible second, the bear-like Andrei flicks his icy blue eyes to the side, detecting the movement. He grunts in surprise, shifting his weight and pivoting out of the path of the lunging figure. Peter's lunge slices through the air, his fingers scraping Andrei's smooth body armor as the Russian commando sidesteps.

Peter gets his feet and spins around, his eyes narrowing.

With practiced ease, Andrei swings his AK-74M assault rifle around. The heavy report of the firearm will bring the others. But Peter's already on the move, his foot swinging up in a sharp arc. There's a solid thwack as he connects with

Andrei's hand. The rifle flies, spinning end over end, clattering uselessly across the concrete floor.

Peter doesn't get everything his own way, however. His momentum carries him into Andrei, and the two grapple, their muscles straining and their breaths coming out in harsh pants. Andrei's superior size gives him the advantage. He wraps his arms around Peter, effectively trapping him in a bear hug. Peter gasps for breath, feeling the squeeze of the Russian commando's steel-strong grip. He can see Andrei's face, grim with determination, his blue eyes cold and calculating. Peter's ribs flex in at the sternum, the bones at breaking point.

Still, Peter is far from defeated. His eyes drop and find what they are looking for. There, strapped to Andrei's thick ankle, a hunting knife glints menacingly.

Getting an arm free, he stretches his hand down, the tips of his fingers brushing against the handle as the air squeezes from his lungs. He forces himself to stretch farther, his joints screaming, the pressure in his chest increasing toward the bursting point. Andrei, mistaking his movements for futile struggles, only tightens his hold.

Finally, Peter's fingers wrap around the handle of the knife. With a swift, desperate motion, he pulls it from its sheath and swings it up.

The blade sinks into the side of Andrei's head at the temple. The Russian commando doesn't cry out in pain. Instead he grunts, like he's confused. His grip slackens, and Peter slips from his grasp, panting heavily, the bloody knife still clutched in his hand.

As Andrei stumbles back, clutching the side of his head,

Peter stands tall, eyes fixed to the big man, until his body crumples to the concrete with a harsh thud.

At the same time, Hashim is battling the odds. His scaffold tower isn't the sanctuary he initially thought it was. Instead it has made him a cornered animal. But he is lethal in his desperation. He fires a rapid succession of rounds, each bullet reverberating through the metal and concrete shell of the building. The commandos have split up in an attempt to outflank him. Hashim's senses snap taut, his gaze sharp as he chooses his prey, the man called Ivan. He locks on to his target, stalking him with calculated precision. The commando lunges for safety, but Hashim's biting bursts from the SA80 rifle doggedly chase him, promising imminent disaster. A bullet finds its mark. Ivan shrieks, crashing to the ground in a tangled heap.

Hashim has barely a breath to savor the victory when he hears the dreaded click of an empty chamber. Glancing down, he realizes with a sinking feeling that the SA80 is out of ammo. Almost immediately, a bullet cuts through the air, buzzing dangerously close to his ear. With no rounds left to return fire, he's forced to pitch himself to the ground as another barrage of gunfire opens up. The other commando, Vladimir, is seeking vengeance from a different angle.

Chased from the scaffold by a deadly rain of bullets, Hashim bolts toward a makeshift shelter of corrugated metal sheets, his every movement shadowed by Vladimir's relentless assault. He ducks into the precarious safety just as a bullet nicks the spot where he stood a split second ago.

It is as he blindly barrels into the skeletal structure that he stumbles upon what seems to be a makeshift corridor, the sides lined with plywood and sheets of plastic serving as barriers against the outdoor elements. The corridor stretches on, the other end just a dim void. Desperation propelling him, Hashim sprints down it, the thumping of Vladimir's boots growing louder and louder behind him, a promise of what's coming.

Suddenly, Hashim skids to a stop, realizing the horrible truth. The corridor has no exit. It's a dead end, and he's trapped.

His heart pounds violently in his chest, filling his ears. He's lived his life in perpetual danger, yet the weight of dread still fills his stomach as Vladimir's footfalls, now steady and measured, get closer and closer. Desperately, Hashim glances around. Above him, he notices a cavity in the ceiling, a possible escape route. But it's a good ten feet above the ground, and the smooth plywood walls provide no obvious foothold.

Hashim takes a deep breath, gathers his remaining strength, and lunges at the wall, trying to use it as a means to propel himself upward. His fingers scramble against the plywood, searching for any grip. But it's slick and unforgiving. His first attempt fails. Desperately, he tries again, his fingers leaving streaks on the plywood as he slides back down.

Vladimir's shadow grows darker and more pronounced at the entrance of the corridor. The glint of the rifle's muzzle slowly edges around the corner, like some sinister sock puppet. Hashim is cornered, and he knows it. The sense of inevitable doom is nearly suffocating. But just as the hope seems to be draining out of him and the shadow of the approaching commando seems its darkest, another shadow drops from above.

Peter, having found an upper pathway, falls from the cavity in the ceiling, crashing onto Vladimir. They grapple on the floor, each man trying to gain the upper hand. Vladimir, caught by surprise, is disoriented for a split second, which Peter uses to his advantage. Drawing Andrei's knife, he drives it deep into Vladimir's neck.

The Russian commando's eyes widen in shock. A gurgling sound escapes his throat as he falls limp. Peter, breathing heavily, pulls the knife free, eyes scanning the area for any other potential threats.

Hashim, meanwhile, slowly joins him, relief evident in his eyes. "You think that's all of them?" he manages to say.

Peter slowly shakes his head. "No. *He's* still out there."

With this portent of the impending face-off with the man who has been at their heels every step of the way, Peter and Hashim move with stealth and caution through the high-rise. They descend the skeletal floors, inching closer to the exit, their senses stretched to their limit. Every sound resonates threateningly through the exposed steel and half-formed walls, sending ripples of unease up and down their spines.

They are acutely aware of the Russian helicopter, the distinctive thrum of its rotors echoing ominously within the building's carcass as it circles.

"You hear that?" Hashim whispers.

"Yeah," Peter replies. "It's getting closer."

"You think he's onboard?"

"I don't know. Let's—It's on us," Peter bellows, his warning swallowed by the crescendoing whir of the helicopter's engines. "Get—"

The dawn is savagely ripped apart by the earth-shaking

roar of the Mi-24 as it surges to their level, hovering menacingly at their side through the open building. The brutal minigun glares in the morning light, wielded by none other than the relentless Hunter himself.

An unholy tempest of bullets roars forth from the relentlessly spinning barrels, tearing through the air and morphing the barren pillars of the skyscraper into a nightmarish war zone. The rain of high-velocity rounds begins to pummel the concrete around them, and they hurl themselves toward any semblance of safety as the chips explode in clouds of dust.

Hashim propels himself behind a sturdy pillar, his breath catching in his throat as the ferocious hail of bullets lays siege to the concrete around him. The once-solid pillar begins to crumble under the unyielding assault, a rapidly shrinking bulwark amidst a maelstrom of flying debris. The frantic thud of his heart beats a matching tempo with the relentless discharge of the minigun, and the cold concrete vibrates beneath him, mirroring the brutal rhythm of the airborne onslaught.

Meanwhile, Peter moves like a ghost among the ruins, darting from one trembling pillar to the next, a dancing shadow under the pale morning light and smoke. As his movement catches Semyon's attention, the devastating barrage swerves to pursue his sprinting silhouette, but Peter's agility and speed prove elusive. When he throws himself behind a steel girder, Semyon returns his attention to Hashim.

The Sudanese can only hunker down, attempting to shrink himself into the smallest possible target behind the crumbling pillar. The concrete disintegrates, laying bare the steel bone beneath, and he can feel every bullet thud against the pillar, each impact vibrating through his body. All the while, Semyon stands there behind the gun, his eyes ablaze with ferocious intent, his left pincer specially designed to hook triggers, enabling him to fire dual-trigger weapons, the ends of the minigun's barrels beginning to glow orange from the heat.

Seeing Hashim's desperate plight, Peter gears up to make his move. Fueled by a surge of adrenaline, he catapults himself around the outer rim of the building, circling to ambush the chopper from a blind spot. When he finally reaches his vantage point, Semyon is too engrossed in his deadly barrage against Hashim to register Peter's approach.

Then he does.

In the final split-second, as Peter levels the Glock, Semyon detects the movement in his peripheral vision and swivels the minigun in Peter's direction. With no time to spare, Peter squeezes off a volley of shots, but Semyon plunges into the safety of the chopper, narrowly evading the bullets. The Glock clicks empty. There's only one course of action left.

As Semyon emerges from the chopper's interior, preparing to reclaim the minigun, Peter hurls himself from the brink of the building. Becoming a human projectile, he hurtles through the air toward Semyon. As the Hunter reaches for the triggers of the minigun with his clawed left hand, Peter crashes into him. The violent collision sends them both sprawling into the cockpit, careening into the surprised pilot.

A brutal melee erupts in the cramped space, the spinning blades of the helicopter casting a whirlwind of erratic shadows within. Fists and feet fly as Peter and the Hunter exchange blows, their bodies locked in a violent ballet, each blow and counterblow a testament to their desperation.

Amid the chaos, a gun manifests in the trembling hands of the pilot. His arm swings erratically, the gun's menacing muzzle wavering between Peter and the Hunter, his eyes wide in an unsettling mix of terror and indecision as he struggles for a clear shot.

Just as his knuckles whiten around the trigger, a bullet hurtles through the windshield from outside, burrowing itself deep into his face. Hashim stands defiant against the danger, his eye narrowed in focus behind the sight of Vladimir's assault rifle.

The pilot's body slumps onto the controls, throwing the helicopter into a violent spin. The sudden lurch unbalances Semyon, his grip on Peter slipping as he is thrown to the side.

Capitalizing on the moment's chaos, Peter hurls himself into a daring plunge from the disoriented helicopter. As the death machine spirals precariously close to the skeletal skyscraper, he falls into the building's gaping maw, swallowed by the construction's towering abyss.

Peter slams onto the unforgiving concrete, a jarring halt that knocks the wind out of him. Dragging himself up, he risks a glance outside and catches sight of Semyon staging his own audacious escape. A tiny parachute unfurls behind him, the Hunter drifting away from the pandemonium.

The shell of the skyscraper shakes with the cataclysmic crash of the helicopter, the impact transforming the aircraft into a monstrous fireball. A towering inferno blazes up the building's façade, casting long, dancing shadows on the surrounding destruction.

Amid the construction site, Hashim and Peter stand, their bodies marred by the aftermath, spirits exhausted but unbroken. They've weathered Semyon's latest onslaught, the taste of survival fresh on their lips. Yet they stand under no illusion. They understand that this battle was just another storm in the brewing hurricane. The war, they know, is far from over.

THIRTY-THREE

HAVING FOUND ANOTHER VEHICLE, THEY HEAD into the rocky mountains of the Green Valley. Ironic, as they see very little green. Mostly beige, like the rest of Sudan.

The Mazda sedan they stole rattles beneath them, the sound of it overtaking the ruckus of battle that is gradually fading into a low hum in the distance. As they ascend into the craggy foothills, the horror of what they have been through lingers in both men, clinging to their minds, the images imprinted, leaving them dazed and shaken. Neither man has spoken since they crawled out of the skyscraper, and a sense of surreal tranquility blankets the journey, as if the mountains themselves were offering a respite from the turmoil.

At the top of a winding track, they pull up to a humble, sprawling farm nestled into the landscape, an idyllic oasis. Chickens peck the earth while goats meander freely, their bleats filling the air. Wooden shacks and a sturdy mud-brick house dot the property, signs of life stirring within.

Exiting the truck, Hashim calls out, his voice wavering with raw emotion. "Awal? Ayla?" After a moment of tense silence, an elderly couple emerges slowly from the house, their faces etched with years of hardship and resilience.

The second they see Hashim, their mouths open in wide, toothless smiles. The reunion is heartfelt, the trio embracing each other, a bond forged in a time when ties mean survival. Peter, a stranger in this intimate moment, stands a respectful distance away. The old couple's eyes meet his, their expressions flickering with uncertainty until Hashim reassures them in their native tongue. Peter watches as their faces relax, welcoming him into their sanctuary.

They step into the refreshing chill of the house, a stark contrast to the sweltering heat outside. The heavy shutters are drawn, plunging the interior into a comforting cloak of shadowy half-light. The elderly woman, Ayla, is in quiet conversation with Hashim, her voice low and reassuring. She is telling him that they have adhered strictly to his instructions—hiding the child at the merest hint of an approaching vehicle and never allowing her out during the day. None of the neighbors have seen her.

The child is hidden even now. They navigate their way into a cramped kitchen where the old man, Awal, makes to unroll a large, woven rug. Hashim intervenes, cautioning him to preserve his back. Together, he and Peter handle the rug, revealing a concealed hatch beneath.

They pry open the hatch, uncovering a small, makeshift hideaway filled with stored supplies. Nestled among some bottles of oil, a pair of wide, brown eyes peer out, the face of a young girl peeking through the darkness. She is the key. The hope.

"Leila," Hashim murmurs, his voice thick with emotion. A rare smile tugs at the corners of his mouth, his gold tooth catching the limited light, gleaming in the dim room. But there's something else—a glistening tear threatens to escape the corner of his eye. It's a sight so rare that Peter can't help but take note before Hashim briskly wipes it away.

With careful hands, they lift the girl from her hiding spot, bringing her into the light. Peter quickly surveys her condition, finding her to be in good health.

Once satisfied, he inquires if the elderly couple possesses a phone, being that he lost Frank's in the river. He is promptly handed a simple, utilitarian Nokia mobile phone and swiftly initiates a call.

"Who is this?" demands Ben Knight's voice from the other end.

"Azrael," responds Peter calmly. "Mission accomplished. I'm with the girl."

Relief resonates in Knight's voice, "Oh, Peter. Thank God. Stand by, I'm verifying your location."

The rhythmic clatter of keyboard keys can be heard over the line as Knight checks the position of Peter's GPS, the one buried in his eye socket. "Location verified. You're stationed at a rural farm, approximately four miles north of Khartoum in the Green Valley."

"Affirmative."

"I've coordinated an extraction team positioned on the border. ETA is twenty-five minutes, but not at your current location. It's still too close to those anti-aircraft guns.

There's a flat expanse of desert approximately two kilometers north of you. Think you can reach it?"

Peter visualizes the surrounding terrain in his mind. "I think I know it. I'll get her to it. Oh, and Knight?"

"What?"

"There'll be three of us."

"Three?"

"Yeah. Hashim Iqbal. I'd be dead if it wasn't for him. He's been the one protecting the girl from the start. He deserves a place on that chopper."

There's a few moments of silence. Then, "I'll see what I can do. How's the girl holding up?"

"She's resilient but visibly shaken. The people she's been with have been good to her."

A sigh from Knight's end. "Poor kid... she's about to be thrust into the heart of a global crisis without the faintest idea."

While Peter converses, back inside the mud-brick house, preparations are underway. Leila is being readied for the journey ahead.

When Peter returns to them, he relays to Hashim, "We have to reach an extraction point a mile and a half away."

After that, the girl shares a tearful farewell with the old couple, her small arms wrapping around each of them. Hashim then scoops her up into his arms, and together with Peter, they set off, leaving Awal and Ayla standing in the morning light.

———

As the three of them arrive at the flat desert expanse, a gust of wind kicks up a storm of sand, stinging their eyes. Moments later, the thunderous roar of a helicopter fills their ears. Its black shape punctuates the clear azure sky as it descends, its rotor blades churning the hot desert air.

Two men in military gear hop off the helicopter, quickly making their way over to Peter, Hashim, and the little girl. One of them, a medic, immediately begins examining Leila, while the other starts to usher them toward the chopper, the girl still in Hashim's arms, the medic jogging beside them.

Peter turns to assist Hashim, who is struggling against the rotor wash. "Give me the girl," he says.

Hashim hesitates, then gives in, handing him Leila. Peter carries the girl the rest of the way, loading her into the helicopter, where the medic takes her. It is then, as Hashim steps toward the chopper, that the other man steps forward, blocking his path.

"We were told only two," he bellows, trying to make himself heard over the deafening roar of the rotors.

"What?" Peter shouts back, incredulous.

"Only two," the guy repeats.

"Bullshit. He's coming."

Peter's gray eyes stare into him.

"I w-was told," the guy stutters, finding it hard to return the relentless stare, "only... two."

"If it's a question of space," Peter growls, "then I vote *you* stay. Now get out of our way and let him on board this helicopter."

The soldier relents, stepping aside to allow Hashim access to the aircraft.

Once they are all aboard, the chopper lifts off, leaving

the barren desert behind. It rises above the terrain, the city and the surrounding desert sprawled beneath them like a patchwork quilt of despair as great whorls of smoke rise up from it all along the horizon.

Before long, they are gliding over a massive slum that catches Peter's eye. It is a giant anthill of humanity, teeming with life, desperation, and squalor; all of it crawling within the shadow of the chopper. The sight is heartrending; bodies move like ants between the network of shanties, each one crafted from discarded materials that have long outlived their intended purpose.

Hills of trash, compressed by countless footfalls into compacted landforms, dominate the landscape, providing an uncanny mimicry of the surrounding mountainous geography. It is a landscape created by desperation, a testament to human endurance and survival in the harshest of conditions.

Peter can't help glancing at Leila. The blood coursing through that little girl will save a billion lives, maybe more. But looking down, he can't help wondering whether Tommy hadn't been right back in that cell. Maybe humanity does need a new start.

Between the serpentine lines of shacks, people are engaged in a battle of survival with stray dogs and brazen crows, each party vying for control over the scant resources the mounds of trash have to offer. The fights are fierce, a testament to the ferocity of life when cornered by need. In the free world, they fight among the supermarket aisles for the last toilet paper roll. Here they fight among the trash. Everything is relative.

As the helicopter thunders over the slum, Peter's gaze suddenly catches a flicker of movement. His heart freezes.

"Pull up!" he roars. A lone figure, shrouded in a ragged hood, stands defiant atop a towering mound of refuse. The object hoisted onto his shoulder glints forebodingly in the sunlight: a rocket-propelled grenade launcher.

With a blinding flash and a plume of smoke, the rocket screams into life, hurling the deadly grenade toward them. Despite the pilot's belated efforts, it detonates just above the rotor assembly, jolting the chopper with a deafening explosion.

With the aircraft rapidly descending, Peter instinctively clutches Leila to his chest, bracing himself against the side of the cabin. As the ground spins dizzyingly beneath them, he times his leap with meticulous precision.

Landing on a cushioning mound of trash, he rolls with the impact, cocooning Leila within his protective embrace. Peter fights with their momentum until they finally stop, skidding to a halt just as the crippled chopper slams into the earth in a plume of dust and debris.

Shaken but apparently unharmed, Leila clings to Peter as he quickly surveys her for injuries. A rustle from the corner of his eye has him twisting around, shielding the girl from the approaching figure.

It's Hashim, bearing a grim expression and two pistols. "I managed to get these from the chopper before I jumped," he says, his voice strained. "They may come in handy."

He hands Peter one of the SIG Sauer P320s. Peter cocks the weapon, chambering a bullet.

"What now?" Hashim asks.

Peter's response is cut short by the stinging whine of bullets ricocheting off their surroundings. Semyon Mikhailovich is bearing down on them from about a hundred meters away, unleashing a hail of AK-74M rounds at them.

With a quick heave, Peter scoops Leila back up into his arms, and the trio bolts into the twisting, narrow passageways of the slum, the harsh sound of gunfire ringing in their ears.

They head toward the refuge of an abandoned warehouse. Leila, the girl at the center of all this chaos, clutches on to Peter for dear life, the world around her erupting into a madness her young mind cannot even compute. Hashim, who is nursing injuries, grimaces through the pain as he prepares for the inevitable confrontation. Peter, with a resolve born of desperation, checks and rechecks the P320, the only line of defense between them and the relentless Hunter.

They reach the corrugated iron of the warehouse. Inside is a metal shop of half-broken-down vehicles, their rusted metal frames looking like the skeletal remains of the desert dead. With adrenaline pounding in their veins, Peter takes a position behind an industrial shear, its round blade hiding them. Leila, scared but determined, huddles behind him. Hashim, peering through a crack in the warehouse wall, sees the imposing figure of the Hunter.

He turns quickly to Peter. "He's here."

And then, without warning, the battle begins. Semyon opens fire, unleashing a torrent of lead, each bullet tearing through the warehouse wall with a primal force, splintering the sturdy timber and transforming the once sheltering barrier into a deadly hailstorm of debris.

Peter and Hashim respond in kind, their SIG Sauers belching out fiery retribution. The air inside the warehouse thickens with cordite and fear, and each echoing gunshot magnifies the claustrophobic intensity of the enclosed battle-field. Yet amid this storm of chaos, Peter remains a resolute pillar, his gaze never straying from Leila, his every nerve, every sinew dedicated to one mission—her protection.

Suddenly, the cruel reality of war strikes home. Hashim's body shudders as a bullet from Semyon's ruthless barrage finds its target on his left flank, inches below his heart. A grunt of pain slips from his lips, a harsh counterpoint to the cacophony around him. His body buckles, but his spirit remains unbroken. Ignoring the red-hot lance of agony from his bleeding wound, he retaliates with a newfound fury, his every shot embodying his undeterred resolve. His pain is intense, his situation dire, but Hashim's determination to survive, to fight, remains undiminished.

Seeing Hashim injured, Peter's heart clenches. "Get into cover!" he shouts.

Hashim obliges, throwing himself out of the way.

There's no time to dwell on it for Peter as Semyon turns his attention to him. He has to protect Leila. He maneuvers her behind a stack of crates, shielding her with his own body as rounds spit from the Hunter's AK-74M and slam into the surrounding machines.

Semyon is relentless, an embodiment of unyielding tenacity. He moves with the lethal grace of a predatory animal, closing the distance between him and his prey with measured, predatory strides while able to dodge their bullets. His gaze is locked on Peter, a relentless focus that promises a lethal endgame.

However, life, even in its most dire moments, is rife with unpredictability. As Semyon steps into the warehouse, out of nowhere, Hashim materializes like a ghost, a primal roar escaping his lips as he charges headlong at the Hunter, his face a contorted mask of determination, a promise of retribution, his eyes alight with a wild, defiant fire.

With the fierce velocity of a bullet, Hashim crashes into Semyon, his body a human battering ram that knocks the formidable adversary off balance. The powerful impact sends shockwaves through the Hunter's frame, disrupting his rhythm momentarily and sending the AK spilling across the ground.

But the victory, while savored, is as fleeting as a lightning strike in a storm. Semyon's recovery is swift, a testament to his brutal efficiency and resilience. It's a chilling display of his predatory instincts, the beast within resurfacing with heightened ferocity.

Before Hashim can brace himself, Semyon retaliates. A flash of silver blurs the air as his claw turns into a knife, a sleek instrument of death that reflects the cold-hearted resolve in his eyes. With a swift, merciless movement, he plunges it into Hashim's chest. The act is so sudden, so unexpected, that it freezes time, the world momentarily caught in shock and horror.

"No!" Peter roars, but it's too late. Hashim slumps to the ground, a satisfied grin on his face. He's bought them some time, but at the cost of his own life.

Driven by rage and grief, Peter sprints out from behind the shear, leaving Leila behind. He throws himself at Semyon. The two grapple, exchanging blows and counterblows, neither willing to back down. Then they're apart.

Chests heaving from adrenaline, their bodies circle one another in the center of the workshop, eyes fixed, the air between them crackling with dangerous intensity. They are apex predators, locked in a lethal ballet, their movements fluid, precise.

As they stalk each other, their gazes never wavering, Peter breaks the silence. "We were once friends, Tommy," he says, his voice resounding through the cavernous warehouse. "Back when we were kids, you had a heart."

Semyon chuckles, the sound low and dark. "And look where it got me, Pete," he retorts. "Caring is a liability. It makes you weak."

"It makes you human, Tommy," Peter counters.

"But humanity is flawed, Pete. Pathetically so," Semyon spits, his eyes flashing dangerously. "We've grown lazy, complacent. X-9 can change that. Teach us a lesson we desperately need to learn."

"By killing millions?" Peter asks, incredulous.

Semyon shakes his head. "You're missing the point, Pete. It's like training a puppy. When it soils the carpet, you rub its face in its mess until it learns. World War Two... the Holocaust... for a while, humanity's face was being rubbed in its mess. We were getting better."

"But that's not the way," Peter argues, his heart pounding in his chest. "You make no sense."

"Oh, but it is the way," Semyon insists, a twisted smile playing on his lips. "We've been too clean for too long, Pete. No real suffering. No real hardship. And look at us."

He pauses, allowing the weight of his words to sink in. "Only through suffering do we evolve, Pete. Only through suffering can we become... better."

With a snarl, Semyon lunges, throwing a vicious right hook aimed at Peter's skull. Agile as a panther, Peter ducks beneath the swing, retaliating with a sharp jab to the gut, born of his training in Krav Maga.

The impact drives the air from Semyon's lungs, and he staggers back, his body bowing under the force. But his recovery is nearly instantaneous, the expression on his face shifting from surprise to a savage grin, a grotesque mask of amusement under the harsh sunlight that floods the warehouse from outside.

A brutal exchange of fists and feet ensues. Their movements are a mix of lethal grace and honed precision, a testament to their brutal training. A cacophony of Muay Thai kicks, Brazilian jiu-jitsu parries, and the ruthless efficiency of Systema, the Russian martial art, reverberate through the confined space, each opponent a dark reflection of the other.

Suddenly, Semyon feints, his left clawed hand, sinister and gleaming under the grimy warehouse lights, drawing Peter into a clever ruse. The trap springs in a blink, Semyon seizing Peter's extended arm, his clawed grip tightening with an unnatural strength around the forearm before he violently twists. A gut-wrenching crunch, as grating as a car crash, resonates around the warehouse as Peter's arm buckles and fractures under the force.

A roar of pain wrenches itself free from Peter's throat, the sounds of agony mingling with the harsh sounds of their deadly melee. Yet despite the fire of torment blazing through his body, Peter's spirit refuses to extinguish. The fight is not over yet. The pain is pushed to the corners.

A flood of adrenaline baptizes his system, a natural anesthetic shielding him from the searing pain as he retaliates with renewed fierceness. His remaining arm whirls, a cyclone of destruction hammering blows onto Semyon, each punch a manifest of relentless will.

But the Hunter shares the same macabre determination as Peter. They are both forged of the same stuff. Each blow is absorbed, the pain held deep within, and soon the two of them part, both heaving air into their lungs, circling once again.

Poised for victory, Semyon, a brutal specter under the cruel sunlight, advances, his clawed hand retracting with a metallic click. With an unnerving certainty, he aims a fatal jab straight for Peter's heart. However, intuition flares within Peter, an animalistic sense of danger. With a swift sidestep, he evades the thrust as the claw shoots out, allowing it to sail harmlessly past.

Without missing a beat, Peter swings his leg in a practiced Muay Thai low kick, connecting with the back of Semyon's knee. Caught off guard, the Hunter's balance falters, his killing strike now a distant echo of failure.

Seizing the opportunity, Peter delivers a swift punch with his remaining strength to Semyon's windpipe, his fist followed by a crushing knee to the solar plexus, a perfect execution of a Krav Maga combination.

But his opponent is nothing if not resilient. Thrown against a workbench, Semyon grabs the first thing he finds—a wrench—and hurls it at Peter. It strikes the top of Peter's eye, cutting it open and causing blood to flow down into it, buying Semyon some time.

He comes at Peter, their movements sharp, precise—a whirlwind of Krav Maga strikes and Muay Thai kicks. The Hunter's remaining hand becomes a blur, each punch carrying a ruthless intention, his stump acting as the perfect foil. He's driving Peter backward, each step a calculated force of domination.

Peter finds his back against a railing, the cold metal biting through the fabric of his shirt as he is pushed against it. Beyond the railing is a ten-foot drop into a skip filled with the jagged shards of scrap metal. It looms ominously behind Peter, each piece a potential executioner's blade. Semyon gets in tight, pressing him into the railing, his left arm's stump pummeling into Peter's face with the merciless rhythm of a war drum, Azrael's flailing blocks and parries diminishing with each blow.

Peter's vision blurs, each strike an assault on his senses. Nevertheless, through the haze of pain, he spots the one element holding him in his precarious perch—a single, rusted bolt that holds the railing in place. With a desperate lunge, his hand clamps around the bolt, pulling with all the strength he can muster as the blows continue to rain down on him.

In a second, the railing gives way with a groan of distressed metal, tilting dangerously. Seizing the moment, Peter twists his body, using Semyon's momentum to maneuver him underneath. With a visceral roar, they both plunge into the maw of the waiting metal below.

The impact is violent, an uproar of pain and shrieking metal. Several jagged shards burst through Semyon, impaling him on the cold, uncaring steel. Peter winces as a piece slices into his side, but he fights through the pain, his determination stronger than the sharp sting.

Beneath him, Semyon convulses, the color draining from his face as blood pools around him. His eyes, once full of predatory fervor, flicker open. He coughs, a gory mix of blood and spit spilling from his lips. The once-terrifying figure lies defeated, a stark reminder of the relentless cycle of hunter and hunted.

Peter gets up off him, grabbing his cut side. Standing at the edge, he looks down at Semyon Mikhailovich the Hunter.

"I think you might have gotten me this time, Pete," the Russian agent says.

Semyon tries to get up, but the pain immediately forces him down, the last vestige of color leaving his scarred face.

"Goodbye, Tommy," Peter says as he grabs the edge and begins hauling himself out.

In the lingering silence of the warehouse, only one man stands victorious—Peter, battered and broken but undeniably triumphant.

He stumbles toward Hashim. The Sudanese lies on his front. Peter turns him over, but he's already gone.

His eyes are still open, staring out, his countenance caught in the emotions of his last, sad second. Peter closes them and sighs. Hashim the Rat Iqbal had been a brave comrade and friend. He had sacrificed himself for their mission. Kneeling beside him, Peter whispers a vow. "Your death won't be in vain, old friend."

Wearily, he rises and moves toward Leila. He finds her where he left her, behind the crates. Wrapping his arm protectively around her, he hoists her up, and they step outside.

Wounded and spent, Peter staggers away from the crumbling shell of the warehouse, the small figure of Leila clasped securely in his arms. Each breath he draws sends daggers of pain ripping through his body, but he continues, propelled by a determination that refuses to dim.

Suddenly, the sound of chopper blades slicing through the air reaches his ears. Peter squints against the dust storm whipped up by the approaching helicopter, shielding Leila with his body as her grip tightens. The bulky silhouette of the craft swoops down, hovering a few feet off the ground.

Just as Peter is expecting more trouble, the side door slides open and a figure leans out, a hand extended. "Ben Knight thought you might need an extra chopper," he shouts above the roar of the rotors.

The sight fills Peter with a sense of relief so profound it almost brings him to his knees. With the last of his strength, he hands Leila over to the man, who whisks her inside the helicopter, before getting in himself.

Exhausted, he slumps in his seat, the last scraps of the adrenaline that has kept him going ebbing away. He glances out of the window as they lift into the air, Khartoum shrinking beneath them. The city of conflict and chaos, of suffering and survival, grows smaller and smaller, until it is nothing more than a sprawling maze of structures shimmering in the midday sun.

Peter leans his head back, his gaze lingering on the rapidly disappearing city. A sense of profound exhaustion washes over him, his body crying out for rest. But there's also a sense of accomplishment, of completion. He's done it. He's gotten Leila out.

Half-conscious, he fixes his eyes to the girl, the weight of the past few days catching up with him as the helicopter cuts a path through the sky, bearing them away from the danger and toward safety.

That's the last he remembers before passing out entirely.

EPILOGUE

USS RAMAGE, RED SEA - 20TH APRIL, 14:10 (EAT)

STIRRING TO CONSCIOUSNESS, PETER FINDS himself swathed in a crisp, sterile white sheet, the metallic tang of antiseptic hanging in the air. He's in the well-equipped medical bay of an American Naval ship, the low hum of engines and the gentle sway of the vessel confirming they are at sea. His body feels like it's been weighted, fatigue and the aftereffects of his injuries bearing down on him.

In a corner, Ben Knight, his lanky frame sprawled in a chair, is engrossed in a book. But as Peter's restless movement draws his attention, he places the book aside, a soft smile of relief forming on his weary face. Pushing the chair back, he strides over, the rubber soles of his shoes squeaking against the polished floor.

"Good to see you awake, Peter," he says, drawing his chair closer, his familiar voice a comforting sound in the featureless room.

"Leila?" Peter croaks, his voice gravelly with lingering pain and exhaustion.

"She's safe, Peter," Knight reassures him, his voice soft but firm.

Peter's gaze, despite his weariness, is sharp. "X-9?"

Knight gives a nod, his face stern. "It's under control. We've managed to use the data on the bacteria in Leila's blood to culture Symbio-B, and it's acting as a probiotic treatment for those infected with X-9. We're also synthesizing Protein Zeta, administering it as a direct antiviral treatment."

Peter's frown eases slightly. "What about a vaccine?"

"Being developed as we speak. They're working on an mRNA vaccine. Thanks to you, the worst of it is over, Peter."

Relief washes over Peter, and he lies back, allowing the pillow to cradle his head. "He saved the world, you know?" His voice is barely above a whisper.

"Who?" Knight's brows draw together in confusion.

"Hashim Iqbal," Peter murmurs, his eyes distant. "He saved the whole world, and no one will ever know what he did. What he sacrificed."

Knight's gaze softens. "The same goes for you, too," he says quietly, his words resonating in the stillness of the medical bay. "And Kamal Osman. None of you will get the credit you deserve. But then, that's always been the deal for guys like us."

Peter considers this, his expression reflecting a thousand unspoken thoughts. "I guess," he finally says. Then his eyes narrow. "You know, there's something I've been meaning to ask."

"Uh huh."

"You said before that the Russians developed three hosts. Why did they need three when they'd only need the blood of one?"

"Fail safes, I guess," Knight replies.

"Or maybe the Russians have given them to other countries."

Knight thinks about it before nodding. "Could be. But that's for another day." He rises from his seat, his eyes never leaving Peter. "Now get dressed and meet me up top. You've got another half a month on assignment. I'd say you've earned a little R&R and have been told by the men upstairs that you can spend it anywhere in the world at your leisure. All of it on Uncle Sam."

Peter snorts. "Isn't most of the world under lockdown?"

Knight gives a half smile. "It is. So your choices are limited. Nevertheless, there are some really nice islands in the tropics that currently aren't affected by X-9."

Peter grins, the gesture slow and slightly painful but genuine. "An island sounds nice."

A Bunker Somewhere in Russia.
24th April, 10:10 (MSK).

In the belly of his fortified bunker beneath the Black Sea, President Putin watches a grainy image flicker on the wall-sized telescreen, the connection not great. The face staring back at him from the video feed is that of Porfiry

Fyodorov, the head of the SVR. Behind Fyodorov, a shadowy figure hovers, an ominous presence in the background. The man is Konstantin, Fyodorov's personal enforcer. His cold, icy gaze is fixed on the proceedings, hands clasped behind his back, waiting like a coiled viper beside his master.

"Mr. President," Fyodorov begins, a worried look on his face. "The Americans... it would appear... have acquired their own host. They're already at work, engineering a vaccine from the girl's blood. I hear that they've recently created an antiviral drug that specifically targets X-9 and are using it in some hospitals."

The news lands like a punch in the gut, but Putin absorbs it stoically, his face a mask of stone. He leans back in his chair, the magnitude of the news sinking in. He finally breaks the silence with a question, his voice echoing in the confines of the bunker. "Casualties, Fyodorov?"

The intelligence chief hesitates, then replies, "Lower than we initially predicted, sir. Globally, no more than a hundred thousand. In America, less than ten thousand."

Putin sighs, the tension momentarily lifting from his hardened features. "Not the end of the world we expected," he says, his eyes narrowing. "Your man failed us."

"Yes, sir." Fyodorov's response is nearly inaudible, but the fatalistic resignation in his voice is unmistakable.

Putin's gaze shifts to the looming figure of Konstantin. With a dismissive wave of his hand, he signals the enforcer forward. Konstantin moves with lethal precision, stepping into the foreground of the telescreen.

Before Fyodorov can react, Konstantin raises a silenced Makarov pistol. A single shot rings out, the sound muffled by the suppressor. The feed flares bright white then fizzes out, leaving only the face of the Russian President reflecting back from the darkened screen.

Putin's hands move swiftly over the control panel, initiating a new call. Moments later, two more faces come into focus on the screen, the video call split between President Li of the People's Republic of China on one side and King Fahad of Saudi Arabia on the other. Their faces are grim, eyes brimming with unspoken discontent.

"Gentlemen," Putin begins, his voice steady despite the heavy air of tension. "I trust your hosts are performing as expected?"

President Li speaks first, his tone curt. "Yes, Vladimir. Our teams have developed effective vaccines and treatments with our host. But"—he pauses, leveling a steely gaze at the Russian President—"the new world order you promised has not materialized."

King Fahad chimes in, his normally warm voice laced with bitterness. "Our people are protected, Vladimir, but the promise of power, the 'new world'... all remain elusive."

Their words hang heavily in the static-laden silence. Putin watches them both, his features hardened into a mask of calculated calmness. But beneath it, he can feel a cold dread unspooling. The tide is turning against him.

"You promised us dominance, Vladimir," Li hisses through gritted teeth, his image flickering on the screen. "We risked everything for your vision."

Fahad's voice rumbles through the speakers, echoing the sentiment. "You've brought us to the brink, Vladimir. This could cost you, cost us all."

The video feed goes dark, leaving Putin all alone in his

bunker, staring at his own reflection on the blackened screen. Their words reverberate in the silence of the room, a stark reminder of the precarious tightrope he now walks.

———

Washington D.C., USA.
April 24th, 07:02 (EDT).

Beneath the shadow of the Lincoln Memorial, the cool morning air swirls around Ben Knight as he waits. He stands alone, the looming figure of Honest Abe casting a watchful eye over the National Mall. The hush of the deserted monument feels appropriate, a silent testament to the world that came close to perishing.

From the darkness, a figure emerges. Director Sandy McLean strides forward, her outline bathed in the soft glow of the nearby streetlamps. She nods in greeting, her stern face softened by a faint smile of relief. "Your man saved us," she acknowledges, her voice barely above a whisper. "It was the right call to get him back on board. Where is he now?"

The ghost of a smile plays on Knight's lips. "A small island in the Tropic of Cancer," he responds. "Decided to soak up some sun."

Sandy McLean nods, her eyes reflecting a hint of warmth. "Well, he deserves it."

The exchange, however, does little to diminish the urgency of the global situation. With a deep breath, McLean drops the next bombshell, her voice dropping to a hushed, grave tone. "I've just had it confirmed. Of the three hosts the

Russians developed, one went to China, the other to the Saudis."

The revelation drops like a bomb. It's not unexpected, but the confirmation brings the stark reality crashing down. "It's an act of war, Ben," Sandy states, her gaze intense, unwavering.

Knight meets her stare, the words hanging in the air between them. War. Again.

"The President wants it kept in-house," she adds. "But I thought you had a right to know. To know what's probably coming. I'll see you in the office."

With that, Director McLean turns and disappears back into the darkness, leaving Knight alone once more under Lincoln's watchful gaze. A chill runs down his spine as the full weight of their predicament settles on his shoulders. This isn't over. Not by a long shot.

———

New York, USA.
14th May, 10:11 (EDT).

As the sun touches the horizon, it casts a warm glow over New York Harbor. A behemoth of an oil tanker is docked, hulking and imposing, a relic of an industrial age. It is almost two months since the ship set off, and among the sailors clambering down the gangplank, one stands out. His silhouette, hardened and defined by years of rigorous training and the countless perils he has endured, emerges from the gangway. Peter Black, his worldly belongings stuffed into a weather-beaten duffel bag slung over his shoulder.

Nearby, a sleek SUV idles, its headlights cutting through the gathering dusk. From the front seats, Michael and his girlfriend Mayu watch in anticipation as Peter approaches. Their eyes track his progress, a stark contrast against the rest of the shipmates with his purposeful strides and an air of barely contained intensity.

Peter slides into the backseat, a wry smile touching his lips as he meets the expectant eyes of his son and Mayu. "Hey, kids," he greets, his voice raspy with weariness.

"Hey, old man," Michael shoots back, his eyes sparkling with relief and amusement. "How was two months on that rust bucket?"

Peter chuckles, adjusting himself in the plush leather seat. "Apart from the virus keeping us out at sea, it was pretty uneventful. Nothing but open water and the occasional storm. How was everything here?"

"The pandemic was pretty rough," Michael says. "That was until they developed the cure."

Mayu turns in her seat to look at him. "Can you believe that it took them all that time to cure COVID, but they literally cured X-9 in a month? It's crazy."

"Technology is getting pretty advanced," Peter remarks sheepishly.

"How was it on the ship?" Michael asks next.

"We couldn't go on land. So when we docked, we had to stay onboard."

"At least you got a tan," Mayu chimes in. "He's very brown, don't you think?"

She nudges Michael playfully. "Yeah," he agrees thoughtfully, narrowing his eyes on his father. "Especially for someone who's been working below deck most of the time."

"Maybe he hasn't," Mayu teases. "Maybe he hasn't been to sea at all. Maybe he's been leading a secret life."

Peter's eyes widen, but then he relaxes as Mayu bursts into laughter. He leans back into his seat, watching his son and his girlfriend with a softness in his eyes. It is in moments like these he feels a strange sense of normalcy, a rare respite from the world of shadows he is often entangled in. For a man who has danced with death on multiple occasions, a peaceful drive through the city, his son's laughter ringing in his ears, holds an inexplicable charm.

With a rev of the engine, the SUV pulls away from the harbor, melding seamlessly with the ceaseless dance of the city traffic. Peter can't help but think as the New York City skyline unfurls before him that this feels like coming home.

Don't miss DARK CORNERS. The riveting sequel in the Peter Black Thriller series.

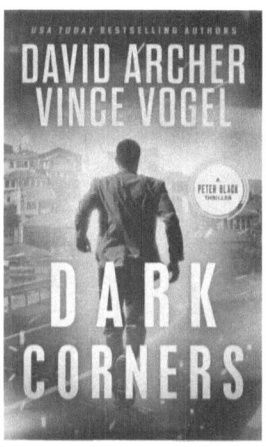

Scan the QR code below to purchase DARK CORNERS.

Or go to: righthouse.com/dark-corners

NOTE: flip to the very end to read an exclusive sneak peak...

DON'T MISS ANYTHING!

If you want to stay up to date on all new releases in this series, with these authors, or with any of our new deals, you can do so by joining our newsletters below.

In addition, you will immediately gain access to our entire *Right House VIP Library*, which includes many riveting Mystery and Thriller novels for your enjoyment.

righthouse.com/email

(Easy to unsubscribe. No spam. Ever.)

ALSO BY DAVID ARCHER

Up to date books can be found at:
www.righthouse.com/david-archer

ROGUE THRILLERS
Gates of Hell (Book 1)
Hell's Fury (Book 2)

JACOB HUNTER THRILLERS
The Kyiv File (Book 1)
The Bogota File (Book 2)

PETER BLACK THRILLERS
Burden of the Assassin (Book 1)
The Man Without A Face (Book 2)
Unpunished Deeds (Book 3)
Hunter Killer (Book 4)
Silent Shadows (Book 5)
The Last Run (Book 6)
Dark Corners (Book 7)
Ghost Operative (Book 8)

ALEX MASON THRILLERS
Odin (Book 1)
Ice Cold Spy (Book 2)
Mason's Law (Book 3)
Assets and Liabilities (Book 4)
Russian Roulette (Book 5)

Executive Order (Book 6)
Dead Man Talking (Book 7)
All The King's Men (Book 8)
Flashpoint (Book 9)
Brotherhood of the Goat (Book 10)
Dead Hot (Book 11)
Blood on Megiddo (Book 12)
Son of Hell (Book 13)

NOAH WOLF THRILLERS
Code Name Camelot (Book 1)
Lone Wolf (Book 2)
In Sheep's Clothing (Book 3)
Hit for Hire (Book 4)
The Wolf's Bite (Book 5)
Black Sheep (Book 6)
Balance of Power (Book 7)
Time to Hunt (Book 8)
Red Square (Book 9)
Highest Order (Book 10)
Edge of Anarchy (Book 11)
Unknown Evil (Book 12)
Black Harvest (Book 13)
World Order (Book 14)
Caged Animal (Book 15)
Deep Allegiance (Book 16)
Pack Leader (Book 17)
High Treason (Book 18)
A Wolf Among Men (Book 19)
Rogue Intelligence (Book 20)
Alpha (Book 21)

Rogue Wolf (Book 22)
Shadows of Allegiance (Book 23)
In the Grip of Darkness (Book 24)

SAM PRICHARD MYSTERIES
The Grave Man (Book 1)
Death Sung Softly (Book 2)
Love and War (Book 3)
Framed (Book 4)
The Kill List (Book 5)
Drifter: Part One (Book 6)
Drifter: Part Two (Book 7)
Drifter: Part Three (Book 8)
The Last Song (Book 9)
Ghost (Book 10)
Hidden Agenda (Book 11)

SAM AND INDIE MYSTERIES
Aces and Eights (Book 1)
Fact or Fiction (Book 2)
Close to Home (Book 3)
Brave New World (Book 4)
Innocent Conspiracy (Book 5)
Unfinished Business (Book 6)
Live Bait (Book 7)
Alter Ego (Book 8)
More Than It Seems (Book 9)
Moving On (Book 10)
Worst Nightmare (Book 11)
Chasing Ghosts (Book 12)
Serial Superstition (Book 13)

ALSO BY VINCE VOGEL

Up to date books can be found at:
www.righthouse.com/vince-vogel

PETER BLACK THRILLERS

Burden of the Assassin (Book 1)

The Man Without A Face (Book 2)

Unpunished Deeds (Book 3)

Hunter Killer (Book 4)

Silent Shadows (Book 5)

The Last Run (Book 6)

Dark Corners (Book 7)

Ghost Operative (Book 8)

JACK SHERIDAN MYSTERIES

A Cross to Bear (Book 1)

The Clay House (Book 2)

Into The Woods (Book 3)

The End is Nigh (Book 4)

A Step Into The Dark (Book 5)

Holier Than Thou (Book 6)

Streetlight City (Book 7)

An Offering for Sin (Book 8)

A Lark on the Wind (Book 9)

A Glass Darkly (Book 10)

Never Came Home (Book 11)

ALEX DORRING THRILLER

Agent 192 (Book 1)

The Hitman's Death (Book 2)

The Wrong Man (Book 3)

Who Dares Wins (Book 4)

The Highwaymen (Book 5)

The Ring (Book 6)

ABOUT US

Right House is an independent publisher created by authors for readers. We specialize in Action, Thriller, Mystery, and Crime novels.

If you enjoyed this novel, then there is a good chance you will like what else we have to offer! Please stay up to date by using any of the links below.

Join our mailing lists to stay up to date -->
righthouse.com/email
Visit our website --> righthouse.com
Contact us --> contact@righthouse.com

 facebook.com/righthousebooks

X x.com/righthousebooks

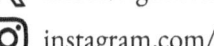 instagram.com/righthousebooks

EXCLUSIVE SNEAK PEAK OF...

DARK CORNERS

PROLOGUE

AFGHANISTAN, 2007

A REMOTE VALLEY STRETCHES OUT, FLANKED BY imposing mountains. As the wind travels over the land, it carries whispers of conversations and unsettled dust, adding an eerie aura to the scene.

Three figures, distinguishable only as men from their size and posture, kneel on the valley floor, their hands cruelly tied behind their backs. The rough ropes bite into their skin and black hoods cover their heads, rendering them faceless. Every short, sharp breath they take rustles the fabric, the world outside muffled.

Six shadowy figures, members of the local Taliban, stand sentinel around the prisoners. Among them, a teenage boy, Ali, stands out starkly. The weight of what's to come makes him appear more like a child lost among wolves than a warrior in the making.

One of the men is fussing with a video camera. He

meticulously checks every setting, ensuring the focus is just right and the view is capturing the entire grim tableau. "Right," he commands in crisp Arabic, his voice reverberating eerily in the vast valley. "Make sure your masks are up."

The men dutifully raise their face veils, revealing eyes that show a mix of resolve, fervor, and—in some—a glimmer of doubt. The father of the teenage boy helps him, lifting his veil and making sure it stays in place. Their eyes meet, and the father offers a gentle, reassuring smile.

"Are you ready to witness the work of God, Ali?" he asks, his voice tender yet laced with an undeniable fervor.

Ali nods, trying to mask his apprehension. "Yes, Papa."

His father's gaze hardens, and he continues with gravity, "It is a gruesome, brutal task. But it is essential for our people's future. For the foundation of the caliphate."

A tense silence stretches, only to be broken by the camera operator. "We're rolling."

As the red recording light blinks to life, Ali's father steps forward, standing ominously behind the three prisoners, assuming the grim stance of an executioner. The wind picks up, a mournful howl that seems to sense the looming tragedy.

"These kuffur," Ali's father proclaims in English with a voice that reverberates across the expanse of the valley, "have trespassed on our holy land." With a swift motion, he rips the hoods off the prisoners one by one. Each face that is revealed reflects a cocktail of emotions: fear, defiance, resignation. "They infiltrated our sacred places, spreading their venomous deceit," he continues. "They masquerade as saviors, as bearers of charity. Yet their true intent is clear—to obliterate our faith, to render us weak and dependent."

Every word he speaks is imbued with conviction, the echoes of his voice underscoring the gravity of the situation. Ali watches on from the sidelines, torn between admiration for his father's command and a burgeoning dread for what is about to transpire.

Addressing not just those present but the unseen viewers of the recording, Ali's father issues a stern warning. "To anyone contemplating alliance with these foreign aid agencies that dare tread on our soil—" he declares, lifting a machete high. The polished blade catches the sun, gleaming menacingly. "You are unwelcome. Your presence is a declaration of war against our faith."

As the machete arcs downwards, intent on delivering its grim message, a sudden, sharp report pierces the tense air of the valley. Before the blade can find its mark, Ali's father is struck in the chest by a .50 caliber round shot from a Barrett M82. The shock is instant. The machete clatters to the ground, the sun now reflecting off a growing dark stain spreading across the gray fabric of his kameez.

Time seems to slow. Birds take flight, their wings flapping in an abrupt and disjointed rhythm. Ali's scream, a mixture of disbelief and anguish, fills the void left in the aftermath of the gunshot. The scene devolves into chaos. The members of the Taliban scramble, searching for the source of the shot, their earlier assurance replaced by panic. The fate of the prisoners, momentarily reprieved from imminent death, hangs uncertainly in the balance of a valley now reverberating with turmoil.

The abrupt gunfire has set the scene alight with frenzy. Men scuttle like cornered animals, their calm veneer shattered in an instant. The dust, previously still, now swirls violently, mirroring the bedlam on the ground. The sun, once a neutral observer, casts long shadows that dance menacingly from the panicked men.

Kalashnikovs, which moments ago lay idle by their sides, are now clutched desperately by trembling hands and everywhere there's movement: men shouting, trying to form a defensive perimeter, their voices a cacophony of confusion and fear. But even as they rally, their invisible assailant begins picking them off. Each shot is precise, calculated—a sharp, resonating report followed by the thud of a body hitting the ground. Dust clouds puff upward with each fallen fighter, making it seem as if the earth itself is gasping in horror.

Amidst it all, Ali, the teenage boy, is paralyzed. His eyes, wide with terror, dart around, processing the unfolding massacre. Close by, one of the Taliban, perhaps only a few years older than Ali, desperately tries to return fire on the unseen force taking them out one by one. But it's clear he doesn't know where to aim. Each burst from his rifle seems more an act of desperation than defense. And then, like those before him, he too crumples to the ground, a red stain blossoming on his chest.

Another, thinking he's found the sniper's location, fires off a full magazine in the general direction of a distant ridge. But his hope is short-lived; he's cut down mid-reload, the magazine falling to the ground, reflecting brief glints of sunlight before being swallowed up by dust.

The camera, forgotten in the melee, continues to record, its lens now smeared with dust and blood splatter, capturing a scene of unbridled mayhem.

Ali, though young, is not without survival instincts. Using the gathering dust as cover, he drops to the ground, pressing his body flat against the earth, as if willing it to swallow him whole. His heart pounds loudly in his ears, each beat a frantic drum of survival. The fallen machete, the instrument meant to execute the captives, now seems to offer a glimmer of hope. Crawling slowly, Ali reaches out and grips its handle, the cool metal instilling a small sense of purpose amidst the chaos.

As the last of the Taliban fighters is gunned down, the valley descends into a haunting silence, broken only by the rapid breaths of Ali and the distant cawing of a bird. The prisoners, still bound but alive, shift uncomfortably, their previous dread now replaced with cautious hope.

From a nearby ridge, a silhouette appears—tall, armed, and daunting. His approach is slow and methodical, a stark contrast to the disarray of the men he's just dispatched.

Ali, clutching the machete, contemplates his slim chances. Does he flee, confront the approaching figure, or continue to hide, hoping the stranger will overlook a lone, terrified boy?

The weight of his decision, combined with the trauma of the past few minutes, threatens to overwhelm him. But one thing is clear: Ali is the last man standing, the sole survivor of a violent interruption to what was meant to be a display of power. Now, with the tables turned, he must decide his next move in this deadly game of survival.

The dust-laden air of the valley churns, giving life to the emerging silhouette, a specter of death, advancing with deliberate intent. Ali's eyes, clouded with a mix of despair and defiance, dart to his fallen father's Kalashnikov. In a last-ditch effort, he throws down the machete, lunges, fingers outstretched, grasping for the weapon that could buy him a chance.

But even as hope ignites, it's snuffed out. A bullet, precision-guided, strikes the rifle, sending it spinning away from Ali's desperate grip, rendering him once more defenseless.

It is then, as he contemplates throwing his body after the gun, that something stops him. From the ground nearby, a feeble voice struggles through labored breaths. "Ali..." his father rasps. Despite his weakened state, he is vehemently shaking his head, the message clear: to grab the rifle will be to die.

So instead, Ali rushes to his father's side, cradling the dying man's head. Hot tears course down the teenager's cheeks, blurring his vision. "Dad, what do I do?" he chokes out, every ounce of his being crying out for guidance.

His father's eyes, clouded with pain but sharp with resolve, lock onto Ali's. "Surrender, my son," he whispers, each word a labor. "Surrender now... and fight to die another day."

Before Ali can process the heavy counsel, his father's life force ebbs away, leaving the boy all alone amidst the carnage.

The sun, now beginning its descent, casts the approaching figure in an almost ethereal glow. As he nears, details emerge: devilish eyes masked behind dark shades, a swathe of pale skin peeking through the dust and grime of the battlefield, and what to Ali seems to be a cruel smirk playing on his lips.

Ali's gaze drops to his father's side, spotting the handgun in its holster. Maybe his father is wrong. Maybe now is as good a time to fight as any. In a blur of motion, he snatches up the pistol, turning on the looming assassin with trembling hands. But his adversary is faster, more experienced. In a swift move, the man has ahold of Ali and disarms the boy, the handgun clattering uselessly to the side. Rough hands then twist Ali around, zip-tying his wrists with brutal efficiency.

Defeated, Ali is pushed to the ground, his face pressed against the dusty earth. The weight of loss and helplessness bears down on him, and he weeps, his tears mixing with the soil.

The assassin, seemingly unfazed by the turmoil around him, activates a cell phone. His voice, cold and emotionless, slices through the valley's mournful silence. "This is Azrael. I've secured the aid workers. Only one survivor among the targets. Some kid."

Through his grief, Ali's mind latches on to that name: Azrael. The Angel of Death. In that heart-wrenching moment, a young boy's sorrow hardens into resolve. He now knows the name of his father's killer, a name he vows never to forget.

CHAPTER 1

BEIRUT, FIFTEEN YEARS LATER - TRINITY SUNDAY

THE STREETS OF BEIRUT, BATHED IN A SILVERY
nocturnal glow, hum with a quiet intensity. Yet beneath the
tranquility of the night, old vendettas silently pulse.

A van, a mere silhouette against the dimly lit streets,
speeds through downtown Beirut. Its engine growls,
mirroring the urgency of the night. Every twist and turn it
takes intertwines with the rhythm of a ticking clock.

Inside, five men sit, their faces obscured by the scant
light. Eyes, sharp and unyielding, give away nothing. The air
within is dense, pregnant with anticipation.

Amidst the night-time hum of Beirut, an auditorium
stands, illuminated by the moon's soft glow. The sound of a
congregation in harmonious chorus flows from the arched
windows of the building. The age-old hymn "Holy, Holy,
Holy! Lord God Almighty!" rises, a beacon of faith in the

deep of night, its purity oblivious to the shadows gathering outside.

The first van slides into the auditorium's parking lot, its tires crunching gravel. Almost simultaneously, two more vans emerge from the night, converging from different directions. The doors of all three swing open in a choreographed cadence.

Figures emerge, their count reaching fifteen. The minimal light paints them in shades of gray, but their collective intent is clear. The juxtaposition of the sacred hymn resonating from within and the gathering assembly outside amplifies the tension, making the weight of the impending moment all the more profound.

The clock, indifferent to the drama unfolding, continues its march, and as the hymn reaches its crescendo, it becomes evident that Beirut's midnight hour holds a destiny yet to be unveiled.

The silver glow of the moonlight paints a deceptive serenity over the old buildings of the city. But in the shadows, chaos unfurls with ruthless precision.

The fifteen men move in concert like a dark tide. As one, they descend upon the security guards at the main entrance with brutal efficiency. Flashes from their AK47s briefly illuminate the night. The unsuspecting guards crumple, the grim harbingers of what's to come.

Three teams splinter off, each heading to a different entrance to the main concert hall. With ruthless efficiency, chains are produced, and they begin sealing the fire doors. Their intent is clear: to ensure there is no escape.

Inside, the sprawling building reverberates with the powerful chorus of "Holy, holy, holy!" The notes rise and twist, creating a cocoon of sound that masks the sinister preparations taking place just beyond.

The doors fastened, the operatives disperse, their movements swift and purposeful. The grand concert hall beckons. Inside, the crowd remains engrossed in their spiritual connection, their unified voices creating a beautiful yet tragically deceptive bubble of security. Four cameramen, their focus on capturing the event, are startled as dark-clad figures appear behind them. The cold steel of a gun barrel pressed against their backs delivers a chilling message.

"Keep filming the stage," a voice, raspy and demanding, hisses in Arabic. The gravity of the situation sinks in, and the camera crew, paralyzed by fear but guided by instinct, comply.

As the gunmen infiltrate deeper into the hall, the veil of safety begins to fray. The once harmonious singing falters, replaced by a rising tide of murmurs and anxious glances. The transition is stark: The spiritual haven is rapidly morphing into a chamber of angst.

Faces, once lit by joy and devotion, now reflect dawning realization and fear. As the clock's relentless ticking merges with the quickening heartbeats of the gathered masses, the grim theater set by the assailants reaches its crescendo. The night, once a refuge, now holds them hostage in its cold embrace, the audience breathless as they anticipate the next phase.

It soon arrives.

The soft glow of the stage lights casts long, menacing shadows as the leader of the group strides onto it and makes his way toward a priest who had been conducting the singing only moments ago. The ambiance, once filled with harmony and devotion, is now tainted with an oppressive dread.

Without hesitation, the leader strikes the priest, a resounding slap that echoes the cold brutality of the moment. The priest's microphone, once a conduit of love and spiritual guidance, is wrenched away.

With a guttural roar, the leader screams into it: "Allahu akbar!" The words, charged with a jarring aggression, reverberate through the auditorium. His gunmen raise their voices in unison, their refrain of "Allahu akbar!" amplifying the chilling proclamation.

Before the terror-stricken audience can fully process the sudden, horrifying shift, the menacing rattle of assault rifles fills the air. A torrent of bullets begins sweeping through the rows, each shot snuffing out a life, a dream, a prayer. The pews, which moments ago held families, friends, and lovers, become monuments to horror.

A panic ensues, raw and primal. The instinct to survive overtakes the crowd, and a frenzied stampede erupts. Bodies press against bodies, the weak trampled by the strong, as terror renders humanity's better angels mute. The cries of the fallen, the pleas of the trapped, form a heart-wrenching counterpoint to the relentless gunfire.

Through this macabre dance, the cameramen, trapped in their own nightmare, continue to roll. The gunmen guarding them, ever watchful, ensure that each horrifying moment is captured, orchestrating a symphony of fear for the world to witness. "Keep filming," they growl like dogs. Directing them with cold precision, they ensure that the lenses focus on the faces of the terror-stricken, the fallen, making certain that the world won't forget this night.

As the clock continues its unforgiving march, the concert hall, once a beacon of hope and unity, is drowned in darkness and despair. The chilling harmony of the gunmen's cries of "Allahu akbar!" the deafening roar of their weapons, and the heart-rending screams of the innocent converge, crafting a nightmare from which Beirut may never awaken.

OUTSIDE THE BELEAGUERED CONCERT HALL, a cacophony of sirens wails into the night, their blue and red lights painting the Beirut streets in urgent, strobing patterns. The very fabric of the city seems to tremble beneath the weight of the unfolding catastrophe.

First to arrive are the ambulances, their drivers wide-eyed, the tires screeching to a halt, leaving trails of rubber on the asphalt. From another direction, police and Special Forces approach, their armored vehicles storming in with tactical precision. Soldiers, dressed in full tactical gear, disembark swiftly, rifles at the ready, surveying the scene with trained eyes, their every movement broadcasting disciplined urgency.

Yet just as they are setting up a perimeter, the roar of military trucks signifies the army's arrival. Troops pour out, their camouflaged forms blending into the night but their intent clear—to take charge and control the situation.

The chaos outside mirrors the devastation within. The multitude of emergency services, each vital in its own right, now seems to hinder more than help. Radios crackle with overlapping transmissions, the myriad of languages and codes only intensifying the bedlam. Leaders from each outfit, chests puffed up with importance, shout orders, often contradicting one another. Hand gestures fly. Arguments ignite. Egos clash.

And in the meantime, in the heart of it all, the auditorium stands silent and wounded, waiting for someone, anyone, to take the definitive lead in its rescue.

————

INSIDE THE CONCERT HALL, an eerie silence begins to settle, punctuated only by sporadic, heart-wrenching screams that echo throughout the vast space. It's a chilling aftermath, the air heavy with the acrid smell of gun residue, blood, and fear. The once grand hall, which had reverberated with melodies of faith and unity only minutes ago, is now a mausoleum of the innocent.

The harsh overhead lights cast a grotesque luminescence over the scene, revealing piles upon piles of bodies, thrown together in a macabre tableau of tragedy. Shoes, belongings, and shattered glass litter the floor. Here a child's toy, there a fallen crucifix.

The terrorists move methodically, their actions cold and calculated. Every step they take, every movement, is deliberate. No rush, no haste, just a mechanical progression through the hall to ensure no survivors remain.

One of them, his boots crunching over shattered remnants, spots a woman's foot peeking out from under the seating. With cold detachment, he aims and fires, the report of his gun echoing loudly. The foot jerks once and then falls limp.

Elsewhere, a faint cough pierces the quiet. It's a fragile,

desperate sound. Another terrorist, attuned to any sign of life, immediately zeroes in on its source. He listens closely, head tilted slightly, narrowing his focus to a wing of seats. Beneath them, the faint, raspy breathing of a survivor is audible.

A man, bloodied and terrified, looks out from his hiding spot, his eyes wide with dread. "No! No!" he pleads, hands raised in a futile gesture of surrender. But mercy isn't on the agenda tonight. The gunshot is swift, its finality ringing in the vast emptiness of the auditorium.

As these final murmurs of life are extinguished, the grim dance of death continues, every corner of the hall a testament to the horrors of this most fateful night, the bodies scattered everywhere.

The remaining cameramen, their faces pallid and slick with sweat, are shadows of their former selves. Trembling violently, they're trapped in a nightmarish scenario that none could have imagined when they arrived earlier to film the joyous occasion. Their equipment, meant to capture moments of faith and unity, is now a tool of terror in the hands of these invaders.

One of the gunmen approaches, his movements deliberate and predatory. "Point it on him," he orders venomously, nodding toward the central figure on the stage.

With shaking hands, the cameramen redirect their lenses, framing the imposing leader on the stage. The sharp glare of the stage lights casts dramatic shadows over him, making his features seem even more menacing.

He takes a deep breath, standing tall and defiant against the backdrop of devastation. "Allahu akbar," he declares with conviction, his voice trembling across the hall like a wave hitting the shoreline.

Before the gravity of his proclamation has a moment to sink in, shots ring out again. The gunmen have turned their weapons on the cameramen, executing the final witnesses with ruthless precision. One by one, they slump to the ground, their bodies joining the grim tapestry of the fallen.

Another gunman approaches the equipment. With a swift movement, he reaches down, switching off each camera.

In the stillness that then settles over the scene, the terrorists exchange glances, nodding almost imperceptibly. They know what comes next. Each man moves to one of three large duffels that they have brought with them. With swift, practiced movements, they unzip the bags.

From inside, they retrieve small, unassuming devices, no larger than a finger. Wrapped securely in condoms for waterproofing and ease of insertion, they glisten ominously under the overhead lights. The true purpose of these devices is not immediately clear, but the methodical manner with which the gunmen handle them indicates their sinister intent.

Two gunmen work together for each victim. One holds open the mouth of the deceased while the other, with a detached efficiency, forces the device down the throat. There's no gentleness in their actions. It's a brutal process, made even more chilling by the lack of resistance from the lifeless victims. The muffled sounds of latex against flesh and the occasional grunt from the gunmen as they ensure the placement are the only sounds that pierce the eerie silence of the hall.

As they move from body to body, there's a palpable

tension in the air. Each insertion, each step, brings them closer to the realization of a plan that remains shrouded in mystery, but its malevolence is clear. Whatever the next phase is, it promises to be as terrifying, if not more so, than what has already transpired.

———

As the clock strikes midnight, the atmosphere outside the building is churning with tension. The hour marks a tangible transition from hope to desperate action. Shadows move surreptitiously, the dim lights reflecting off helmets and visors. On one side of the concert hall, the special forces are assembled, instruments of penetration at the ready, every breath syncing with the heartbeat of the operation.

Hushed whispers intertwine with covert hand gestures, commands traveling swiftly through a cadre of unyielding gazes. Expert hands place explosive charges with precision along the formidable wall of the concert hall.

The night is shattered as the explosives detonate, a symphony of concussive blasts rendering the wall vulnerable. With engineered precision, a breach forms, a wave of debris and dust mushrooming into the midnight air, heralding the onset of the next phase of the operation.

The muted hum intensifies, climaxing with the sharp sizzle of gas canisters launched inward, hurtling through the breach. They skitter across the hall's floor, spinning and releasing their contents, filling the air with thick, white clouds designed to incapacitate. The special forces are finally ready to breach the building, the newly created opening serving as their gateway amidst the clouds of incapacitating gas.

The fight is instantaneous.

As soon as the special forces move in, their progression is immediately halted by the terrorists, equipped with gas masks, prepared for this exact scenario. The hall, filled with an eerie, foggy glow, becomes an arena of fierce combat as gunfire erupts, reverberating through the vastness of the building.

Bullets ricochet off walls, bright muzzle flashes punctuate the smoky darkness, and shouts of commands intertwine with the screams of the wounded. The battle is intense but brief, the superior training and tactics of the special forces quickly overcoming the terrorists.

As the smoke begins to clear, the magnitude of the operation starts to take shape. While scouring the fallen terrorists they discover high-tech comms earpieces, still warm from the terrorists' ears.

One of the men places an earpiece into his own ear. Muffled static comes back and something else: a man's breathing. Then it goes dead.

The revelation sends a chilling ripple through the unit. They've managed to secure the building and neutralize the immediate threat, but a lingering unease remains. The puppeteer, the one orchestrating this horrific act from the shadows, is still out there.

CHAPTER 2

BEIRUT, THE NEXT DAY

THE SUN RISES OVER BEIRUT, CASTING A MUTED orange hue over the city. The normally bustling streets are eerily quiet, weighed down by the grief of the previous night's horror. Birds that usually serenade the dawn seem stifled, as if even they sense the city's latest sorrow.

Throughout the day, the grim task of accounting for the deceased has ensued. The once-vibrant auditorium now resembles a war zone, scarred by violence and filled with the remnants of chaos. Emergency workers clad in white overalls move with a somber precision.

The sheer number of victims is staggering. Body bags line up row upon row along the auditorium's parking lot, each one a life, a story, a family shattered. The sight is gut-wrenching, even for the most seasoned first responders, some of whom take occasional breaks, stepping outside the broken building to catch their breath, wipe away tears, or simply stare into the distance.

The city's morgues are woefully ill-equipped to handle such a mass casualty event. As a result, vans and trucks are dispatched, shuttling between the auditorium and multiple morgues throughout Beirut. It's a haunting caravan of death, winding its way through Beirut's narrow streets, an unending procession that seems to go on for hours.

At each morgue, grim-faced workers receive the bodies, their facilities quickly overwhelmed. Refrigeration units fill up rapidly, forcing some to make use of makeshift cold storage solutions, while others have to turn to neighboring cities for assistance.

As for the populace, throughout Beirut, there's an undercurrent of tension. Rumors circulate, some born of genuine concern, others the product of fear and speculation. Whispers of other potential threats keep everyone on edge, and security checkpoints mushroom throughout the city. Beirut, a city that has known its fair share of violence, finds itself in the throes of a nightmare once again, a chilling reminder of the fragility of peace.

In a corner of a discreet rooftop café, one man, however, sits among the city's trepidation with an air of nonchalance.

The warm aroma of his freshly brewed tea mixes with the faint scent of jasmine from the nearby trellises. The wrought-iron chairs and tables around him are mostly empty, an unusual sight for a place that is generally abuzz with patrons this time of the day.

Given last night's horror, though, it's not surprising.

The man's eyes flit to the screen of a sleek smartphone. On it, a sophisticated app displays several pulsating dots, scattered strategically across a map of Beirut. Each dot is connected to a GPS signal. And each signal is nestled deep within a victim, who now lays motionless on a gurney in the basements of seven hospitals scattered across the city and its neighboring towns.

Yet it isn't only GPS tags inside the bodies of those poor people. Something else is nestled deep inside. Something that the world will soon find about.

The man's lips curl into a slight, self-satisfied smirk. While the city is consumed by grief and chaos, he finds himself in the eye of the storm, quietly orchestrating what comes next.

He leans back in his chair, taking one last look at the wounded city unfurling all around him. The final phase of his plan is about to begin—the cherry on the cake, if you will —and Beirut, still reeling from last night's terror, has no idea of the further devastation that awaits it in just a few seconds.

His fingers move swiftly across the screen, typing a six-digit code with precision: *40*—the age of the Prophet Muhammad when he received his first revelation—*99*—for the ninety-nine names of Allah—and *37*—the age his father was when he died.

He barely has time to set the phone down when the first blast shatters the relative calm. It is followed by another, and another. Each explosion is a thunderous testament to his meticulous planning. The sound waves bounce off buildings, creating an ominous chorus of destruction that reverberates throughout Beirut's neighborhoods.

Columns of smoke rise rapidly, merging into a thick, ashy veil that begins to obscure the once-clear evening sky. The familiar chaotic soundtrack of the city transforms.

Honking horns and yelling street vendors are replaced with the shrill of a million car alarms, screams of panic, and the relentless wailing of emergency sirens.

At the café, the man remains unmoved. There is grim satisfaction evident in the taut lines of his face and the glint in his eyes. From his central location, he has a panoramic view of the devastation unfolding. Fire, smoke, and the cries of the city erupt all around him. A waiter, initially frozen in shock, approaches hesitantly, his face a mask of fear and confusion. "Sir, we need to evacuate. It's not safe here."

The man doesn't respond immediately. Instead, he takes one last, sweeping look at the city, as if imprinting this moment forever in his memory. Then, standing up, he nods at the waiter. "Of course," he says, his voice betraying no emotion. Leaving a few bills on the table, he moves with purpose, descending a set of stone steps into the street and disappearing into the tapestry of Beirut's bustling labyrinth.

Without hurry, he walks past the frightened bystanders, not one of them acknowledging him in any way, their focus elsewhere, on the plume of smoke and dust rising from the direction of the nearest hospital, on the cries and sirens echoing up to the heavens. The man fades into the streets, another faceless figure in a city that has just been irrevocably changed.

He pulls out his phone once more and dials a number he knows by heart. Almost immediately, as if the person on the other end has been eagerly awaiting his call, the line connects. Without preamble, he speaks. "It is done."

A brief pause ensues, filled with the ambient noises of sirens, distant screams, and the inescapable noise of devastation. Then a voice, chilling in its calmness, responds, "Allahu akbar."

There's a tangible satisfaction in that voice, a pleasure derived from chaos. It continues, reveling in the moment, "Today is a great day for the caliphate."

The man takes a deep breath. "But tomorrow will be greater. Now make sure Hezbollah pay the rest of the money into the account."

"Of course. I'll get on the phone now, get them to release the funds." The voice on the line, as if sensing his thoughts, delivers a final statement. "Now it is time for you to come home, Musa."

"Yes," Musa replies as he drifts past the stunned people. "It is time for us to paint our masterpiece, *Ali*."

Scan the QR code below to purchase DARK CORNERS. Or go to: righthouse.com/dark-corners